To my editor, Sandra Harding,
and my agent, Jessica Faust.
Every author should be so lucky.

THE DIVA
DIGS UP THE DIRT

KRISTA DAVIS

WHEELER PUBLISHING
A part of Gale, Cengage Learning

Detroit • New York • San Francisco • New Haven, Conn • Waterville, Maine • London

LIBRARY OF CONGRESS CATALOGING-IN-PUBLICATION DATA

Davis, Krista.
  The diva digs up the dirt / by Krista Davis. — Large Print edition.
    pages cm. — (Wheeler Publishing Large Print Cozy Mystery)
  "A Domestic Diva Mystery."
  Also issued in standard print: New York : Berkley Prime Crime, 2012.
  ISBN 978-1-4104-5434-8 (softcover) — ISBN 1-4104-5434-7 (softcover)
  1. Winston, Sophie (Fictitious character)—Fiction. 2. Missing persons—Investigation—Fiction. 3. Large type books. I. Title.
PS3604.A9717D545 2013
813'.6—dc23   2012037081

Published in 2013 by arrangement with The Berkley Publishing Group, a member of Penguin Group (USA) Inc.

Printed in the United States of America
1 2 3 4 5   17 16 15 14 13

ACKNOWLEDGMENTS

I am deeply grateful for the information and suggestions I received from Luci Hansson Zahray, fondly called The Poison Lady by mystery writers. She was so very knowledgeable and enormously helpful. Any mistakes, of course, are entirely my own.

The gorgeous house on the cover of the original edition is loosely based on the Rosemary House Bed and Breakfast in Pittsboro, North Carolina. Thanks to Karen Pullen, who so graciously allowed me to share with my cover artist a beautiful photo taken by Dr. John Shillito. I knew it was Roscoe's house the moment I saw it.

Which brings me to Teresa Fasolino, the incredible artist who always paints the most wonderful covers for Sophie and Natasha. Her covers are like special gifts every time. Thank you, Teresa.

Huge thanks to Mary Wheeler Jones for allowing me to use her other name and especially for being such a great sport about it.

I would be remiss if I didn't thank my friends and fellow authors Avery Aames, Janet Bolin, Peg Cochran, Kaye George, Janet Koch, and Marilyn Levinson. They're always available for silly questions, serious opinions, and professional advice. I would be lost without them.

And last, but more certainly never least, I am always grateful for the unflagging support of my mother, Marianne, and my friends Susan Erba, Betsy Strickland, and Amy Wheeler. I count myself unbelievably lucky to have such wonderful people in my life.

Join us for the annual

**PLANTER'S PUNCH and
BACKWOODS
Picnic and Open House**

*Bring the whole family for fun, games,
and our famous ice cream bar!*

**At the Greene Homestead
Sunday at 4 p.m.
Chicken Lickin' Attire**

Roscoe Greene
Mindy Greene
Audie Greene

GREENE FAMILY PICNIC
GUEST LIST

Roscoe Greene
Mindy Greene
Audie Greene
Cricket Hatfield
Violet
Francie Vanderhoosen
Nina Reid Norwood
Mars Winston
Natasha

Note: Picnic is an open house. Friends and family are welcome.

Per Mindy, Olive Greene is not invited this year.

CHAPTER ONE

Dear Sophie,
My mother-in-law is an avid gardener who makes her own herbal teas. She grows a lot of poisonous plants like rhubarb, lilies, irises, and bleeding heart. How do I know she's not offering me poisonous tea?
— Suspicious in Lily, Kentucky

Dear Suspicious,
Bring your own tea bags.
— Sophie

"I'd like to hire you to find my daughter."

The woman's request caught me by surprise. I'd been deadheading geraniums in pots by my front door in the early morning and held flower snippers in my hand.

Pouffy dark hair framed her face. It wanted to curl but had been firmly set into a helmet by a hairdresser. Her clothes were equally impeccable. Full-figured from top to bottom, she made no effort to hide her shape under black garments. Her skirt and matching short-sleeved top bore a festive purple, pink, and yellow print. I guessed her to be in her midsixties, but she oozed energy.

My hound mix, Daisy, sniffed the woman's dainty purple and yellow shoes. Kitten heels weren't the best footwear for Old Town's uneven brick sidewalks. Daisy's tail wagged with restraint.

"I'm sorry," I said. "You must have the wrong person."

"Aren't you Sophia Winston?"

Close enough. "Sophie, actually. But I'm not an investigator."

"That's okay. I've heard about you." She dug in a leather purse big enough to hold four large loaves of bread and pulled out an envelope stuffed with cash. "How much do you charge?"

I splayed my fingers and waved my hand at her. "You don't seem to understand. I don't know anything about finding people. I'm an event planner."

"Please." She tucked the money away and pressed her palms together. "Maybe I could tell you a little bit about my Linda?" Her gaze swept to the salmon-colored geranium blooms. "I called her my little Anemone because she loved flowers and gardening. She was such a gentle soul, almost timid. Her father and I made a mistake by pushing her to study accounting. I see that now. We wanted her to make a good living. We only wanted the best for our little girl. She would have been so much happier studying horticulture." The woman plucked a tissue from her pocket and wiped her teary eyes.

I couldn't help noticing that she spoke of her daughter in past tense, as though she didn't expect to find her alive. I wasn't in the habit of inviting strangers into my home, but this woman didn't look like an ax murderer. I considered offering her a cup of coffee.

She looked up at the second story of my house. "This is quite a place for a single girl."

Red warning flags jumped up in my mind. "How did you know I was single?"

For the most fleeting instant, panic crossed her face. So briefly that I wondered if I had imagined it.

She reached out to me. "Your finger, dear. No wedding ring."

The red flags drooped. My mother would have made the same observation, and she would have referred to me as a girl. Still,

15

the woman had crossed some imaginary line and left me wary. "I'm terribly sorry, but you must have misunderstood someone. I've never searched for a missing person. I don't even know anyone who could help you. Good luck to you."

Her mouth twisted to the side. She issued a huge sigh, turned, and trudged away, heading toward the center of Old Town.

My best friend and across-the-street neighbor, Nina Reid Norwood, crossed the street to my house, causing Daisy's tail to spin in an excited circle. "Who was that?"

Without prompting, Daisy sat and offered a paw. "You're such a good girl." Nina pulled a treat from the pocket of her loose drawstring pants and offered it to Daisy.

"I have no idea. She wanted me to find her daughter."

"Your reputation is growing. After all, you *have* solved a few murders." She followed me into the house and stroked Mochie, my Ocicat.

"That's way different from locating someone." I stashed the flower snippers and poured each of us a latte.

"A lot of missing people have been murdered . . ."

"I'm not a private investigator. I wouldn't dream of taking anyone's money for something I'm not qualified to do." I set the lattes and a white platter of chocolate croissants on a wicker tray and carried it out to the backyard.

Daisy and Nina followed me.

I set the tray on a small table in the shade. I'd found the old-fashioned wrought-iron furniture ages ago when I was still married, painted it white, and sewn bright floral cushions for it that matched the gorgeous Blaze roses in bloom by the fence.

I settled back on a chair, cupping the latte in my hands and listening to the birds twitter.

"It's going to be another scorcher." Nina helped herself to a croissant. "This is the only time of day when the temperatures are still bearable. What are you wearing to Roscoe's picnic?"

I hadn't given it any thought yet. It had been a busy month so far. Everyone claimed that the event-planning business slowed down in the summer months, but that hadn't been true for me. I had wound up a big Fourth of July extravaganza and run a weeklong international radiology expo. I was also working on Roscoe's event, but his annual picnic on National Ice Cream Day was tiny in comparison. And when it was over, I was taking time off for two glorious weeks. I

17

didn't plan to do anything but laze around, with a margarita in my hand and flip-flops on my feet, and throw a cookout for my friends.

"The invitation said something cutesy, didn't it?" she asked.

I groaned. "Chicken lickin' attire."

Low snickering arose on the other side of the fence.

"Do you want to ride with me, Francie?" Nina raised her voice to be sure my elderly neighbor, Francine Vanderhoosen, heard her.

"Not going," came the response from the other side of the fence.

"Do you feel okay?" I asked.

"For pity's sake, it doesn't have anything to do with how I feel. Olive Greene is my friend. I wouldn't dream of making an appearance there."

She didn't have to say more. A longtime resident of Alexandria, Roscoe Greene was CEO of *Planter's Punch*, a catalog that catered to southern gardeners. His parents started the business, but he had expanded it to include *Backwoods*, for hunting and fishing enthusiasts. Roscoe had set tongues wagging all over Old Town when he'd replaced his wife of forty-five years with one of his employees. Their destination wedding

18

in Ireland ten days before had been the talk of the town. Roscoe had at least twenty-five years on his bride, who reportedly played the role of the trophy wife to the hilt, complete with tiara.

We heard Francie shout, "Hey! Can I help you?"

"Oh, pardon me. I must have counted the gates wrong. So sorry to intrude." The voice seemed vaguely familiar to me, but I couldn't quite place it.

I didn't need to. Moments later the gate at the rear of my yard opened. Daisy loped toward the back as a full-figured, dark-haired woman stole inside. She closed the gate behind her and stepped gingerly across my lawn, evidently not having noticed us in the shady corner by the fence.

Her forehead creased, Nina threw me a questioning look.

I placed a finger over my lips. I wanted to see what the woman planned to do.

She patted Daisy in a dismissive manner and continued to pick her way toward my house. Almost comical, she hunched over and stepped carefully to avoid lodging her kitten heels in my lawn. She studied the windows like she was checking to see if anyone was watching.

When she reached the patio, I asked, "Are you planning to sneak into my house?"

CHAPTER TWO

Dear Sophie,
We moved into a new house and need to plant some decorative beds. My husband says buying the smallest plants is best. I think he's being cheap. How can I convince him that big plants are the way to go?
— Mrs. Miser in Tightwad, Missouri

Dear Mrs. Miser,
Sorry, but I have to agree with Mr. Miser. Although large plants give you instant oomph, the roots of small plants have an easier time getting established when planted. In two or three years, they will have caught up.
— Sophie

She screamed and dropped her purse. Clapping her right hand over her heart, she threw her left hand into the air. "I didn't see you there." She staggered over to the table and slid into a chair. "You almost gave me a heart attack."

I hoped that wasn't the case. She seemed to be the dramatic type, so I assumed she was exaggerating.

She fixated on Nina. "Hello, dear." She extended her hand, and Nina dutifully shook it. "I'm Mona." She tugged her colorful top into place and patted her coif. "Desdemona, actually. I can't imagine what my parents were thinking. Today you'd probably be reported for child abuse if you named an innocent little baby Desdemona."

"Nina Reid Norwood."

"Three names. You're clearly a southerner."

Nina laughed. I could tell she liked Mona.

Mona placed a pudgy hand over mine. "Sweetheart, I don't like to impose . . ."

Oh no? What did she call prowling into my backyard?

"But do you think I could have a glass of water?"

Nina leaned toward her. "How about a latte?"

Mona held up both hands in protest. "Oh no. I couldn't." Her left shoulder lifted in a teeny shrug. "Maybe a little one."

She was too cute. Like a nosy aunt that

everyone adored. I reminded myself that people weren't always what they seemed. Still, it wasn't as though I didn't have everything ready in the kitchen. It wouldn't take long to make coffee for her. She'd left her purse in a heap on the patio, so I didn't imagine she intended to pull out a gun. I left her with Nina while I fetched two more lattes. When I returned, Mona was mmm-ing over a chocolate croissant like it was the best thing she had ever eaten.

I set a latte in front of her, which prompted her to say, "Thank you, darling."

I carried the other latte to the wooden privacy fence that separated my lot from Francie's, stepped on a wobbly old stump, and held the latte out across the top. Francie's hand readily snatched it.

When I returned to the table, Mona was gabbing with Nina, but her sharp eyes hadn't missed a thing.

"Now see? That was such a nice thing to do — bringing a coffee to your neighbor. I can sense that you're a kind person. Your friend, Nina, has been telling me about your adventures solving murders." She gestured toward Nina, who sputtered latte. "I'm certain you girls could find my Linda."

I wasn't going there. "Mona, I'm very sorry about your daughter. You have to understand that I have no expertise in finding missing people. You really should go to the police."

"You think I haven't talked to them?" Her mouth pulled back in irritation. "They have too many cases to care. She was an adult, so they won't do anything. Meanwhile, I lie in bed every night wondering if she's in a ditch somewhere, if she has food to eat" — Mona released a big sigh and her shoulders sagged — "or if her bones are bleaching in the sun."

A shudder hit me full force. No matter how sneaky or forward Mona might be, she shouldn't have to live with that thought hanging over her. "She lived in Old Town?"

"She lived in Alexandria, outside of Old Town proper, but she worked here in town. She disappeared one evening and was never seen or heard from again. Next week she will have been gone for five years."

"Sounds like someone nabbed her," said Nina.

I flashed her a warning look. We were *not* getting involved!

Mona placed her fists on the table. "Wouldn't you think someone would have noticed something?"

Uh-oh. I could tell where this was going. "No you don't." I spoke firmly, because

Mona struck me as the kind of person who kept at you until she achieved her goal. "I see what you're doing. I am truly sorry about your daughter, and I hope you find her. However, I am not in the business of locating missing persons." No matter how sorry I felt for her, I knew nothing about finding people. It would be wrong, wrong, wrong to mislead this poor woman. She needed a professional criminal investigator, not an event planner.

Mona drained her latte. "Is she always this stubborn?" she asked Nina.

Nina had the nerve, *the gall*, to wink at her. "Sophie balks at first, but she usually does the right thing." She looked at me, fighting a grin. "She'll come around."

"Not this time. So sorry."

"I'll walk you out," said Nina. To me she said, "I'll see you at Roscoe's around four."

Mona picked up her purse and returned to the table to pluck two more chocolate croissants from the platter and wrap them in a handkerchief she pulled from her handbag. "For the road. But don't think I'm through with you yet, young lady. How would your mother feel if you disappeared, and she didn't know what had happened to you?"

Ouch. Her question hit home. My family

25

would be frantic if any of us were missing. I felt like a crumb when I watched them walk away.

My phone was ringing when I returned to my kitchen. I answered only to hear an agitated voice yelling, "Stop that. I said stop that! Oh no! How could this have happened?" The connection went dead.

"Hello?" I checked the caller ID — Mindy Greene, Roscoe's new wife. I hit the button that redialed the number.

Busy. Due to the wedding, Roscoe had given me a free hand in setting up his picnic. Mindy had been busy in Ireland, so I hadn't spent much time with her yet.

It was going to be a long day. I walked Daisy and tried calling Roscoe. When he didn't answer, I left a message.

Hurrying, since I didn't know what was up over at Roscoe's house, and I figured I should get over there, I showered and slipped into a loose-fitting, coral-colored sundress. I pinned my hair up with a clip and skipped makeup altogether. If I was out in the heat most of the day, it would only slide down my face and give me dreadful raccoon eyes. But that reminded me to wear a hat. A coral hat with an extra broad brim matched my dress nicely. I skipped sandals and went for turquoise Keds, not elegant, but practical for someone who would be on the run all day. I clipped on heart-shaped earrings that had been a gift from my ex-husband, and I was out the door.

Just then, Wolf's car eased into a parking spot in front of Nina's house. We had met almost four years ago, on Thanksgiving weekend. It had taken us a while to date, but we had been an item for about three years. Wolf's irregular hours as a homicide investigator with the Alexandria Police Department and my late hours as an event planner hadn't made it easy to get together. Much of the time our dates consisted of late-night dinners relaxing at my house after work.

He stepped out and whistled at me appreciatively.

I whistled back, jealous that silver hair looked so handsome on men. It gleamed in the sunlight, accenting his temples in the perfect places, as though a beautician had done it. Our efforts to eat healthy from the vegetable garden we had planted were paying off, too. He'd definitely shed some pounds.

"Where are you off to?" he asked.

"Roscoe Greene's picnic. Want to come?"

"Is that today?" He planted a delicious

27

kiss on me.

"You'd enjoy it. He always has a fabulous ice cream bar, and I believe we're allowed one scoop today, aren't we?" I hoped so.

"Ice cream — yes!" Wolf closed an eye and squinched up one side of his face like Popeye. "Roscoe — not so much. I used to go to his picnics. Not interested."

Nina appeared at her front door. Dressed in turquoise cropped pants and a matching top, she looked ready for the beach.

"Actually," said Wolf, "I'm here to see Nina."

She sashayed over to us. "You've finally come to your senses, and it's me you want?"

"Shh. Not in front of Sophie!" he teased.

I left them to their business and walked four blocks to my parked car, wishing, as I did in the winter, that I had a garage. Off-street parking was a precious commodity in Old Town Alexandria. The sun beat on my shoulders, and the pavement reflected the heat. Bake and broil, I thought, glad that I had opted for a light dress and a hat.

Roscoe's Colonial Revival house was quint-essential Americana. Three stories high, with dormer windows in the third floor attic, it was perfectly symmetrical. Gleaming black shutters accented windows in white walls of wood siding. A perfect lawn of lush grass sprawled in the front, not a single dandelion in sight. An old oak tree offered relief from the sun. A walk of herringbone-patterned bricks led to a porch that ran along the entire front of the house and around to the sides. Black rocking chairs beckoned. I felt as though lemonade might magically appear if I sat in one of them. An American flag fluttered gently by the steps to the porch.

Leaving room for vendors in the driveway, I parked on the street. A powerful smell hit me the second I stepped out of my car.

CHAPTER THREE

Dear Natasha,
We have a vacation home that we try to keep low maintenance. It's folly to leave nets or equipment outside when we're not there because they blow away. What outdoor game can we erect in the yard that doesn't have to be removed and the whole family can play?
— Hubby Checkers in Lawndale, Pennsylvania

Dear Hubby,
Install a permanent game board in the grass. Make sixty-four concrete pavers about two feet square each. Paint them two colors and arrange in a checkerboard pattern. Or get the kids involved and make a large version of your favorite family board game. Buy large inflatable dice and have fun!
— Natasha

I had grown up in a small town in the Virginia countryside, and I knew that stench well — manure. More specifically, cow manure.

I rang the bell at the front door. It swung open. The housekeeper, Violet, scowled at me. Then again, I'd never seen her with any other expression. As usual, she didn't say a word. I'd been arranging the picnic for years and she had yet to utter anything to me. She shut the door behind me and walked away. On the left, oak stairs led to a second floor. A simple pine chest of three drawers stood against the right wall. A large painting of dogs hunting quail hung over top of it. Huge purple gladiolas stole the show in a majestic bunch on top of the chest. Was I supposed to follow Violet or wait there? I hurried after her, through a family room. She opened a door to the back garden and stared at me with cold black eyes. Was she just putting me outside?

I stepped out onto the flagstone terrace, where I found Roscoe and Mindy, wrapped in matching fluffy white bathrobes. Mindy's thin lips formed an angry slash in her pasty face. Bone thin, she wasn't as young as everyone described her. In her forties, probably. Her platinum hair flipped up at the ends, reminiscent of a popular 1960s style.

Pale skin suggested she avoided the sun at all costs. Not a single wrinkle marred her face. Either avoiding the sun helped more than I thought or she'd been Botoxed.

There had been no lack of scandalous gossip about Mindy's dogged pursuit of Roscoe. The classic case of an employee who set her sights on her married boss. Stealthy as a thief in the night, Mindy had spent a few years working her way into the coveted position of Roscoe's assistant. Her next promotion came with a wedding ring.

Roscoe sported an ample girth that led me to suspect he liked the fried chicken he served at his picnics. His hair had thinned, exposing the top of his head, but the additional pounds filled out the wrinkles on his pleasantly round face. For the first time since I'd known him, his normally ruddy complexion looked sallow and unhealthy.

"This is a fine mess!" he said, gesturing at his garden.

The garden was remarkable. Beds of colorful flowers surrounded a plush green lawn almost big enough for a baseball game. Towering trees lined both sides of the property, blocking any view of neighbors. At the opposite end, the grass gave way to a stone path that meandered to a pond. Tall trees clustered behind it like a magical forest. But the stench was awful.

"What happened?"

"We were still fast asleep when Violet came upstairs and told us the gardeners were here. Didn't think a thing about it." He held out a sheet of paper.

I glanced at it. A bill for manure, ordered by none other than Mindy Greene.

"I am horrified," she spat. "My first party as your loving wife and" — she stopped her rant and pointed at me — "this is your fault."

My fault? Okay . . . *I* didn't order the manure, and I wasn't present when it was delivered. She needed someone to blame, and I happened to be handy.

"Now, honeybunch, don't blame Sophie. By the time we got up and realized what they were doing, they'd spread it all through the garden," said Roscoe. "But Mindy called a mulch company, and they're coming right out. I figure dumping mulch on top of the manure will help tamp down the smell."

"You managed to get a mulch company to deliver and spread on a Sunday?" I asked.

For a moment, I thought Mindy had stopped breathing. "They had better show up. That's all I can say. And by the way, I did *not* order that manure. Roscoe! Why don't you believe me? It had to be Violet or

Olive. They'd love to spoil this party to make me look bad."

I sought to soothe her. "The mulch seems like a good idea. Which way does the breeze blow in the afternoon? Maybe we could set up big fans."

Mindy stared daggers at me.

What did she expect me to do? Dig it all up?

"We could move the party over near the guest house."

"Ugh! Absolutely not! That place is unusable as it is."

"That was my ex-wife's retreat," said Roscoe. "I told Mindy it's all hers now, but she refuses to go in there. She says she can't use it unless it's completely redecorated."

"You have two choices. Cancel the party, or move the party. It's late to do either, but we could try. It's your decision."

"We'll have the party here. The smell's not that bad. It reminds me of my grandparents' farm." Roscoe wrapped one arm around Mindy and hugged her to him.

"Should I follow up with the mulch company?" I asked.

"No!" Mindy cried out, appalled at my offer. "I'll handle that."

The door to the house opened, and Harry Jenkins, always on time with event equipment like tents and chairs, vaulted out onto the terrace. I could only imagine that Violet had given him the same heartwarming treatment I had received on arrival.

"Sophie! Thank goodness. Who is that witch who answered the door?"

"You see, Roscoe," said Mindy, "I am not the only one who finds her creepy."

I walked around the house to the front with Harry, glad he'd brought the tables and chairs so we could get set up. After a great deal of huffing and pouting from Mindy, Harry's men unloaded the picnic tables along the side of the house, underneath a gorgeous row of arching trees. I hoped we wouldn't be moving the tables.

The day wore on, and with each passing hour, the heat and the stench grew. One of my suppliers offered to send over five huge outdoor fans, but Roscoe declined them, saying he would rather smell something real than have the view of his gorgeous gardens blocked by big blue boxes. It was his party.

At two thirty, the tables had been draped with traditional blue and white checked picnic tablecloths. The caterers had taken over the kitchen, and they yammered at me about Violet presiding over their every move, threatening them silently with her scowl.

Matt Godadski, also known as the Barbecue Prince among event-planning circles, leaned toward me to kiss me on the cheek and whispered, "The new wife is a nightmare. You should have seen the fight over the ice cream bar. The princess wanted a crepe station. At a picnic? Not to mention that the ice cream bar is a tradition."

I was on the side porch when I heard rumbling. Matt burst from the kitchen in a panic. We ran down the stairs and around to the backyard.

Two huge dump trucks, one on each side of the yard, emptied their contents unceremoniously on the lawn, just missing beds of giant Shasta daisies.

Mindy ran to the one on the left, her screams not quite drowned out by the noisy engines.

In a remarkably calm voice, Matt said, "I'm moving the buffet to the side of the house and the ice cream sundaes and watermelon to the porch. I will *not* serve people back there where it stinks."

He walked off, and I didn't bother stopping him. I was in full agreement.

Just before four o'clock, the musicians I had hired strolled onto the grass strumming their guitars. The trucks drove out, and notes of "Sweet Caroline" reached me as the drone of the engines diminished.

Mindy stomped toward me ready to start World War III. "They're not spreading the mulch! They said they can come back in the morning. I told them not to bother ever showing their faces around here again." She folded her arms across her chest. "I swear we're moving. I can't put up with this rotten old house and this park of a backyard. We're moving, and that's that. I cannot entertain here. I thought if I paved it over with concrete and put in a swimming pool that it would be . . . tolerable. But this is the last straw."

That was Roscoe's problem, not mine.

The face painter and the magician arrived. A team of kid's party game pros set up croquet and sack races on the front lawn, and waitresses began to circle with trays of icy drinks. I relaxed a little bit. The odor was the only real problem, and Mindy had no one to blame but herself, even if she did try to blame me for it. I hoped the wind would shift.

It didn't. My ex-husband, Mars, showed up with Natasha. He looked terrific in shorts and a black cotton polo shirt with tiny red and white stripes and the Dior bee logo. I knew he still ran every morning, because I saw him jogging by my house with

Daisy on the weeks he had custody of her. I'd been avoiding him since we shared a romantic moment that left me shocked to my core. I'd been so sure everything was over between us. I was perfectly happy dating Wolf, and I knew I didn't want to be the other woman with my ex-husband! The mere thought was enough to send me over the brink — even if he hadn't married Natasha yet. She had done everything possible to put a ring on her finger, but Mars had managed to dodge her. They continued to live together, though, so as far as I was concerned — they were a couple.

"Is that cow dung?" he asked.

"I'm afraid so."

"I haven't smelled anything that bad in years. Can't you do anything about it?" Natasha's robin's-egg-blue dress skimmed her perfect shape. I had managed to break two nails setting up the party, but hers shone like she had just come from having them done. She wore a matching blue hat with a brim that curled up at the edges to reveal a white side underneath. Natasha and I had grown up together, competing at everything, except the beauty pageants she adored. We both wrote newspaper advice columns on domestic matters, which irritated Natasha, since we had different styles.

I couldn't help tweaking her. "We're asking everyone to pitch in and shovel mulch over it. You don't mind, do you?"

She stared at me in horror.

At that precise moment, a towheaded little boy who looked like a blue-eyed angel ran by chanting "Poop, poop, poop!" and swiped his dirty hand on Natasha's silk dress.

She stood stock still except for her trembling hands. "Mars, take me home to change clothes." She swung around and marched out.

Mars sighed. "We'll be back."

I followed them out to the front porch, pleased to see that the rest of the party was in full swing and going well. Francie and Nina walked up the steps. A blue cotton jacket topped Francie's long dress, a floral print the colors of the ocean. She wore anklet socks that revealed just an inch or so of her bare legs, and chunky white running shoes.

"I thought you weren't coming!"

She leaned toward me and whispered, "What kind of friend would I be if I didn't spy and report back to Olive?"

She must have noticed me looking at her shoes because she said, "I have to be able to sneak around!"

Roscoe rushed up and held out his arms.

"Francine Vanderhoosen! Darlin', you have made my day by coming. You don't have to be a stranger. I didn't divorce you, you know!" He embraced her, but I could see her mouth twist to the side. She halfheartedly patted his back.

"Mindy!" he bellowed.

She sidled up to us.

"Honey," said Roscoe, "this here is Francie, one of Olive's and my best friends."

The mention of Olive's name wiped a pretend smile off Mindy's face. She maintained her composure, but there was no mistaking the frostiness in her tone when she greeted Francie.

"Y'all come on in," said Roscoe. He waggled a finger in front of Francie's nose. "I've got somethin' to show you that'll turn you plumb green." Roscoe motioned them inside. We wedged through the throng of people and followed him into the foyer.

A waiter passed by with a tray of drinks. "Which one's the sweet tea?" asked Roscoe.

The waiter politely pointed at different colored drinks in highball glasses. "Sweet tea, lemonade, Arnold Palmers."

Roscoe plucked a glass of tea off the tray and cocked his head at us. I went for an Arnold Palmer, a refreshing blend of half tea and half lemonade.

We followed Roscoe to the left, through a sprawling but comfortable living room furnished with a mix of 1970s furniture and stark antiques with simple lines. He showed us into his den and barked, "Audie! How many times do I have to tell you that you'll get that desk and everything that goes with it soon enough?"

Roscoe's son, Audie, didn't seem upset by Roscoe's outburst. I'd seen Audie at a lot of chic Old Town functions, but if I hadn't known who he was, the similarity between him and Roscoe would have told me they were related. Comfortably midforties, Audie looked like a slimmer version of Roscoe with a little bit more hair.

Cricket, Roscoe's assistant and Audie's fiancée, who would have been perfectly at home on Hugh Hefner's arm, sat on the desk, her legs crossed seductively. She had a figure like a Barbie doll and waves of cascading copper tresses. Audie waved a hand at his dad and led her out a back door.

Roscoe shook his head at his son. "Well, Francie? Do you see it?"

I gazed around.

Old paneling lined the walls, giving the room a dark feeling — cozy in winter yet a welcome, cool respite from the blistering sun of summer. The scent of burned wood

41

lingered from the brick fireplace. Bookshelves covered one entire wall. Duck decoys and statuettes of hunting dogs dotted the shelves between books.

Tan leather furniture looked to be soft and cushy from years of use. Outside the window, next to a mini meadow of daisies, Audie wrapped an arm around Cricket.

"Soph?" Nina's voice held a tinge of impatience.

"Sorry. I was admiring your garden."

Roscoe sipped from his tall glass of iced tea. "That was my Olive's pride and joy. She lived for that garden and it still shows. People tease about having a green thumb — I swear that woman has green fingers and toes. She never did meet a plant that wouldn't grow for her. Now ladies, not a one of you sees it? You know, they say the best place to hide something is right out in the open."

CHAPTER FOUR

Dear Natasha,
I would love to have a gazebo, but my funds don't stretch that far. What can I do as a focal point in the middle of my garden?
— Hostess in Willow Springs, Missouri

Dear Hostess,
Build an outdoor floor out of treated lumber. It should be large enough to accommodate an umbrella table and chairs. Paint a rug on the floor, and make some bright cushions for the chairs. Place a potted spiral topiary on each corner. Voilà! An elegant outdoor space!
— Natasha

"Roscoe!" Francie spoke his name softly. "It's the Havell. The mallard Havell!" She shuffled closer to the bookshelf and focused on a print of ducks in a simple gold frame about three feet wide and two feet tall. Two male ducks with the hallmark emerald green heads of mallards and two plain female mallards were depicted in a marsh-type setting. At the very bottom, the words *Mallard Duck* were printed in a scroll font.

I looked over at Nina, who shrugged.

"Does Olive know about this?" Francie's tone had become harsh and accusatory.

Roscoe laughed heartily and placed a hefty arm around Francie's tiny shoulders. "You're a good friend, Francie. You bet Olive knows about it. After the divorce, she bought herself a new house, and I bought myself four ducks."

Francie snorted her disapproval.

"Roscoe." The voice was low and clear. Not demanding or insistent. Simply there.

I turned and found Violet in the room with us. I hadn't heard her enter, and calling his name was the first time I'd ever heard her speak. She stood by the door, her mouth set in an angry slash of a line, her dark eyes blazing with a fury that I hadn't heard in her voice. Hair the color of coffee grounds was pulled back into a tight bun.

Roscoe nodded. "Excuse me, folks. Y'all go on out and help yourself to our finger-lickin' chicken."

When Roscoe headed for the door, Francie spoke up. "You're not going to leave the mallards unguarded with all these people roaming around, are you?"

Roscoe gazed fondly at his print. "It's a little bit big to stick in a purse or under a coat. Good to see you, Francie. Don't be a stranger." He walked by me and paused for a nanosecond. "I'd like to talk with you privately. How about lunch day after tomorrow at noon?"

He didn't wait for an answer and walked out the door in a rush. Violet flicked a disapproving look over me and Nina before turning and following him.

His failure to wait for my response didn't bother me. He probably needed to set up another event.

"Was it just me, or did that woman remind you of Mrs. Danvers?" asked Nina.

I smiled at her apt reference to the dour and sinister housekeeper in *Rebecca*. Just like Mrs. Danvers, Violet lurked about, casting her critical gaze on people. With one glance she reduced them to insecure children about to be scolded.

"That's just Violet. She's been with Roscoe for ages." Francie took a close look at the print again and sighed. "You can bet *I* wouldn't leave something like that out for anyone to take."

"At the risk of seeming supremely stupid, what's the big deal about the mallard print?" I asked.

Francie clucked at me. "I suppose you don't know, either?" she asked Nina.

"It's just an old print of some ducks."

"It's a two-hundred-year-old hand-colored engraving of an Audubon — worth roughly one hundred thousand dollars. Possibly a bit more. It's in excellent condition."

"I knew Roscoe had money, but that's twenty-five thousand dollars a duck!" Nina marched up to the print and peered at it.

Francie scratched her head. "I always liked Roscoe. In spite of his wealth, he's so down to earth. An everyman's man. Did you know that each office in his headquarters is the same? The corner rooms with extra windows are conference rooms, lunchrooms, things like that, which everyone uses. He and Olive could have moved to a fancy place, but they stayed right here, in the house Roscoe's parents bought before he was born."

"Like throwing a low-key picnic for families instead of a formal event at night," I murmured.

"Exactly. It was a huge disappointment when Roscoe dumped Olive for that minx Mindy." Francie's tone emphasized her bitterness.

I opened the door Audie had used earlier, and we stepped out onto the slate patio.

"Whoa!" Nina cupped her hand over her nose. "That's brutal."

"Manure." I sighed. How many times would I have to explain?

Francie smiled. "I think it's wonderful!"

"At a party?" I asked.

Her smile grew.

"Why do I think you might know something about this?"

"Me? Don't be silly."

In past years, the picnic had been held in the expansive garden. This year, only a few brave souls wandered out to the pond in the back.

Nina waved her hand in front of her face. "This is terrible. Where is everybody?"

We followed the sound of voices to the far side of the house. Matt had set up the buffet in the grass. Not an ideal location, but the breeze didn't seem to carry the stench to that part of the lot. Old oak trees offered shade, but I worried about what might drop onto the food.

The clang of a cowboy triangle dinner bell rang out, and the crowd turned to look at Roscoe and Mindy, who stood on the porch overlooking the side yard like they were the king and queen holding court.

"First, I want to thank you all for coming, and I apologize for the strong farmyard scent," said Roscoe. "I'm grateful to all my employees for another banner year, and I'm equally grateful for the friendship everyone here has extended to me. This picnic is always the biggest highlight of my year."

Mindy nudged him.

"Oh! I guess this year the picnic has to be the second highlight. Marrying Mindy takes first place."

Laughter rippled through the guests.

"Now, you know I'm not one for speech-making, but there's been a lot of speculation about my retirement. Audie there can't wait to move from heir apparent into my seat. But I want you to know that I'm not planning to retire just yet. I've got a new wife to support! However, I have been listening to my new sweetheart and Audie, who keep telling me it's time for me to take up golf and leave work behind."

I looked around at the faces. Audie focused on his dad expectantly.

"I bought a retirement home! Yup, and I want all of you to come visit with us. We won't be there full time yet, but I know you're all going to love it, and there's room for plenty of visitors."

Mindy's mouth dropped open. "Sweetheart! Did you buy the house in Palm Beach?"

"I did you one better, honeybunch. I bought us a five-hundred-acre bed-and-breakfast lodge in the best hunting and fishing wilderness in the mountains! We're headed there later this week."

Clearly not adept at hiding her initial reactions, Mindy looked as though she had taken a bite of a luscious éclair only to find glue inside. Her head bobbed with shock. She recovered quickly, forcing her thin lips into a smile as the crowd applauded and whistled.

An elbow poked me in the ribs. Nina stood beside me and cocked her head toward the woods in the back of the house.

A woman had dressed to blend with the dark greens and shadows of the trees. Oversized sunglasses and a dark straw hat concealed her face. If the sun hadn't reflected off a shiny belt buckle, I never would have seen her there.

"Think it's Olive spying on the party?" Olive generally avoided black-tie events and anything involving a crowd. The hat and sunglasses prevented me from identifying her, but I couldn't imagine that anyone else would want to linger on the fringes of the party.

Nina nudged me and whispered, "Look again."

Behind the royal purple spikes of a butterfly bush, I spotted a man dressed to blend in with the trees. His dark green T-shirt and trousers hid him well. Only his sandy hair gave him away.

"Not there!" hissed Nina.

How many people wanted to spy on Roscoe's picnic? My eyes breezed past the man in green and the woman in the hat until I picked up Nina's target.

Mona's colorful outfit almost blended with the huge blue and purple blossoms of a cluster of hydrangeas. "You don't think she's following us?" I asked.

Nina heaved a sigh. "It's a little peculiar that she happened to turn up here, don't you think?"

I thought exactly that. I knew she would turn out to be one of those dogged people.

When we were indulging in ice cream sundaes, mine sweet pink peppermint with heavenly fudge sauce, Nina ever so casually asked Francie, "So how is Olive?"

"She can't believe that business about the bed-and-breakfast. That was her dream, not Mindy's."

I grinned at Nina. Evidently it *was* Olive

whom we saw lurking in the woods behind the house. "That explains Mindy's horror. It's probably not the life for everyone."

After most of the guests departed, I took a little stroll through the gardens collecting trash. Why would anyone throw paper napkins on the lawn? I paid little attention to murmuring voices until I heard a sob. Through a cluster of bamboo, I could see into a private garden. Two white wicker chairs sat comfortably side by side, adorned with seat cushions that matched the blue delphiniums and hydrangea behind them. Although Roscoe never served alcohol at his picnics, a pitcher and drinks that looked suspiciously like mint juleps dominated a white table spread with a Battenburg lace cloth. An ice cream sundae melted next to a slice of watermelon. I imagined Olive had spent many happy hours there. She probably never dreamed that she might someday find her son there — with his arms around Mindy, his new stepmother. Yet I could swear that's what I was seeing.

Waves of guilt pelted me for spying. Whatever was going on was none of my business. Feeling like I'd seen something I shouldn't have, I lowered my head and tiptoed away.

■ ■ ■ ■

I took a long, hot shower that night to wash the dreadful stench out of my hair. Poor Roscoe and Mindy would have to live with the smell. It was after midnight when I wandered out to my own garden wearing flip-flops and an oversized T-shirt that came to my knees. I carried a cool, refreshing lemon drop to drink and had Mochie on a leash. At the table where Nina and I had sat in the morning, I relaxed with my feet up and watched Mochie sniff nighttime delights. He pawed at fireflies while Daisy explored and I basked in a balmy summertime-and-the-livin'-is-easy atmosphere. The manure nightmare was over, and except for lunch with Roscoe, I had two blissful weeks of nothing to do. I drank in the scent of lavender.

But my thoughts kept veering to all the little tasks that needed to be done. I could finally tackle the renovation of my bathrooms. No! I deserved a couple of weeks of lounging. No major projects. No drudge work. I would take in a movie. Even better, maybe a play. I could finally spend some quality time with Wolf. We could take some short trips to the mountains or the beach. It seemed like Wolf and I were always in a hurry. Being too busy for each other had led to the eventual demise of my marriage to Mars. I wasn't going to let another relationship go down that path.

Every time we sat out here, Wolf spoke wistfully of an old Blaze climbing rose in his yard that had died. Now that I was a lady of leisure, I thought it would be a nice gesture to surprise him by planting one where his had died. That wasn't a big project. It would only take a couple of hours and would give me pleasure to boot.

I woke early, earlier than I wanted, to someone pounding the brass knocker on my front door. I forced one eye open and looked at the clock. Six? I was on vacation. I rolled over, but the pounding continued.

With great reluctance, I slung on a thin cotton bathrobe and stumbled down the steps. I opened the door to find Leon, Natasha's assistant, in the street, waving his arms. Ever since he showed up at my Halloween party dressed as Frodo, the hobbit, I had trouble seeing him as anything else. Leon loved food almost as much he loved gossip. Unfortunately, he wasn't particularly good at hiding his emotions. His expressive face told all. Like a kindly hobbit, he would give away his last bit of food to a hungry child or dog.

Chubby Leon looked over at me and ran back to my stoop, panting heavily. "I had nothing to do with this. I didn't even know about it until five minutes ago. Change clothes and do your hair. Now!"

CHAPTER FIVE

Dear Sophie,
My garage faces the street and is painfully prominent. There's little room for plants along the driveway. How can I dress it up?
— Hopeless Garage in Morning Glory,
Kentucky

Dear Hopeless Garage,
Buy a bench and paint it an eye-catching color. Place it near the garage, and surround it with colorful potted plants like geraniums. If there's room, stick a trellis in a pot along the front of your garage and plant a mandevilla. People won't be seeing the garage anymore.
— Sophie

The words had barely left his mouth when Leon shrieked. "They're here! How do I look?"

The rumbling of a large engine drowned his words. An eighteen-wheeler truck rolled toward us, overwhelming the narrow old street. It stopped before my house, blocking early traffic. Green and blue covered the side of the truck in an abstract version of grass and sky. Brightly colored flowers and leafy trees formed a frame for the words *"Tear It up with Troy!"*

Nina ran across the street to me, and Francie joined us from next door. Of course, this was the one time Nina wasn't wearing one of her elegant silk bathrobes. I didn't even know she owned green yoga pants, much less ones that were so unbecoming and appeared to have been partly shredded by a cat. Her boxy shirt didn't do much for her, either. Her hair bushed out to the side in a bad case of bed head. Francie was no better. I hadn't seen a housedress like Francie's since I was a child. From the looks of it, she might have worn it when I was a child. She wore kneesocks and shabby bedroom slippers on her feet.

Troy, whom I recognized from his popular TV show, bounded out of the truck. The person who coined the phrase *tall, dark, and handsome* must have meant this guy. Athletically slender, he wore an intentional scruffy shadow of a beard. He pushed back masses of tousled coal black hair, revealing the deepest blue eyes I had ever seen.

Spellbound, Nina, Francie, and I stared in silence. He flashed us an easy smile.

I spluttered, "Tha, tha . . ."

Nina gently smacked me without taking her eyes off of him. "She, she, um, she . . ."

"Hubba, hubba!" said Francie. "If I were ten years younger . . ."

Thankfully, Leon hadn't lost his ability to speak. He trotted to Troy and squeaked, "You're him! I mean, he's you! I mean . . . Well, I'm just your biggest fan. I can't believe you're here!"

Troy turned his dazzling smile on Leon. "Troy Garner." He extended his hand. "It's a pleasure to meet you."

Leon pumped Troy's hand. "Stay here. Right here. I have to get my camera. You'll take a picture with me, won't you?"

"Sure thing. Do you know Sophie Bauer?"

Leon aimed his forefinger at me.

Troy slapped him on the shoulder. "Thanks!"

Nina gripped my arm. The closer Troy came, the tighter her fingers clenched. His stunning smile paralyzed us like deer in headlights.

"Which one of you lovely ladies is Sophie Bauer?"

Francie giggled and offered the back of her hand as though she expected him to kiss it.

He did. "It's a pleasure to meet you, Sophie. I understand you need a garage!"

"Yes. Yes, I do!" said Francie.

At that moment Natasha made her grand entrance, dashing across the street and fluttering into our midst, ending our besotted daze. Unlike Nina and Francie, Natasha was camera ready, her hair coiffed and her face perfect in what I suspected was full TV makeup. She wore a tailored white dress, complete with pantyhose and five-inch heels. "Francie! What do you think you're doing? Cut! Cut! That's not Sophie."

Cut? I'd been so mesmerized by Troy's blinding good looks that I hadn't even noticed two guys with cameras.

Natasha stopped just short of pushing Francie out of the way. She flicked her hands at her, like she might at a rabbit in her garden.

In spite of Natasha's agitation, Troy kept his cool. "You must be Natasha."

She flipped her black hair over her shoulder and coquettishly touched the silver choker that lay on her neck. Her long, slender legs posed in an ever-self-conscious beauty queen position. She reached both of her hands out to him.

Troy never missed a beat. Evidently used to hugging strange women, he embraced her.

When she released him and patted her hair, Natasha said, "*This* is Sophie."

Troy blinked at me for one second, then shook my hand and introduced himself. "I hear you need a garage."

I wasn't sure how to answer that. I didn't have a garage, but I had seen his show. *Tear It Up* was exactly what he did.

Natasha called, "Cut! Cut!" She tilted her head like a confused puppy. "You're supposed to act happy, Sophie." She sighed and turned her attention to Troy. "Are people always this clueless?"

I glared at Natasha before directing my attention to Troy. "Hold everything. I don't quite understand what's going on here."

Troy beamed like he thought I was the most charming woman in the world. *No wonder he had a TV show.* He wrapped an arm around my shoulder and bent his head to speak with me. "Sophie, sweetheart, we're going to rip out your backyard and give you the garage you so desperately need."

I scooted out of his grasp. "That's what I was afraid of. I like my garden."

"Sophie!" Natasha spoke as though she was scolding a child. "Don't be impolite."

Seizing the moment, I held out my hands, gesturing toward Natasha. "There you go. Tear up Natasha's yard."

Oh, the priceless mixture of astonishment and fury on her face!

"No!" she protested. "That wouldn't be fair to you. I already have a garage."

Troy's dazzling smile had disappeared. He looked up and down the street and cast an appraising eye over me. "I thought Natasha said you come home late at night because of your job and that you have to park blocks away and walk to your house alone."

Okay, that part was true.

Troy cocked his head in the direction of my house. "Let's look at this backyard of yours."

Leon opened the gate and mouthed at me, "I didn't know. I swear."

We trooped to the backyard.

"Did Natasha also say I was a little old lady?" I asked Troy.

"Yeah, something like that."

So that was why he thought Francie was me. The picture was becoming more clear. I eyed Natasha. *She had never said a word to me about my safety. There must be something in this for her.*

Troy studied my garden. The irises and my beloved peonies had long given way to cheerful daisies, bright sunflowers, rich blue delphiniums, and black-eyed Susans.

He chewed on his lower lip. "Lots of flower beds. Good foundation plantings. Vegetable garden. Cute and practical garden shed, but you don't have much in the way of outdoor living space. And you *do* need a garage, even if you're not the little old lady I expected."

I didn't want to be rude, so I tried to weasel out of the situation as politely as possible. "I'm very sorry if Natasha misled you. We could probably help you find someone more deserving of a yard makeover."

He nodded and made a little whistling sound. "What if we built you a fire pit?"

"I *have* a fire pit." True, it was the kind you buy ready-made and plop on a terrace, but it served my purpose.

"Um hmm." He cast an unappreciative eye at it. "Outdoor kitchen."

I laughed. "I have to give you credit for trying. In a few hours it will be hot and humid. Who would want to spend time cooking out here unless it was on the grill? I don't need an entire outdoor kitchen for that."

Natasha nudged me. "Could I speak to

you for just a moment?"

We walked a few feet away, and I braced myself.

"You're embarrassing me. You're supposed to be thrilled and excited. Nobody turns down a star like Troy!"

"I can't help it if you misrepresented the situation. I happen to like my backyard, and I'm not interested in having Troy and his troops dig it up with a bulldozer." I eyed her with suspicion.

She winked at Troy. Was she *flirting?* Had she finally given up all hope that Mars would marry her?

"Look, Sophie. You need a garage. You know you do. I cannot imagine why you would turn down a garage. It's a big yard. You have" — her lips bunched up like it pained her to say it — "this big double lot. The garage will only take up a little corner. And think how wonderful it will be not to have to carry groceries from your car in the rain."

She had a point. I hated to admit that, though. And I still didn't want my yard torn up.

Troy ambled over. "Excuse us, Natasha." He motioned to me, and we strolled toward my potting shed.

"What if I said I could give you a garage

and a fabulous outdoor living space you would love — without ripping out your flower beds. The only thing you would lose is that left back corner, which is mostly bushes anyway. Whadda ya' say?"

It was tempting. I felt guilty, though. Someone else probably needed a garage much more than me.

A truck thundered along the alley that ran behind my fence.

I looked up at Troy. "It's too late to change your plans, isn't it? I'm on the schedule, and everyone is already here, ready to work."

He grinned at me. A genuine grin, not the dazzling smile he used before. "Pretty much. They count on me talking people into it."

He was good at his job. "Has anyone ever turned you down?"

"Not yet. C'mon, you're getting a new garage!"

I didn't trust him. I wanted to, but I had seen the show, and I had a very bad feeling that his backhoe would run right over me if I tried to protect my beautiful plants.

Nina poked me from behind and whispered, "Are you nuts? You're the only person in the whole world who would turn this down. No nightmares with contractors who don't show for work and no having to find people to finish or fix what someone else started."

"What if I don't like what they do? What if they build something that looks like a gleaming steel tin can?"

Troy held up his palms. "I have the design guidelines for Old Town. They're fairly specific for these historic blocks. It will be a good change for us. We like to vary the shows, and I see this garage and backyard looking like they've been here as long as the house." He clapped my back. "Have a little faith in me."

I relented. After all, how bad could it be? Nina was right, at the very least I would get a garage out of it. "All right."

"Roll cameras!" shouted Natasha.

Troy quickly covered up his surprise at her audacity. Even if she had her own local show, it wasn't her business to direct Troy's show. I had a hunch we were in for some entertaining clashes.

After I signed a stack of papers we shot an opening for the show in which I pretended to be both surprised and delighted. I hoped I would be.

Troy asked Natasha to supervise the unloading of the bulldozer. As soon as she was out of earshot, he rolled his eyes. "Is she always like that?"

I had to laugh. "Oh, yeah."

He lowered his head as though thinking. "Okay. I need to come up with little tasks to keep her out of the way. Good to know."

The engine in the back stopped running. In the abrupt quiet, the sound of my gate slamming open had all the impact of a gun being fired. A man barged through and loped determinedly toward Troy. Natasha followed behind him, her heels slowing her progress as they caught in the grass and soil.

Although his face was stormy with anger, he was almost as good looking as Troy. Sandy hair fell into his forehead. When he pushed it back, he revealed green eyes that matched the color of his T-shirt and pants.

Nina yanked on my arm, her eyes wide.

I knew why Nina was surprised.

CHAPTER SIX

Dear Natasha,
I love pots of annuals because they're so practical. I'm bored with terra-cotta, though. I've tried painting it, but it never looks quite right. How can I dress up my pots?

— Crafter in Pansy, Ohio

Dear Crafter,
Break some dishes! Use tile snips to cut chipped dishes or tiles, and adhere them to your pots in bright mosaics. Add grout and you're done!

— Natasha

There was no doubt about it — this guy had been one of the party watchers in the woods at Roscoe's house.

Troy gestured toward him. "Ladies, this is Heath Blankenship, my number two man. If you need something and I'm not around, you just ask Heath."

Heath brightened up. "I aim to please. Which one of you is Sophie?"

I wiggled my fingers at him.

He acknowledged me by bobbing his head. "Pleased to meet ya."

Natasha finally caught up to him, her nostrils flaring with fury. She pushed her hair out of her face and glared at Heath. "Excuse me. Troy put *me* in charge of unloading the bulldozer."

Heath's long dimples disappeared when he turned an amused gaze on Natasha. "No problem, darlin'. You go right ahead and put the backhoe wherever you want."

Natasha sputtered. I couldn't recall having seen her speechless.

Watching Troy and Heath side by side was an interesting study in contrasts. Heath didn't have Troy's polish, nor, apparently, his deft touch for dealing with the public. Heath didn't sport an expensive haircut. In fact, he seemed a little bit scruffy. His face bore weathered creases surely brought on by too much time outdoors in the sun. Yet I had no doubt that his rugged I-just-chopped-the-wood appearance brought women to him like puppies chasing bacon.

Troy slung an arm around Natasha's shoulder. "You have to help me with Heath.

He can get a little bit testy, but he's a good guy." He walked her away from us and continued talking.

Heath looked heavenward, as though he'd seen Troy do this song and dance before. He flashed those dimples at us — "There's one at every shoot" — and headed in the direction of the backhoe.

Wolf strode into my backyard as Troy was steering Natasha toward the street. I suspected Troy used the dazzling smile on him. They nodded at each other.

"What's going on?" asked Wolf. "Should I be jealous?"

Nina snorted. "Any man would be a fool not to be worried about Troy. It's like having a Roman god walk into your life. And that other guy has a certain untamed charm. I bet he's the bad boy of the group."

Wolf pretended to be appalled. "I can't leave you alone for a second."

I wrapped an arm around his waist and laughed. "Only in our dreams. Troy must have loads of women running after him." Wolf might not be as young, slender, or drop-dead gorgeous as Troy, but he was a good guy, which was far more important to me.

"Is he the fellow who rips up people's yards?"

I wished he hadn't put it quite that way. "I'm afraid so."

He pointed at the climbing rose near the table where Nina and I had talked with Mona in the morning. "Just be sure they don't tear that one out."

"It should be safe. They're going to work on the other side of the yard."

"I stopped by to beg off dinner tomorrow. Meet me for lunch at The Laughing Hound instead?"

"Sorry, I have a meeting. How about dinner tonight at my house?"

"I thought you were taking some time off."

"I am, but Roscoe Greene wants to see me tomorrow."

Wolf's face grew stony. "What does Roscoe want now?"

I continued in our jolly vein. "Don't tell me you're jealous of him, too?"

"Stay away from him." Wolf wasn't joking.

"Don't be silly. He just got married. I'm sure he wants to talk about another event."

"Then turn him down."

Just past Wolf, I could see Nina, her expression showing the bewilderment I felt. "I gather you have some kind of issue with Roscoe?"

His hands balled into fists. "Isn't it enough

69

that I ask you not to get involved with the man?"

I thought about it and took a step back. "No, it's not enough. If you expect me to refuse to do business with someone, I want to know why. What's wrong with Roscoe?"

Wolf turned so red I was afraid he might have a coronary on the spot. Instead, he turned and walked toward the street. I watched as he disappeared along the side of my house, but I had no desire to run after him.

"That was weird," said Nina.

We returned to my kitchen, and I put on a pot of coffee. "Wolf never acts like that. Do you know any gossip about Roscoe?" Nina knew everything. If there were stories about Roscoe or his family, she would have heard.

"Nothing other than the new wife. I gather Olive was extremely put out about the divorce and Roscoe's relationship with Mindy."

"Surely that wouldn't bother Wolf."

Angry voices outside drew us to the kitchen door. Daisy, Nina, and I crept toward the backyard.

Someone shouted over the sound of the engine, and Natasha staggered through the gate in a panic. A backhoe crashed through my fence, knocking down a substantial portion of it. I grabbed Daisy's collar to keep her out of harm's way.

"Oh, this is going to be fun," said Nina.

"That's not nice. They just destroyed my fence!"

"Yeah, but look who he's after."

Natasha stumbled toward us, a bit disheveled in her effort to dodge the big machine.

Heath drove the backhoe, his grin revealing too much joy in scaring Natasha and ruining my fence.

I retreated to my kitchen, already ruing my decision. I was pouring coffee for Nina when Natasha barged in.

"Did you see that? The nerve of that man! He's a menace!" Natasha patted her hair in place with trembling hands. "I don't know what they're so upset about. Honestly, I think men are intimidated by me."

She paused at the kitchen sink, gathering her composure. When she turned around, the old, confident Natasha was back as though nothing had happened. "Sophie, you're not allowed to see your backyard unless they ask you." She opened my cabinets and pawed through dishes, selecting some. "I'm supposed to keep you from looking. We're going to do all kinds of projects."

So much for a relaxing week off. Appar-

71

ently, she had never watched Troy's show. The owners were periodically taped showing their dismay over the wreck in their yards. "What are you doing with my dishes? Are you feeding the guys?"

"We should do that! How thoughtful of you to make coffee for them. The plates are for our first project. Your terra-cotta pots are so drab. We're going to dress them up by breaking plates and adorning them with the pieces. Some of these are very colorful."

I whisked my dishes away from her. "Not with these plates, you're not! Besides, you're in luck this morning, Natasha. I have plans, so you can help Troy instead of watching me."

"That's sweet of you. I'd much rather be outside helping Troy. Maybe we can dress up your pots another day?"

My job for the next week became clear. Troy would invent tasks for Natasha, and I had to invent reasons to send her back outside to him.

Ordinarily, I would have whipped up breakfast, but I had no desire to linger out of fear that Troy would turn the tables on me again. I popped yogurt, blueberries, and bananas into a tall jar and used my immersion blender to puree it into summery fruit smoothies. I poured one for each of us, making sure Natasha stayed in the house for a bit so that Troy wouldn't realize what I had done to him too soon.

I whispered to Nina to keep Natasha busy, took the stairs two at a time, and changed into gardening clothes — khaki skorts, a sleeveless pink top, leather deck shoes, and a straw hat — as fast as I could.

Tiptoeing, I dared to sneak into a back bedroom and peek out the window. I slapped a hand over my mouth to stifle a shriek. My entire back fence had been knocked down. Ugly bulldozer tracks churned up the lush green grass. My potting shed had been lifted from its base and now rested at an odd tilt far too close to my house.

It took all the strength I had to resist the temptation to run outside and stop them from any further destruction. I had made my bed, and now I would have to deal with whatever nightmare they created in my lovely, peaceful backyard. I was about to leave when I spotted an onlooker in the alley.

Mona peered into my yard. Her hair as perfect as the day before, she wore a short-sleeved yellow dress, but she had wised up and worn white running shoes. *The better to follow me with, eh? Not if I could help it.*

I grabbed a pair of small hoop earrings from my bedroom and put them on in the kitchen.

"Where are you going dressed like that?" asked Natasha. "You look like a young version of Francie! I really should go through your closet and help you weed out some of your homely clothes."

Nina giggled until Natasha said, "I could do the same for you. Those pants aren't even worth saving as dust rags."

Mochie had nestled on the window seat for his post-breakfast snooze. I filled a small bag with a few gardening items and clipped a leash to Daisy's collar. We left by the kitchen door, Natasha heading to the backyard while Nina and I went in the opposite direction. Nina crossed the street to her house, and Daisy and I turned the corner to the sidewalk that ran along my fence. We walked to the alley and came to a halt. I peered around the corner of the side fence and saw exactly what I had hoped for — the back of a woman in a yellow dress. Daisy and I sped across the opening of the alley. I looked back briefly to be sure Mona hadn't seen us. We were in luck.

We jogged down the block and looked back to check on Mona one more time. No sign of her. Hoping I'd managed to dodge

Mona, I tossed the bag in my car and took Daisy for her morning walk.

Just my luck, as we strolled by Café Olé, Wolf shoved open the door and stepped onto the sidewalk. There was no avoiding him. I tried to use a dazzling smile like Troy did, but I had a feeling it just looked goofy on me.

Wolf must have noticed because a twisted grin crossed his face, and he bent to kiss me on the cheek. "I'm sorry I was an ogre."

"Me, too." *Oops.* That wasn't exactly what I'd meant to say. "I mean I'm sorry we had a spat."

"Are you still going to meet with Roscoe?"

My breath caught in my throat. *Not again!* "I don't want to argue about this, Wolf."

"Can't you just trust me?"

"I trust you more than just about anyone I know. But it's not like I'm meeting a known drug dealer on a loading dock at midnight." I lowered my voice, in case anyone was listening to our conversation. "Roscoe is a respected member of the community."

"He's trouble, plain and simple." Daisy pawed at Wolf, and he rubbed her ears. "Is that good enough for you?" He didn't wait for an answer. Something behind me distracted him.

I turned around to see Cricket, the bombshell copper-haired woman who'd been seated on Roscoe's desk the day before, Audie's fiancée. She strode with confidence, her chin high, her long legs elegant. Men stopped to stare at her. She didn't return their gaze, but she tossed her hair as if she knew she was being admired. "Do you know her?"

He nodded. "Cricket Hatfield. We go way back. I haven't seen her in years."

"Way back? Like you dated her?"

He inhaled deeply and let out a slow breath. "It was a long time ago."

Why did my skorts feel tight? Why hadn't I worn makeup? I immediately scolded myself for being so insecure. Nevertheless, I turned my head and looked at her again. Nobody could compete with that. Either she'd had a lot of work done or nature had been stunningly kind to her.

Wolf still watched her. At least she'd distracted him from his anger about Roscoe. I wondered if he knew she was engaged to Roscoe's son. Oh! Maybe that was the source of the problem. He wouldn't have wanted to tell me if there had been some kind of argument over another woman. Maybe Wolf had a run-in with Audie, and Roscoe came to his son's aid.

I said good-bye and headed back toward my car.

In any event, I had no plans to cancel my meeting with Roscoe — no matter what Wolf said. Although my little vacation wasn't turning out quite the way I had envisioned, I had the day to myself, and I looked forward to leisurely browsing through the nursery and finding a rose for Wolf. It would be less nerve-racking for me if I wasn't home, watching as Troy hacked up my yard. Besides, while I didn't feel I needed to apologize to Wolf, I thought he would appreciate it.

Daisy jumped into the back of the car and we were off, feeling the freedom of summertime without any immediate obligations. On the outside chance that Mona had miraculously managed to follow us, I drove through Old Town in a roundabout way before I hit Duke Street, watching the cars behind me to be certain she hadn't followed us. The next time I saw her, I would have to turn the tables and tail her to her car so I would know what she was driving.

At the nursery, Daisy snuffled bark chips lining the grounds as we strolled through greenhouses that looked like there had been a run on plants. Nearly wiped out, they had tightened their supply of annuals into one greenhouse. Ribbons of color undulated as far as the eye could see. I strolled through but resisted the desire to buy. Troy would only tear it up.

In the rose corner of the nursery, I found exactly what I had in mind — a classic Blaze climbing rose. Bright red blossoms would bring some color back to Wolf's garden, and the plant wouldn't need much care.

I paid for the rosebush and placed it in the back of my car, crowding Daisy a little bit. I merged into traffic, Daisy standing in the back, panting near my shoulder as I drove toward Wolf's neighborhood. Heavily treed lots dominated the area. Most of the bungalows and colonials had been expanded over the years, making each house unique.

Wolf's Arts and Crafts–style home featured three stone steps leading up to the front door, which was flanked by two narrow windows. Fish scale shingles adorned the three gables in front, and cedar siding clad the rest of the house. A giant rhododendron that had bloomed purple in the spring hid the right front corner of his home. A sugar maple and azalea bushes blocked the view of the side yard on the left. The lawn was neatly mowed, and white-edged hostas thrived in the shade around the front steps.

I pulled into the driveway and let Daisy jump out of the car. Wolf was surely busy with work, so I could take my time planting, and the new rose would be a welcome surprise when he came home. I slung my bag over my shoulder and carried the rose to the rear of the yard, where the temperature was still bearable, thanks to the shade of towering yellow poplars. Although the grass had been neatly mowed, the gardens showed neglect. Wolf had dutifully dumped masses of mulch on them, but some plants had withered and died, while others seized the opportunity to grow out of control. A red trumpet vine had bunched over the top of a garden shed, and a wisteria had taken hold of a pear tree and climbed it like a trellis.

Bare branches of the deceased rosebush that Wolf had loved so much still stood in a bed in the very back of the yard near a trellis, with mulch heaped around it.

I set the new rose plant on a nearby bench, slid on my gloves, and grasped the old rosebush, hoping rotted roots would allow me to simply pull it out. No such luck. I grasped it closer to the base, chiding myself for wearing a sleeveless top. My arms would be scratched by the thorns. It still didn't give. I needed a shovel.

Daisy followed me to the shed covered by the trumpet vine. The door squawked when I opened it. I peered into the darkness, snakes on my mind. How long had it been since anyone had opened the door? My eyes adjusted to the lack of light, and I was surprised to find the little shed in fairly good order. I plucked a shovel from a corner that I could reach easily and hightailed it out of there.

But a movement to my left caught my eye. I froze in my tracks. A snake? I shivered at the thought. I held my breath and watched for any sign of life. A branch jiggled, and Daisy barked.

CHAPTER SEVEN

Dear Sophie,
I love colorful flowers. Each August, it seems like everything stops blooming. Is there a perennial that will provide color in that hot month?
— New Homeowner in Sage, Arkansas

Dear New Homeowner,
Try planting crepe myrtle. They come in a variety of bright colors and are very low-maintenance plants. They thrive on lots of sun and extended summer heat.
— Sophie

"Who's there?" The voice was gruff, but it sounded like a woman. Blue eyes peered at me from under the brim of a grungy yellow hat.

Thank goodness. It was only a neighbor, not a snake. "Sophie Winston."

"What are you doing in Wolf's yard?"

"I'm his girlfriend. I'm planting a rose bush."

The woman squinted at me before sliding on sunglasses and pushing past brush and overgrown viburnum. She wore a loose, long-sleeved shirt over golf shorts. Heavy lines cut through her face, and she sported a deep tan — Olive Greene, Roscoe's ex-wife. I didn't know her well. Olive avoided major social events, reportedly preferring the tranquility of her own garden. She had always made appearances at Roscoe's picnics, though.

She kneeled by Daisy. "Well, aren't you the sweetest thing? What's your name, sugar?"

"Daisy."

"My favorite dog name!" She laughed when Daisy licked her cheek. Still kneeling on the grass, she said, "Didn't you do some work for my husband?"

"I usually arrange his annual picnic."

"Oh, yes. Thank goodness you did that nonsense. I can't stand all that hullaballoo. Give me a quiet garden and a pretty puppy like Daisy any day over all that pretentious fraternizing. So you're Wolf's girlfriend, huh? You're either brave or stupid."

She took me by surprise, even though she wasn't the first person to make that sort of comment. What was I supposed to say? Thank you?

When I didn't respond, she said, "You *do* know about his wife, don't you? They say he murdered her."

A gossip. Just what I needed. I knew very well what *they* said, whoever they were. But I had dated Wolf long enough to know that he wouldn't kill anyone. Wolf didn't like to dwell on the subject of his wife, and I fully accepted his explanation — his wife simply left one day. It had happened more than four years ago and was old news by now. Wolf said he had searched for her in the beginning, but as time passed and he found no leads, he'd moved on with his life.

It happened. He wasn't the only person whose spouse had run away. Her unexplained disappearance had concerned me in the beginning, but Wolf had proven himself to be honest and gentle. Well, up until he got so huffy about Roscoe. But then, I had my moments of anger, too. Everyone did.

"If you knew Wolf, you would know that he didn't murder anyone."

She looked toward his house. "He's never home. He mows the grass religiously, but other than that, I never see him. Besides, as a homicide detective, he surely knows how to hide a body."

That was what the gossips always said.
Poor Wolf. It must eat at him to realize
people viewed him that way. Why did everyone look past the fact that he worked hard
and was a kind and decent man? I should
have controlled myself better, but I couldn't
help tweaking Olive a little bit. "I know how
to poison you with a plant in this yard, but
that doesn't mean I'm going to."

Her hat fell off when she threw her head
back and laughed. Without the hat, wiry salt
and pepper hair fell around her face.

"Touché! A lot of people have asked me
how I dared to buy a house next door to a
wife killer."

"Why did you?"

She picked up her hat and slapped it onto
her head. "I liked the lot. These deep
wooded grounds aren't easy to find around
here anymore." She stood up and stretched
before extending her hand. "Glad to meet
you, Sophie."

I slid off the gloves. "If I'm not mistaken,
you were at the chicken lickin' picnic
yesterday." I delicately omitted the fact that
she had watched from the woods.

She smiled demurely. "What an awful
name. *Mindy* has no taste whatsoever. What
did you think of my replacement?"

She'd said Mindy's name as though it

tasted bitter. Nothing like putting me on the spot. "I thought she was threatened by you."

Olive preened, evidently very pleased. "Was she? My presence as his wife certainly didn't deter her from putting her moves on Roscoe during our marriage. I don't know what's wrong with that man. You'd think an old coot like Roscoe would realize he'd been snagged by the worst sort of gold digger."

She tilted her head to look at my hands.

I held them out to show her. "No rings. No plans to marry. You'll have to come over sometime to get to know Wolf better."

She scratched Daisy behind the ears. "Mmm." Her mouth puckered as though the mere thought was sour. And then, as quickly as a cloud breezes past the sun, she was all smiles again. "I believe I'd like that," she said as she headed for the brush separating the properties.

Returning to the stubborn dead rosebush I needed to remove, I pulled on my gardening gloves and planted the shovel about eighteen inches away from the trunk. Giving it a good shove with my foot, the shovel slid into the deep mulch easily. I tilted it backward to loosen the soil. Moving the shovel over a bit, I repeated the procedure. The soil and mulch didn't pose a problem, but I didn't seem to be moving the dead roots of the plant. On the fifth stab into the ground, the shovel hit something hard — a rock, I presumed. I backed up a few inches and tried again to see if I could slide the shovel around the edge of the rock and come up under it to dislodge it. I put more pressure on the handle of the shovel, using it like a lever. The mulch shifted.

With renewed vigor, I slammed the shovel into the mulch, stepped on it, and pressed on the handle as a lever again to loosen the soil. Daisy helped by digging, flinging dirt underneath her.

Something gave way, and I fell back on the mulch.

Daisy continued her frenzied digging. I scrambled to my knees and crawled closer. "Stop, Daisy, stop!" I placed a hand on her coat, looking more closely at the dirt-encrusted corner of something . . . leather?

CHAPTER EIGHT

Dear Sophie,
I hate my garden! The previous owners never weeded. The weeds are just everywhere. What to do?
— Desperate in Weedville, Pennsylvania

Dear Desperate,
Cut the weeds so that they're relatively short. Place newspaper over them, about half an inch thick. Wet the newspapers thoroughly. Cover with mulch. You may have to repeat this for a few years to kill all the weeds.
— Sophie

I grabbed hold, and the object yielded slightly under the pressure of my grip. Clearing soil away, I kept pulling until the ground relinquished it. Clumps of dirt clung to a strap. I brushed it off. In spite of the dirt, I recognized the fob with a soil-encrusted logo. There was simply no question — I had dug up a woman's purse.

My heart pounded as I opened it. The bag was an expensive brand, made of good leather that lasted for years. In contrast to the outside, the interior was surprisingly clean. I reached in and removed a wallet. The plastic-encased driver's license inside left no doubt about the owner. "Anne Fleishman," I whispered. Wolf's wife.

A shiver shook through me. I closed my eyes and winced, wishing I could turn back time so that I would never have found it.

The implications flicked through my head like a kaleidoscope. No matter how the facts twisted and turned, the presence of Wolf's wife's handbag buried in the dirt had to mean she was dead. I couldn't think of a single innocent reason to bury her purse in the garden. My hands trembled. They held evidence that pointed to Wolf as Anne's killer.

I placed the bag on the grass, jumped up, tore off my gardening gloves, and threw them on the ground. I knew what I had to do. I knew *exactly* what I *should* do. But I didn't want to. Daisy bounding along next to me, I ran to my car for the cell phone I'd left inside it. My fingers shook so hard I had trouble pressing the digits to call Nina.

"I'm at Wolf's house, and I have a problem."

"Need a mediator for a lovers' spat?"

My voice broke. "A *big* problem."

"I'll be right there."

I walked back to the purse, wishing it would have vanished. If it had been a snake, it wouldn't have frightened me more. In a way, it was a snake. If I did what I should — if I turned it in to the police — that purse would bite Wolf. Just because I had never known Anne, and I loved Wolf didn't mean I should hide evidence to protect him. *Did it?*

I paced the contours of Wolf's backyard, fretting.

Maybe I was wrong. Maybe there was a very good reason for burying the purse in the garden. I'd been in shock and hadn't taken the time to think it through. I sucked in a deep breath. I needed iced tea to cool off. I could go buy some. But I couldn't take the purse with me. I would contaminate it. Could they get fingerprints off a purse? Off leather? Of course they could. They could take them off almost any surface. But Wolf's fingerprints wouldn't mean anything, after all, he'd been married to Anne. Husbands touched their wives' purses, didn't they? I felt certain Mars had held my bags for me, or handed them to me, or looked for keys in them.

But he had never buried one in the yard.

Why did her driver's license and wallet have to be in it? If they hadn't been in the purse, the bag would be almost meaningless. No one would know for certain to whom it belonged. But her IDs changed everything. If she was alive, she'd surely have taken them with her wherever she went. Wouldn't she?

I collapsed to the grass, far from the horrible handbag. Daisy licked my face, and in spite of the oppressive heat, I buried my face in her fur.

And that was how Nina found me.

She placed a gentle hand on my shoulder. "Soph? You okay?"

"No."

She extended her hand and helped me stand. I led her to the handbag. "It belongs to Wolf's wife. Her driver's license is inside."

Nina's eyes widened and horror spread over her face. The two of us stood over the handbag, looking down at it like it was a bomb. *It was!* It was a nightmare wrapped up in good leather.

"You opened it?"

"Of course."

"Do it again."

I pulled the gardening gloves on, reached

inside the bag, withdrew the wallet, and held it out to her.

Nina screamed. She slapped a hand over her mouth and whispered, "This can't be happening. I can't believe it. I was completely convinced that Wolf was innocent." She gasped and looked toward his house. "Where is he? What if he finds us here?"

"Relax. He's at work."

She took a deep breath. "What are you going to do?"

"I think *we* have to turn it in to the police."

"Yes. It would be wrong to re-bury it and pretend it never happened." She looked at me in all earnestness. "Right?"

"I don't *want* to turn it in!"

Nina held up her hands, palms toward me. She bit her upper lip. "Let's think this through. Are you willing to *ever* be alone with Wolf again now that you've found the purse?"

It was a valid question, no matter how much I hated hearing it. "Maybe." That was partly a lie. Alone with Wolf? I didn't know how I would react. I feared it would never be the same.

"When he kisses you — what will you be thinking?"

I frowned at her.

"When he wraps his arms around you for a hug, will you be afraid his hands might creep up to your neck and strangle you?"

"Stop that!"

"Well?" She wobbled her head around and gestured aimlessly. "I don't want Wolf to have killed his wife, either. Soph, we don't have the power to change his past. If he did it, then I don't want you going out with him anymore. And I don't want any other women to suffer his wife's fate."

My voice came out much smaller than I'd have liked. "I couldn't live with the guilt. But what if we're wrong?"

She opened her mouth and shut it again like a fish out of water.

"Turning the handbag over to the police doesn't mean we're accusing him of murder," I said.

"Right. *You're* not even suggesting that Wolf planted the purse there."

"Exactly. It just happened to be there."

"No one is making any accusations."

Daisy barked and we swung around to look at Wolf's house. Had he come home?

No. But Mona, who had invaded my yard only the day before, chugged toward us, her gait odd and unsteady. "I knew you would find her." She stared at the bag on the grass. "That's her purse," she cried. "I would know it anywhere!" She fell to her knees and hugged the handbag like it was her baby.

"No!" I screeched. "You're contaminating it. It doesn't belong to your daughter."

Mona held it at arm's length. "Yes, it does. She saved for this bag. Wolf thought it was too expensive, but I came through with a little cash. It's definitely her purse."

"Wolf?" The kaleidoscope in my head swirled again. I still held the wallet and looked at the driver's license photo again. Anne Fleishman had been very attractive, with rich cinnamon hair, and a frightening resemblance to Mona. I knew the answer, but I asked anyway. "I thought you said your daughter's name was Linda."

"I couldn't exactly tell you that I'm Wolf's mother-in-law, now, could I? I had to lie."

I stared at her kneeling on the ground with the handbag clutched to her breast. "What if I had agreed to look for her? I would have been chasing after someone who didn't exist."

Mona tightened her grip on the handbag. "I was going to wing it. The important thing was that you could get me inside Wolf's house to search around."

Her plan made no sense to me. Either she was delusional or, more likely, so desperate that she hadn't thought anything through.

"What's that? Anne's wallet?" Mona's eyes blazed with fury. She thrust her hand toward me. "Give it!"

Against my better judgment, I handed it over.

Mona whimpered and cried out like a wounded animal. "My baby! He killed my baby!"

Tucking the wallet inside the bag, Mona staggered to her feet. "He's not home. This is our chance to go inside and look for clues."

"I think we can officially scrap the business about no accusations," said Nina.

My heart sank. We were kidding ourselves to wish for even one moment that Wolf wouldn't become the prime suspect in his wife's disappearance. Once the handbag was in the hands of the police, everything would change. But I had no choice. Sometimes one had to do the right thing, even if it led to disastrous consequences.

I struggled to sort my mixed feelings. The last thing in the world that I wanted to do was hurt Wolf. Yet, if he'd killed his wife, the police had to know. This wasn't something that could be overlooked — the handbag was too incriminating. My feelings for Wolf were something *I* had to deal with.

They couldn't impact my actions, though I did wish I could have a redo of the entire rotten day. Who would have ever thought the notion of planting a rose in Wolf's backyard would lead to this?

"Sophie! Please. There's no telling when Wolf will return." Mona stumbled toward the house, still clutching Anne's handbag.

Chapter Nine

Dear Natasha,
I have a brand-new house and not even one blade of grass. I don't know where to start! Everything has to be done!
— Too Much to Do in Plantersville, Texas

Dear Too Much to Do,
Start with a plan. Draw a sketch of your property and plan your gardens. Begin with trees and foundation plantings. Layer other plants in, large to small. Use a color wheel to be sure you're planting complementary colors. Then sketch a three-dimensional view from all sides. It's crucial to do this for each of the four seasons. Now you're ready to dig!
— Natasha

I ran after Mona. "We're not going inside Wolf's house."

"We have to."

Nina caught up to us. "How would you like it if someone snooped around *your* house?"

Mona stopped walking. "How would you feel if you didn't know where your daughter was?"

I could understand Mona's motivation. If I were in her shoes, I would move heaven and earth to find any tiny bit of information that might lead to my daughter. But I wasn't about to let her into Wolf's house, even though I knew where the spare key was hidden. *If* Wolf had killed Anne, it would be highly unlikely that the murder weapon would be under the mattress all these years later. Besides, in the unlikely case that there was some sort of evidence in the house, if we entered, we might disturb it. "I'm sorry, Mona. Two things are clear to me. Whether I want to or not, I have to report the purse to the cops. And whether you like it or not, we are *not* going into Wolf's house to snoop."

She lifted her right hand to her forehead. "The heat. I feel dizzy."

Nina grabbed Mona's elbow and ushered her to Wolf's back deck, where she helped her sink onto a teak patio chair.

It *was* hot. No doubt about that. Yet I had a feeling Mona's dizzy spell had more to do with her desire to get inside Wolf's house.

She certainly hadn't loosened her grip on Anne's handbag.

"Do you need an ambulance?" I asked.

"Good gracious, no. A glass of iced tea and an air-conditioned room would do nicely."

My guess had been right on target. "If you'll give me your keys, I'd be happy to start up the air-conditioning in your car for you." Did that sound as mean as it felt?

Nina gaped at me like I'd lost my mind.

"She's faking! Can't you see that?"

The words were barely out of my mouth when Mona slid off the chair and collapsed in a heap on the deck. I dashed to her side. She still hadn't lost her talon hold on Anne's purse. I placed my finger over my lips in a signal to Nina to not speak. Nina gripped her head with her hands, like a mime who thought I had gone nuts. Sure enough, in a matter of seconds Mona opened one eye and looked up at us.

While Nina helped her into the chair again, I dialed Wolf's number on my phone. I might have to report the handbag to the police, but I could at least let him know about it so he wouldn't be blindsided. After all, the Wolf I knew wouldn't have murdered his wife. Couldn't have. Then why was doubt pounding at me like a jackhammer?

Although I hadn't intended to, I walked away from Mona when he answered. I just couldn't bring myself to tell him in front of her. "Wolf, we have a little problem. I brought over a rose to plant in your yard, and when I dug in your flower bed" — I paused, trying to read his reaction, which was silly, because he didn't say anything — "I found Anne's handbag."

He didn't speak for what seemed a very long time. When he did, it was terse. "I'll be right there."

Although I'd been out of earshot, Mona screamed at me. "Did you call Wolf? Are you insane? He'll leave. He'll skip town!"

If she was right, it would bring everything to a head immediately. I decided to give him half an hour. If he bolted, like Mona thought he would, thirty minutes wouldn't give him enough time to leave the metropolitan Washington, D.C., area. I supposed I had put him on notice, though. The minutes ticked by painfully.

He arrived ten minutes later. I hurried out to the driveway to warn him about Mona's presence.

He bent to plant a kiss on my cheek. "What's this about Anne?"

I explained what had happened.

"Where is the handbag?" he asked.

"Out back." Before I could tell him about Mona, he loped around the house.

I jogged after him. He stopped short when he saw Mona. I had to give him credit, though. He didn't fly off the handle or act angry.

"Hello, Mona," he said. "I didn't know you were in town. Is that the bag Sophie found?"

I couldn't help noticing that Wolf didn't seem perturbed by Mona's presence, but she glowered at him. He pulled out gloves and slipped them onto his hands. For a moment, I thought she might not give him the bag, but she relented.

He examined it thoroughly. I watched his expression for signs of panic. He appeared grim and deadly serious but said nothing until he set it on the table. "Show me where you found it."

We left Mona sitting on the deck, but Nina and Daisy crossed the expanse of lawn with us.

Wolf studied the hole in silence, then glanced at the dead rosebush, which lay on the grass, tipped over. Instead of expressing anger or annoyance or worry, his jaw tightened and he stared into the trees. His Adam's apple bobbed a couple of times, and I thought he might be choking back tears.

I wrapped an arm around his waist but he was stiff as a corpse toward me. He pulled out his phone, walked a few steps away, and made a call, explaining the situation briefly and ending with, "We'll wait for him."

Nina's wide eyes met mine. We'd been so worried about turning him in, and now it appeared he'd done that dirty work for us.

He took a deep breath. "You always think they'll come home." He bit his upper lip and winced. "After all this time, I still thought I would come home from work one day and find her on the porch with a frosty root beer in her hand. Then something like this happens, and it grabs you in the pit of your stomach, because you know it was just wishful thinking, and she's never coming back."

I wanted to be kind, to soothe him in some way, but instinct told me this wasn't the time, and I wasn't the right person.

Wolf walked away from us. He crossed the yard, his head bowed.

Nina peered at me with a questioning look. I shook my head at her. He deserved to deal with his grief privately.

His solitude didn't last long. Detective Kenner lunged around the side of the house, his long legs moving so fast that the uniformed cop with him had to run to keep

101

up. Wolf strode across the grass to meet them.

Kenner had made no secret of his romantic interest in me, but with his sour attitude, he ought to look for someone more like Roscoe's housekeeper, Violet. His sunken cheeks and weathered skin gave him a haggard appearance. As far as I could tell, he never slept. He seemed to turn up everywhere I went, which I found a bit disconcerting.

Mona miraculously recovered from her fainting spells and sped out to them.

When Nina and I reached them, Wolf was explaining that *the evidence* had been handled by Mona, Nina, and me.

"*Au contraire*, my friends," cried Nina. "*I* have not touched anything. And Sophie wore garden gloves when she handled it."

"I suppose your fingerprints are all over it?" Wolf asked Mona. For the first time since he arrived, I heard a tinge of anger in his tone.

She smiled pleasantly. "Of course. I had to find out if it was Anne's."

Kenner motioned to me. "Let's see where you found it."

For what seemed like the hundredth time, I crossed the lawn and told my short story.

Daisy trotted along with us, keeping a

sharp hound eye on Kenner. For some reason, she had never liked him. When we stopped at the site of the hole, she sat down and lifted her lip at him. She didn't growl, but her skin sagged loosely, so when she snarled, she made quite a frightening face.

Kenner took a step back, away from Daisy. "Did you call Mona?" he asked.

It had all happened so fast that I hadn't given Mona's fortuitous arrival much thought. "No. Now that you mention it, she just showed up."

"What did she do when she saw it?"

"She fell to her knees and clutched it to her like a baby."

"So she knew what it was right away?"

Why this line of questioning about Mona? I thought back. "Yes, she knew instantly . . . or she acted like she did. She looked inside it, of course, but she immediately recognized that it belonged to Anne."

Kenner wrote something on the back of a business card and handed it to me. "If you need anything, that's my cell number."

"Thanks." Kenner was the last person I would call, but it would hurt him to know that. I tucked his card into my pocket and started to walk back to the others.

Kenner caught my elbow, causing Daisy to growl at him. "Sophie, be careful."

That sent a new shudder along my arms. In spite of the heat, little goose bumps popped up.

Kenner conferred with the uniformed officer, who had bagged the purse. The words "Tape it from the bench all the way across the rear garden" hit me like a punch in the stomach.

Wolf had been so calm that I'd begun to think finding Anne's purse wasn't a big deal. But if they were cordoning off the back of Wolf's lot, it was the alarming development I had feared.

I wanted to apologize to Wolf, but my original concerns about his involvement in Anne's disappearance flooded back to me like a tidal wave, and I didn't know what to say or do. There wasn't any protocol that I knew of for a situation like this. "I guess I'll get going. You, too, Nina?" I asked. When I pulled my car keys out of my pocket, Kenner's business card fluttered to the ground.

Wolf picked it up, glanced at it, and handed it to me. "See you tonight."

I nodded. Though we'd planned to have dinner together at my house, after all this, it just seemed — odd.

Nina said good-bye and propelled me toward our cars. Daisy ran ahead of us and waited by my car to jump in.

"He's coming to your place tonight?" whispered Nina.

"It was already planned. Just dinner."

"I don't know what to think." Nina jiggled her keys nervously. "He could have done it. He's too calm. Just to be on the safe side, I'm coming to dinner, too."

"I appreciate your offer, and I love you to death for worrying, but maybe it would be a good time for me to feel him out. Do you know any of the details about Anne's disappearance?"

"No one does. No one I know anyway."

That was saying a lot. Nina had some impressive connections when it came to information.

She cocked her head at me. "I don't want anything to happen to you."

"Wolf has always been very kind. That's probably why I feel so torn. The Wolf I know couldn't have killed anyone, but that handbag . . ."

"If I weren't married and you weren't dating Wolf, I'd be dating him myself. I love the guy! There isn't one other man who swings by the shelter every single week to donate food for the animals. I never believed the idiotic rumors about him — but I can't imagine anyone except Wolf burying that purse under the rose bush like that."

CHAPTER TEN

Dear Sophie,

I plant a fabulous vegetable garden each summer. My mother-in-law keeps telling me to bury a fish under each tomato plant. I think she's pulling my leg. Please tell me it's a joke or some kind of kooky superstition.

— Dubious in Tomato, Arkansas

Dear Dubious,

Sorry to side with your mother-in-law, but this is a common practice. Dig a hole deep enough to bury the fish or fish head, and cover it with about one inch of soil. Plant the tomato over top of it. As the fish breaks down, nutrients are released that will feed your tomato plant.

— Sophie

"Soph, I'm not letting you be alone with Wolf."

Logic and emotion were colliding within me. I hugged Nina. "Thanks for looking out for me. I'll let you know what happens tonight."

Thanks to heavy tourist traffic, I parked five blocks from my house. During the walk home, I decided a garage wasn't such a bad idea after all. It would be a delicious luxury to be able to pull into my own garage and avoid the extra trek. I unlocked my front door, and Mochie strolled into the foyer. With typical cat composure, he yawned and stretched before circling my ankles to let me know he was glad I had returned. Normally, I would have ushered him into the kitchen, but today I couldn't wait to see what had happened in my backyard.

Daisy and Mochie accompanied me to the sunroom overlooking the back of my property. All the shrubs, trees, flower beds, and grass on the left side were gone. All of it. I kicked myself mentally. It wasn't as though I had never watched the show. *Tear It Up* was Troy's thing. He'd lied to me. What a surprise. He'd promised to build on the right side and yet they had dug a trench for footings that extended all the way to my house on the left. I tried to comfort myself with the notion that my angle wasn't the best, but if that became the slab for the garage, I could park four Hummers in it.

A noisy truck was pouring concrete, and Natasha appeared to be shouting instructions to everyone. She waved her arms wildly at the driver of the concrete truck, but from my vantage point, I could see that he was watching the hand signals of a very calm man who was part of the crew.

I returned to the kitchen, fed Mochie leftover chicken breast, and gave Daisy a dog cookie. Troy knocked on the kitchen door.

"Could you come out a minute?" I followed him to the backyard.

"What do you think?"

This time I was painfully aware of a camera filming us. I tried to keep my cool. "It's much larger than I expected. You *do* realize that I don't own four cars?"

He laughed. "Not to worry. It will be wonderful. Trust me."

I knew better than to trust anyone who could turn on the charm like Troy. "Didn't you say it would be on the right?"

"Sorry, last-minute change."

Last-minute? I didn't think so. I was willing to bet the plans he submitted to the town showed everything on the left. Did they lie on purpose to get a rise out of the homeowners?

"Sophie! You're not supposed to be out here." Natasha barreled up behind me holding a clipboard. "Oh! You're on camera." Whispering, she said, "Isn't this the most fun? I know what you're going to say, but you don't have to thank me. Getting to work with Troy is like a dream come true."

She smiled at the camera, stood at an angle, and lifted her chin. "Honestly, Troy, I don't know how you manage to get anything done with that crew of yours. They were all just standing around, so I put them to work raking what's left of the grass."

Troy barely missed a beat, but I thought I saw one second of shock. "I'm sure they were waiting for more concrete to be poured." He grinned. "We, um, need to pick up some things this afternoon."

Natasha straightened her top. "Will the cameras be coming with us?"

Troy smacked his forehead. "How stupid of me. We'll need someone to stay here and accept deliveries."

"I could do that." Natasha waved the clipboard.

"I don't know," said Troy. "It really ought to be someone strong enough to stand up to the delivery guys. You're so pretty that they might give you a hard time."

"No! I can do it. I'm very firm with my employees, right, Sophie? No one messes with me."

Troy was slick. He knew exactly how to get her off his back. I watched with amusement as he reluctantly agreed to leave her behind. Natasha promptly ran toward Troy's crew to tell them of her new and oh-so-important role.

"Thanks," I muttered sarcastically.

He dragged his fingers over his face, pulling his features so he appeared demented. "I have spent the entire day with that woman telling me what to do. I deserve a break. Besides, there's not a thing *anyone* can do until the concrete sets up. At this point, I would pay to get away from her."

I chuckled at his mock desperation.

"I do feel a little bit guilty for sticking you with her, though."

That was nice. If he hadn't lied to me and torn up my backyard, I would have thought he was a good guy. He gave me a little two-fingered salute and strode away, waving his hands over his head at his crew.

In fairly short order, the concrete truck departed, leaving my world blissfully quiet. With Natasha hovering over them, Troy's crew finished smoothing the concrete, packed up their belongings, and headed out.

I had to assume that Natasha was worn out. She eased wearily into a lawn chair, took off her shoes, and slouched with her eyes closed. Her hands fell to her sides. I had never seen her in such an unladylike position before. When I looked out the window a few hours later, she had left.

At precisely seven o'clock, Wolf rapped on the door to my kitchen and opened it. "Think it's cool enough to eat outside?"

"Have you seen the mess back there? They poured concrete earlier today. I think we could cook on the grill, though. They didn't tear up the patio."

"Sounds good to me." He was dressed to relax in navy shorts, a red polo shirt, and flip-flops. "Feel like a margarita? After the day I've had . . ."

"Yes, please!" I sliced sweet, juicy pine-apple chunks to thread on skewers with onions, red pepper, and pork seasoned with sea salt, pepper, and rosemary. Rice cooked on the stove, along with spicy black beans.

Icy margaritas in hand, we ventured outside. The table, chairs, and closed grill needed serious dusting before we could use them. That chore behind us, I put the shish kebabs on the grill and joined Wolf at the table, exhausted from the events of the day. Wolf and I stared at each other for a few minutes in silence. I couldn't imagine how he must feel.

"I didn't expect quite this much concrete in your backyard."

"Me, either. How much do you think it will cost to rip it all out?"

He licked a bit of salt from the rim of his glass. "Maybe it won't be so bad. What's the deal? Will they undo it if you hate it?"

"I don't think so. I could clobber Natasha for starting this nonsense. I thought I'd have two weeks of leisure. Now I'll be getting up before the crack of dawn for construction."

"I'll be glad when you can park safely inside your own yard, though. It always worried me when you had to walk for blocks in the dark after work."

I gazed at the expanse of concrete. I hoped the garage would prove to be worth it after all.

When the meat had finished cooking, we sat down to eat. I pondered how I could gently broach the subject of his wife. Other than talking about vegetables and concrete, though, I couldn't think of anything that wouldn't upset him. I was itching to ask questions about Mona, but I guessed she might be a giant thorn in his side. I was also dying to know what happened after I left. Had they really roped off the back of his yard?

I returned to the subject of my own yard; surely that was innocuous enough. Maybe I could work my way over to his marriage. "Think I made a mistake letting Troy tear it all up?"

"The homeowners on his show generally act appalled in the beginning, but it turns out well in the end."

"I wonder how much they cut. Those homeowners might not be as happy as the show indicates." I couldn't stand the pretense any more. "Wolf, I'm so sorry that I dug up Anne's handbag. I . . ." I wavered. I couldn't say what I wanted — that I never meant to bring him harm.

Wolf stopped eating. "Can we not talk about that? I spent most of the day reliving the biggest nightmare of my life. For just a few hours, I'd like to think about something else."

I could understand that. It had been thoughtless of me to expect him to dwell on his problems. I wanted to know more, and I believed I deserved to know. After all, I'd been accepting of his simple explanation up to this point. But if we were going to continue dating, I had a right to be in the loop. I just had to wait a little bit longer before I pressed him.

"I'm sorry." Wolf sat back in his chair. "Maybe I shouldn't have come tonight."

"It's fine. This has been a horrible day for you. Let's just focus on something else."

"I never thanked you for the rosebush."

"I hope we'll get to plant it soon. Did you water it?"

"No. Maybe Kenner will do it tomorrow if I tell him the request came from you."

I laughed, relieved the tension had been broken. "I'd like to see that!" I couldn't imagine dour Kenner immersing his hands in soil or caring about a plant.

"When Anne planted roses, she watered them with diluted beer." Wolf sipped his iced tea and smiled at the memory. "I used to tease her about it, but it worked."

"I've heard of planting fish under tomato plants, but beer is a new idea to me."

"Something to do with the yeast. She had a lot of old-timey tricks when it came to gardening. It was her passion. She had a thing for ladybugs. She was always releasing ladybugs and praying mantises in our yard. They eat bugs or something."

He was speaking of her in past tense. Still, I didn't dare launch into questions. It wasn't easy for me to wait and hope he would talk about her disappearance.

He didn't seem to notice me. "We were

married in the azalea garden at George Washington's River Farm. You know how women are about their weddings. I thought Mona would blow a gasket. She hated the idea of an outdoor ceremony, but the azaleas were in full bloom. It was unforgettable. Anne knew her plants."

The pain in his eyes told me everything I needed to know.

"I could use some mustard." Wolf rose and walked toward my house, while I studied our meal, noting that nothing required mustard.

He stopped, his head bowed, and turned to face me. I could see his discomfort. "I don't want to be dishonest with you, Sophie. The worst thing is not knowing. It would be terrible if Anne were dead, but at least there would be a resolution. I look for her in every crowd, in every picture, on the news, and on Facebook. Until she turns up somewhere, or I die, I'll be looking for her."

He turned again and rounded the corner, headed in the direction of my kitchen. Maybe it would be good for him to have a few minutes alone. I certainly needed a minute to digest what he'd said.

For the very first time, I understood that there were three people in our relationship. Anne would always be there, unless he discovered what had happened to her and could move on. As hard as that was to hear, I appreciated his honesty. Wouldn't I have felt the same way if Mars had disappeared?

Something scratched against the fence. Daisy whined, and whatever it was rustled in the dying light of day.

CHAPTER ELEVEN

Dear Sophie,
I've nearly given up on gardening. I love geraniums and impatiens, but every summer when they're at their peak, a water shortage is announced, and we can't water our plants. I fear it's hopeless. Do you have any ideas?
— Withering in Dry Branch,
South Carolina

Dear Withering,
We throw out a lot of clean water every day. Keep a bucket or a couple of gallon jugs in the kitchen. Fill them with water from the kettle, water in which you've cooked vegetables or eggs, the dog's water bowl, and other "clean" water, instead of dumping it down the drain. Use that water on your plants! It's recycling and green living at its best.
— Sophie

Daisy dashed toward the noise, running straight through the wet concrete. I heard a grunt on the other side of the fence as Daisy placed her front paws against the weathered wood.

"Francie?" I hissed.

Moving quietly, I skirted the wet concrete by balancing on the wood frame at the end closest to my house. Hopping off, I joined Daisy on the other side. I stepped on the old stump to peer into Francie's yard. Her outdoor dining table had been set with hurricane lanterns. Open cartons of Chinese food were scattered about the table, and precisely on the other side of the fence from me, I could see Mars sheepishly rising from the grass and dusting himself off. In the growing darkness, I could make out Nina and Francie.

"Please tell me that you haven't been eavesdropping."

"Perish the thought!" said Francie.

"We're just having dinner," added Nina. "We would have invited you, but we knew you had other plans."

Mars must have stepped onto a bench on Francie's side of the fence, because I was suddenly face-to-face with him.

"Just know that you're not alone," he whispered. "Are you devastated?"

"By your nosiness?" I whispered back.

"Because he's still in love with his wife."

The notion caught me by surprise. It wasn't as though I hadn't known about Anne and accepted that he had loved her. But I never considered that Wolf might still be *in* love with her. Such a tiny difference in semantics, but in reality, the implications were mind-boggling. Wolf could never truly love me as long as he was still *in* love with Anne. Would he ever be able to be *in* love with anyone else? Would I always be second best?

I teetered off the stump and fell backward into the wet cement. Groaning, I tried to sit up without using my hands so I wouldn't damage more of the slick concrete but Daisy immediately jumped onto the concrete, knocking me back. Her nose went down and her rump went up — universal doggy language for "Let's play!" She barked happily.

"Soph!"

I twisted around to see Wolf running toward me.

"Are you okay?" He skirted the concrete exactly as I had, stood on the narrow strip of grass in front of me, and held out his hands.

I stood up with his help, the wet concrete weighing me down. Fortunately, Wolf began laughing. I couldn't help myself, I slid my finger over a gob of concrete and wiped it on his nose. We laughed hysterically, no doubt releasing tension and stress. Tears ran down my cheeks.

When I let go of him, Wolf said, "Hey, Mars! Get over here, and help me smooth out this cement."

"How did you know?" I whispered.

Wolf kissed me, sweet and light and a little bit grainy from the concrete. "You're totally oblivious about the men around you. Your discovery of Anne's purse buried in my backyard triggered all the old suspicions. I knew your friends wouldn't leave you alone with me."

Of course, I wasn't as unaware as he thought. But I'd done my level best to put a damper on the situation with Mars. I honestly didn't think anyone else had noticed, except perhaps Nina.

The spotlights on my house turned on, illuminating the mess Daisy and I had made. Wolf grimaced. "You'd better hose that stuff off Daisy before it sets on her. Or on you."

Mars, Nina, and Francie charged around the corner of my house. When their laughter subsided, Mars and Wolf found tools left by Troy's crew and started smoothing the impressions we had made in the concrete.

Nina and Francie were all too happy to spray down Daisy and me with the garden hose. It reminded me of being a kid and playing in the yard. After the brutally hot weather we'd had, the cold water actually felt good. Daisy shook herself damp, but I dashed to the house and changed into a dry T-shirt and shorts.

When I returned to my yard, Mars and Wolf had finished smoothing out the concrete. As soon as they saw me, a cheer went up.

"Finally!" said Francie. "She's here! Hit it."

Only then did I realize that Wolf held Mochie in his arms. He kneeled and dipped Mochie's paw into the concrete of the garage floor. Next to him, Mars pressed Daisy's paw into the newly smoothed concrete.

"Don't look so worried." Nina held up a butter wrapper. "We massaged butter on their signing paws so the concrete wouldn't stick."

After oohing and aahing over the paw prints, we carried Mochie and the dinner dishes into the kitchen.

"Anyone for dessert?" I asked.

It was a universal no. They all headed for the door. Nina and Francie were wet from hosing Daisy and me down, and spots of concrete clung to Mars and Wolf. The whole gang left in a hurry.

Before I washed the dishes, I took a few minutes to be sure Mochie and Daisy's paws were clean. I certainly didn't want them ingesting any concrete.

Wolf dominated my thoughts as I tidied the house. I had realized that he still loved Anne, but until Mars put it so bluntly, I hadn't considered that Wolf was still *in* love with his wife. No wonder he'd been so touchy. He wasn't just dealing with the worst thing that had ever happened to him, he was coping with the very real fear that his wife was dead. I had found the evidence that forced him to revisit his hope that she was possibly still out there somewhere — alive.

He had come for dinner, seeking relief from his own thoughts and the terrible reality of his situation. What an inconsiderate dolt I'd been to think I could weasel information out of him.

I slid between cool, crisp sheets, more tired than usual because of Troy's early arrival. I hoped he and his crew wouldn't be quite as early the next morning.

The phone woke me from a deep sleep. The

minute I answered, the caller hung up. I was too tired to check the caller ID. With a most undignified grunt, I turned over and fell back asleep, only to be wakened moments later by an annoying banging sound.

Daisy and Mochie flew off the bed. I managed to sit up and could hear them thumping down the old wooden stairs. Grabbing a cotton bathrobe, I stumbled downstairs and found them waiting impatiently by the front door.

I picked up Mochie and opened the door to find Francie.

"Good gracious, you look awful. No wonder Mars divorced you."

"You woke me up." I motioned her inside and shuffled toward the kitchen. "Good grief, it's not even seven yet."

"I tried to call but you didn't answer."

Eh, wasn't worth explaining. "What's so important?"

"Olive called. They're digging up Wolf's backyard. I think we'd better check on him."

Moving as fast as I could, I opened the door to let Daisy out in the backyard, then remembered about the mess and missing fence. I called her back in, fed her and Mochie, then flew up the stairs to dress. Francie was right, I looked a mess. I didn't have time to deal with what was clearly a bad hair day. I threw on a simple yellow sun-dress and white sandals. Twisting my hair up, I used a big banana clip to hold it in place and let the ends fall over it. Not the best look, but it would have to do. I grabbed hoop earrings and put them on as I raced down the stairs.

Francie had made tea and poured it into travel mugs for the two of us.

"You're a doll!"

"Don't get used to it. It's just that I'm worried about Wolf."

"I haven't had a chance to walk Daisy. She'll have to come with us."

Police vehicles lined the street in front of Wolf's house. At Francie's direction, I parked in Olive's driveway. I hopped out, attached Daisy's leash, and immediately suspected that I would be able to see more from Olive's yard. The cops would probably block me from entering Wolf's backyard. Daisy loping beside me, I ran along the shrubs and trees separating the two proper-ties. An engine rumbled in Wolf's yard. I recognized the sound, since I'd heard it at my house the day before — a backhoe.

I could make out Wolf's potting shed between the branches. I stepped into the brush, wondering what had possessed me to wear a dress. I needed jeans and sneakers. Pushing branches down, I peered through them. Kenner watched the progress of a backhoe, his arms folded over his chest, his expression grim.

I scanned the little group for Wolf, but didn't see him. Mona, on the other hand, stood only feet from the soil that had been turned over, inspecting it carefully.

As though he had Sophie radar, Kenner looked in my direction. He strode over casually, like we were at a baseball game. Using one hand, he moved branches on his side. "What are you doing?"

"Are you digging for Anne?"

The hollows under his cheekbones seemed even more pronounced today. "Yeah. Unless you have a better idea."

"Me?"

He sighed so hard I could hear it in spite of the noisy backhoe. "Mona thinks Wolf told you the truth."

"In the first place, I'm not sure I'd believe anything Mona says. She's done nothing but lie to me. She even pretended to collapse yesterday. And second, if she's right and Wolf told me the truth, then the truth is that he doesn't know what happened to Anne. So there!"

Daisy's growl punctuated my ire.

"You brought that vicious dog again?"

"She's not vicious!" But she didn't like Kenner. Not that I could blame her. The man was sour, stiff, and forbidding. "Besides, what is Mona doing in the crime scene? Aren't you afraid she'll contaminate it? She messed up any prints on the purse big time yesterday."

"She's behind the yellow line in the grass. We combed it, but after all these years, it's unlikely we'd find much there unless it was buried. Plus, Mona is Anne's mom. She deserves to be there and see what's happening. It would be cruel to expect her to sit in a hotel room waiting for word that might never come."

"When did you become so sensitive?"

"Always have been."

Not to me!

I could barely bring myself to ask, but I had to know. "Have you found anything?"

"Not yet. We've just gotten started, though. It's a big yard."

"You're not digging up the whole thing?"

"I hope we don't have to."

I hoped he would have to. That would mean they didn't find anything.

He swung around, his attention on Wolf's house. "Now we'll get some answers."

"What happened?" I crouched, trying to see.

"The cadaver dog has arrived. He'll be able to tell us where Anne is buried." Kenner ambled off.

"Sophie!" I could barely hear Francie calling me, but Daisy tugged in her direction.

Francie beckoned to me frantically. Olive stood next to her, also motioning to me.

I ran toward them.

"Wolf won't come out."

"What?"

"We've knocked and rung the doorbell," said Olive.

"We even peeked in the windows," added Francie.

"Maybe he left."

Olive shook her head. "I don't think so. His car's in the driveway."

CHAPTER TWELVE

Dear Sophie,
Aphids are feasting on my roses. I hate to use chemical sprays because I have dogs and children. Any suggestions?
— Worried Mom in Rose, Nebraska

Dear Worried Mom,
Ladybugs think aphids are a gourmet delight. You can order them through garden supply centers. Or go out in the morning when the dew is still on your roses, and dust them with flour. The aphids will die.

— Sophie

My heart pounding from running in the increasingly warm morning air, and out of concern for Wolf, I rushed toward his house with Daisy.

To my complete dismay, reporters already clambered in his front yard. I scooted by them, aghast at their questions about whether I knew the victim or — the killer.

I ducked around the rhododendron, only to be blocked by a cop whom I didn't know. I introduced myself and told him I was there to check on Wolf. Daisy wagged her tail and sniffed his knees.

"I don't think so." He pointed to the front yard, evidently meaning that was where I should go.

"But I know where the spare key is. Someone should check on him."

"Good try, lady."

"Do you really want me to bring Kenner in on this?" I asked.

He flinched and his eyes narrowed. "Come with me." He led me to the back of Wolf's house. "Which one is Kenner?"

Too easy. "Blue shirt, sleeves rolled back, leaning over to look at the dirt."

"Okay, where's the key?"

Part of me wondered if I should give away the location. On the other hand, I wanted to go inside. Wolf would have to find another hiding place. Daisy and I walked over to the side door. I lifted a concrete bunny that nestled among the leaves of a hosta and pulled off the key taped to the bottom. "Happy now?"

He took the key from me and tried it in

the lock. "Doesn't fit."

"Of course not." I held out my hand for the key.

He gave it to me with some degree of reluctance.

I walked around to the back deck and unlocked the sliding glass door. Daisy and I barged inside. I dropped her leash and locked the door immediately, the cop looking in at me from the other side. Mona caught wind of what was going on and chugged across the lawn toward us. I pulled the drapes closed.

"Wolf?" The grandfather clock ticked steadily. Dark and cool, the house offered a comfortable breather from the sun. The family room, an addition to the original bungalow, featured high, beamed ceilings and a stone fireplace, in keeping with the Arts and Crafts style. Everything appeared to be in place. I took off Daisy's leash, so she wouldn't drag it over the hardwood floors.

"Wolf?" I called out louder.

I wandered to the kitchen. No coffee brewing. No sign of breakfast at all.

Where had Daisy gone? I should have followed her.

No one in the dining room or the living room. I walked up the stairs. "Wolf?"

His bedroom appeared untouched. Maybe he wasn't home.

A thudding sound pulled me down the hallway to another bedroom. I knew that sound — Daisy's tail hitting something.

I peered inside. "Wolf?"

He sat on a bench at the foot of the bed. His elbows on his knees, his head bent forward. Daisy had wedged her head between his knees, demanding his attention.

Gauzy white curtains couldn't block the sun — or the view of the backyard. I'd never paid much attention to this room before. In fact, I'd thought it was a guest room. But now that I saw Wolf here . . . "This is the master bedroom, isn't it?"

He didn't move. My heart went out to him. When Anne disappeared, he'd abandoned their bedroom. What could I possibly say to console him? Everything seemed trite or vapid.

Mostly, I was angry with myself. How could I have dated Wolf without giving Anne much thought? Somehow, I'd imagined him as being single. I knew about her, but I'd managed to compartmentalize her in my mind — because I thought she was dead. My left hand swooped up to cover my mouth in horror. *I'd been dating a married man.* People asked me about marriage and engagement and rings. Everyone acted like he was single. I hadn't given any thought to marriage, but I wished I had because I'd have given his current marriage more thought.

I walked over to him and gently pried Daisy away. Kneeling on the floor, I looked into his face. "I'm sorry, Wolf."

He rose and took a step toward the windows. "I'm sorry, too, because you're about the last person in the world I want to see right now."

"Because you feel like you've been cheating on Anne?"

He clutched the windowsill with both hands and bent his head again.

"Isn't there anything I can do?"

"Go away."

"Have you eaten anything? I could make you an omelet."

He turned toward me. "Food isn't going to fix this, Sophie."

And just like that, I turned into my mother. "Of course not, but you have to keep up your strength."

I retreated downstairs to his kitchen and put on the kettle for tea. Coffee might be too strong for him right now. I'd left my tea in the car, and I needed another little morning jolt.

Wolf must have been to the grocery store not too long ago. In his refrigerator, I found leftover asparagus that was already cooked, sliced deli ham, and Cablanca, a nice salty goat Gouda. While I heated the pan for the eggs, I could hear Francie arguing with the obnoxious cop outside. I opened the kitchen door and hissed, "Francie!"

She and Olive piled into the kitchen.

I shut the door in the cop's face and locked it. "Tea?"

"Where's Wolf?" asked Francie.

"Upstairs. It's probably not a good time to talk to him. He's . . . shaken."

I whisked the eggs and poured them into the hot pan. Rustling through a drawer, I found a wood-handled steak knife that sliced through the asparagus and ham like they were butter.

Francie and Olive sniffed hungrily.

"No one has had breakfast?" I asked. "Get the other eggs out. I'll make more omelets as soon as I'm done with Wolf's."

"So what did he say?" asked Francie.

"Go away."

"That's sort of rude."

"He's devastated!"

Francie frowned. "That boy needs to buck up."

Boy? Wolf passed boy a long time ago. It

was all relative, I guessed. I loosened the edges of the omelet and shifted the pan to allow excess egg to run underneath and cook. Using a vegetable peeler, I sliced the Gouda into thin, wide strips and laid them on top of the cooked eggs with bits of asparagus and ham. Loosening the edges again, I rolled the eggs gently into an omelet and slid it onto a plate.

"Stay down here. I don't want to upset him any more than he already is." Taking a deep breath, I loaded a mug of tea, a napkin, a fork, and the omelet onto a tray and marched it up the stairs.

He sat on the bench again, holding a small pillow in his hands.

"Where would you like to eat?"

"Sophie, I don't know of a nice way to say this, and I don't think I have it in me to be kind to anyone right now. Please, leave me alone. I need to deal with this by myself."

I placed the tray on the bed, took the pillow, tossed it on a chair, and handed him the plate and fork. "I'm not going to pretend that I understand your pain. But you have friends, Wolf. We're not going to abandon you." Well, not unless they proved him guilty of murder. Then I might have to reconsider. Was it terrible of me to feel that way? "Come on, you know you're hungry."

To my surprise, he ate a bite. And then another. I perched on the edge of a cushy barrel chair. The curves and floral fabric contrasted nicely with the stark dark wood furniture. Anne's touch, I guessed. I picked up the pillow Wolf had held. It was made of yellow gingham with a white fringe. On it, someone, presumably Anne, had embroidered a ladybug sitting on a daisy. It was darling. Summery and sweet — the sort of personal imprint that made a home cozy. Examining those careful stitches brought Anne alive to me.

Lest I say something that would cause Wolf to lose his appetite, I kept quiet company with him while he ate. Francie and Olive could wait a bit. I was totally parched and couldn't wait for my own cup of tea. I should have brought one up with me.

Wolf finished the omelet. "Thanks, Soph."

"Do you want to talk about it?"

He shot me a look hotter than the pan I'd cooked the eggs in. I collected everything except the mug of tea, which he held, and retreated in silence, glad that he'd eaten.

At the bottom of the stairs, I passed the entrance to the family room addition and backed up. A pile of pictures had been left on a side table. Bracing the tray on my hip, I scattered them with my free hand. Anne and Wolf camping. Anne and Wolf's wedding. Anne and Wolf at the beach. He must have looked through them last night. No wonder he was so short with me — I wasn't Anne. I swiped the picture of them at the beach and slid it into my pocket. Chances were that she was dead. But if I was going to help him, a picture might come in handy if someone claimed to have seen her.

Francie, Olive, and Nina sat around Wolf's kitchen table, gabbing. "Where did you come from?" I asked Nina.

"I cannot believe that you didn't call me this morning so I could come along."

"I was in a bit of a panic. How did you find us?"

Francie waved my cell phone at me. "You left your purse in the car. That didn't seem safe, so I carried it with me. When the phone rang, it only seemed polite to answer it."

"So how's Wolf?" asked Nina. "Maybe he'd feel better if he came down here with us."

I was about to say that I didn't think so, but Olive spoke first.

She rose from her seat. "Maybe I should go. My presence might make things worse."

"You sit right down and tell them." Francie drummed her forefinger on the table.

I poured hot water for tea and cracked more eggs for omelets. "Tell us what?"

Olive sat down. "I feel uncomfortable talking about this in their kitchen."

"Sophie deserves to know," said Francie.

Nina placed the mugs of tea on the table. "What am I? Chopped liver?"

"You aren't as close to Wolf as Sophie. For heaven's sake, Olive, if you don't tell them, I will!"

"You have to promise you won't tell anyone else." Olive looked straight at me.

Yeah, right. Why did people always say that before they spread gossip they knew they shouldn't tell?

"It's just that —" Olive seemed flustered. "Okay, I'll cut out everything except the pertinent part. Anne was involved with another man when she disappeared."

"What?" I drifted to the table. "I'm stunned."

Nina frowned, creating a deep crease between her eyes. "That can't be. Everyone would have known and talked about it. No way."

"It's true," said Olive. "For various reasons, it was kept very quiet. Are those eggs burning?"

I whipped around and rescued the omelet. While Nina and Olive discussed the news

137

about Anne's affair, I made four more omelets and served them, glad that Wolf was upstairs and couldn't hear our discussion. I joined the others at the table, and savored my tea.

Nina squinted at Olive. "And why is it that you happen to know this when no one else does?"

Olive took a bite of omelet. I got the distinct impression that she was buying time to consider how she would word her answer.

"My family was involved. I really can't say more than that."

Suddenly it all made sense. That's why Wolf had such a fit about Roscoe. Anne must have had an affair with Roscoe or Audie. My money was on Audie. If Roscoe had had an affair with Anne, surely Olive wouldn't report it so unemotionally.

Francie tapped my arm. "Great omelet. But you haven't said anything about Wolf."

Hadn't I? They all watched me. "Well, Anne's affair certainly explains a lot. No wonder Wolf didn't want to talk about it — especially with me. It must have crushed his male ego. Maybe he doesn't want to admit it."

Olive waggled a finger at me. "I suspect you're right."

I finished the last savory morsel of omelet

and wished I had more. "It also explains why he thought she left. If she was in love with someone else, she might have taken off with him." Assuming, of course, that it wasn't Audie.

The grinding hum of the bulldozer came to a halt. We all noticed and listened, the silence of the machine ominous. No one said a word. My gaze met Nina's anxious eyes. Why hadn't the machine resumed its noisy work? My heart beat faster. Surely it didn't mean . . . couldn't mean . . .

Outside, someone screamed. It had to be Mona.

Wolf's footsteps thundered down the stairs, with the clatter of Daisy's right behind him. We jumped to our feet and dashed through the family room to the sliding glass door. I pulled the drapes open. As far as I could tell, Wolf didn't even notice us.

Kenner strode across the lawn in our direction.

Wolf opened the door. "Did they find her?"

CHAPTER THIRTEEN

Dear Sophie,
My brother built one of those big composting bins and spends his weekends adding manure and turning it. I don't have time for that, but I'd like to add some organic matter to my garden. Isn't there an easier way?

> — Too Tired to Compost in
> Parsley Bottom, West Virginia

Dear Too Tired to Compost,
Grandma Bauer didn't call it composting, but she buried her organic kitchen waste in her vegetable garden each day. She covered it with soil and a screen to keep the raccoons out. It biodegraded without any help, adding nutrients to the soil.

> — Sophie

I wished Wolf had thought through his

words before he asked. It was such a simple question, but it made him sound as if he *expected* them to find Anne's body buried in his yard.

Kenner's eyes took a quick inventory of us. "Will we find her, Wolf? It would go a lot quicker if you would tell us where to dig."

Nina gasped, and although I'm not a violent person, I wanted to punch him. Wolf didn't seem to hear.

He looked in the distance, over Kenner's shoulder. "They're bagging something. What did you find?" He didn't wait for an answer. He just took off running.

Daisy ran along beside him.

"Where's the cadaver dog?" I asked.

"It didn't find anything," growled Kenner.

Hope restored, I ran to join the others.

I panted worse than Daisy after jogging in the humid air. Nina grabbed my shoulder for support and whispered, "I have got to start working out."

I leaned forward to see what Wolf was looking at. A cop held a knife in his gloved hands. My heart sank. It had an extra long blade and a hefty weight to it. I knew because I had just used an identical one in Wolf's kitchen.

"It's just a rusty kitchen knife." Nina released me for a closer look.

With a very sharp point. It could have easily been used as a murder weapon.

"That's not rust!" exclaimed Mona. "It's blood!"

"Nonsense." Olive spoke in a matter-of-fact tone. "I've buried a good dozen of my kitchen knives by accident over the years. I bring them out to cut a vegetable off the stem, or they fall into my compost, and I bury them along with the peels."

Wolf nodded at the cop — a silent message to put the knife away. "They'll be testing it. We'll know soon enough."

"Or you could just tell us what you did to her!" Mona screamed.

Wolf ignored Mona's outburst. His back ramrod straight, he ignored everyone and didn't turn his head once on the way back to his house. I arrived two minutes after him, but he'd already locked the door and was in the process of drawing the drapes. He couldn't have made himself more clear.

"He locked us out?" asked Nina, breathing hard. "He's in a serious clinical depression. This isn't like him at all."

"Wolf?" I tapped on the glass. No response. I tried louder "Wolf? You have Daisy in there with you."

The curtain swung to the side, the door slid open, and Daisy walked out. I thrust one foot inside, just enough to prevent him from getting rid of me right away.

"Listen. I know you don't want to talk, but you can't stay here. The press is already gathering and going nuts on your front lawn."

He motioned me in and slid the door shut. "I have a place to stay, but I need help getting out of here without being followed. Would you swap cars with me?"

"Absolutely. As long as you don't mind Daisy in your car."

"Right now I like Daisy a whole lot more than most people. She's welcome to drive it if she wants to."

It was a silly thing to say, but I was glad to see he hadn't lost his sense of humor. "Here's what we'll do. I'll go out to your car with Nina and Francie. That ought to get the attention of the people out front — at least for a minute or two. While we're doing that, you dodge through the bushes to Olive's property."

"Olive?" He choked out her name like she was the devil.

"My car is in her driveway."

He rubbed his forehead and turned, like he hoped he might find a better solution behind him. "Okay. Wait here." He charged upstairs and returned with a duffel bag. *He'd clearly planned ahead.*

We exchanged keys. It felt oddly final, like I might never see him again. "Are you . . . Is there anything I can do?"

He shook his head. "Are you ready?"

I took his duffel bag, in case anyone in the backyard, like Mona, was watching. We stepped outside, and he locked the door behind us.

In a low voice, I said, "Francie and Nina, come with me. Olive, you go with Wolf. He'll explain."

We walked toward the side of his house. When we reached the big rhododendron, I passed the duffel bag to Wolf. I didn't wait to watch him. We needed to appear out front to distract the onlookers. I ducked around the rhododendron, with Daisy leading the way on her leash.

In seconds, we were surrounded by people asking questions. I pressed the button to unlock Wolf's car from a distance so we could climb in without delay. Daisy hopped into the driver's seat and jumped over the middle console to the backseat with Nina as though she understood what we were doing. To my delight, when I adjusted the driver's seat so I could reach the gas pedal, the car was very nearly surrounded. No one, but no one, was over by the rhododendron.

Nina and Francie cackled wickedly when they realized what we had done. After they high-fived, Nina asked, "So is Wolf going to your house?"

"Nope. He didn't say where he's going."

"Does he have family around here?" asked Nina.

"Not that I know of. His sister lives in Maine, and his parents are in Pennsylvania."

Even though I was driving, I caught the odd expression on Francie's face.

"What?"

"He must have another girlfriend." Francie always spoke her mind. No pussyfooting around, no matter how much she might hurt someone.

"I don't think so." *I didn't!*

"You don't have the best record for noticing another woman moving in on your men. Natasha scooped Mars before you realized it."

"You lose one husband to someone else, and no one ever lets you forget it," I jested. "That would make Wolf a real worm, and he's just not like that."

From the backseat, Nina said, "Do you think Mars is a worm?"

Her question took me by surprise. "No!"

Okay, she'd made her point. Maybe I *was* blind to it when the men in my life strayed. For years I believed that my marriage to Mars was over before he moved on, while my friends and family insisted that Natasha had targeted him while we were still married. Mars and I certainly grew apart on our own. But I wasn't so sure anymore that Natasha hadn't sped it up a bit.

"We should have followed Wolf," said Francie.

"I think he would have recognized his own car tailing him."

We fell silent until Francie asked, "Did we just aid and abet a murderer in escaping?"

I slammed on the brakes in shock. "Of course not!"

"I like Wolf as much as the next person, but you can't deny that the buried handbag and knife look incredibly bad for him. If he killed her, he's probably on the lam right now, getting out of Dodge before they find the body." Francie twisted in her seat to see Nina.

"In your car," said Nina. "The cops will be looking for *his* license plate. Pretty slick of him."

They couldn't be right. Had he just pulled a fast one? Had I been a willing dupe? "He wouldn't have taken my car . . ."

146

"Why not?" asked Nina. "His car is pretty snazzy. He probably thought it was an even exchange."

"Just you wait," added Francie. "I bet you'll find your car parked near your house. He knows you'll tell the cops that he's driving it. He'll know he can't keep it for long."

I hated their theories. "Aha! Caught you. On the one hand you're claiming that he snookered me, yet on the other hand, you're claiming he's so decent that he would leave my car where I can find it. I don't think you can have it both ways."

Francie grumbled under her breath. "That boy is in big trouble."

She was right about that. I parked Wolf's car in front of Francie's house.

"How are they coming on your garage?" asked Francie.

I stifled a shriek. I'd been so absorbed by Wolf and his problems that I had forgotten all about it. Who knew what Troy and his crew had done in my absence? Hustling from the car, I could barely wait for Nina and Francie to get out so I could click it locked. As soon as I had, Daisy and I dashed to my house, only to be met in the foyer by Natasha.

"Is something wrong? What are you doing here?" I asked.

"Troy sent me to wait for you so you wouldn't see the backyard. I used our key. Knew you wouldn't mind."

What a sneaky guy. I would bet anything Troy had sent Natasha inside to get her out of the way of his crew. I smiled pleasantly and chatted about the brutal heat while I walked directly to the sunroom to see what was happening in my backyard.

Natasha blocked me but let Nina and Francie through. "Sophie! You know you can't fool me."

I sighed. "You're right. I have to meet Roscoe for lunch, so I'm going upstairs to shower and dress."

Natasha planted her hands on her hips and eyed me. "Why would you lie about your lunch date? Did you think I would leave and you could sneak back to see what Troy is doing?"

"I'm not trying to trick you. I *do* have a lunch date with Roscoe."

"You picked the wrong lie, Sophie. I happen to know that Mars is having lunch with Roscoe today."

Mars was invited? Interesting. Roscoe must be planning something for one of Mars's clients. I couldn't help tweaking Natasha a little bit. "Or is it Mars who is lying about his lunch date?"

I didn't wait for an answer. *What had gotten into me?* I wasn't usually so wicked. Daisy and Mochie followed me upstairs. On my way to the shower, I snuck into the bedroom overlooking my backyard. Ack! They'd torn down part of the fence between my yard and Francie's. The garage had been partially framed but there were additional posts in places that I just didn't understand.

Fortunately, they had set my potting shed right, and it looked fine in its new location.

After a quick shower, I dressed in a cool, pale-green linen sheath with a V-neck. Since Roscoe was fairly informal, I thought I could get away with thong sandals in a similar green. This time, though, I did bother with a little bit of makeup and took the time to blow my hair into a passable style that curved inward around my throat.

Dangling peridot earrings and a gold bangle dressed it up a notch without being too formal.

When I returned to my kitchen, Natasha gave me the sort of look my mother used on me when I wore ratty sweats around the house. "That's hardly appropriate luncheon attire. Sandals?"

"It's hot. Haven't you heard? Pantyhose are out." I forced a smile.

"Haven't you heard? They're back! You're

always a step behind, Sophie." Her smirk faded and she gasped. "Oh my gosh, it's no wonder that you're testy." She held her arms wide and came at me like a locomotive. She hugged me to her and patted my back. "I just heard about Wolf." She let go. "I can't believe he killed his wife! You could have been next!"

"We don't know that he killed her."

"Don't worry, Soph. It's only natural that you're in denial."

"I'm *not* in denial." I didn't know what I was in. I'd never been so conflicted in my life. I wanted to defend Wolf. I *had* to defend him. Yet, in my heart of hearts, deep down, Anne's handbag had left a big, fat stinking doubt in me.

"Oh, sweetie. Now that they have the murder weapon, it will only be a matter of time before he's arrested and convicted. He won't be able to fool anyone anymore."

I wanted to say something that would contradict her in an unassailable way. But I feared she was right because I couldn't come up with a single clever idea. I left her in my kitchen nursing a tall glass of ice water.

At eleven forty-five, I drove into the circular driveway in front of Roscoe's home. In the brutal summer heat, the old trees and white house looked like the perfect place for a cool respite.

I parked in the shade of a tree and left the windows open. The charming porch beckoned. No wonder Roscoe had remained in his comfortable house instead of moving to a mansion. I rang the doorbell and waited. Hurried footsteps approached the door on the other side.

Violet opened the door and stared at me. Her black hair was drawn back so tightly it pulled her skin taut. She frowned at me but said nothing.

"Sophie Winston. I have a meeting with Roscoe."

She scowled and stepped aside. Without uttering a single word, she turned and walked through the foyer into a hallway. I guessed I was supposed to follow her. Once again, she led me through a family room with a brick fireplace. Decorated much like Roscoe's study, it had a masculine feel, with cushy, old leather furniture. I knew the drill this time and opened the door to let myself out on the terrace.

Across the green lawn, a door slammed shut at the guest house. Cricket, Roscoe's assistant and Audie's fiancée, walked toward me, her copper hair gleaming in the sun.

Unlike me, she wore office clothes — pantyhose, a chic navy suit, and heels so high that I would have toppled over and broken both ankles. I suspected she was aerating the lawn with the spiked heels as she walked.

"Did Violet throw you out here in the sun? I'm so sorry. We're all in a bit of a frenzy around here this morning."

"Oh?"

She motioned to me to follow her. "I'm afraid something rather valuable has been stolen."

CHAPTER FOURTEEN

Dear Natasha,
The neighbor's cat keeps coming to my yard to hunt birds. I treasure those sweet birds, and it makes me very angry when I see that cat bothering them. How can I keep it out of my garden?
— Birdwatcher in Catnip, Kentucky

Dear Birdwatcher,
Turn on the sprinkler.
— Natasha

Cricket stopped for a moment, rested her hand on a patio chair for balance, and scratched her calf. "Roscoe is beside himself. He may want to cancel lunch."

"Of course. We can reschedule it for any time that suits him."

"Thank you for being so understanding."

She opened the exterior door to Roscoe's den. I couldn't make out a thing. My eyes had to adjust to the dark interior.

"Cricket! Did you call Audie?" I recognized Roscoe's deep voice before I could see him clearly.

"Audie's in meetings all day. You know how he is about turning off his phone." She turned to me. "Audie's company policy — he goes wild when he's talking to someone who keeps reading texts or taking calls. I don't know how you think Audie can help, Roscoe, it's not like *he* would have taken it."

"Sophie, I'm sorry this had to happen right before our lunch. What I want to know is who hates me enough to steal from me? I'm good to my people. Real good."

Mars murmured, "Hi, Soph."

The paneled room had finally come into full focus. A huge empty space in the bookcase clued me in about what was missing. "The mallard print is gone?"

"Where's Mindy?" barked Roscoe.

Cricket didn't seem to be the least bit disturbed by Roscoe's demanding tone. "She's dressing to go shopping. She needs some things for your trip tomorrow."

"Sophie, sugar," said Roscoe, "Mars says you're something of a sleuth. How did the burglar get in here?"

I glared at Mars. "I've just gotten lucky a

few times. I'm not a professional. You need the police, Roscoe. They can fingerprint —"

He cut me off. "No police! Good heavens, I've got a reputation to maintain. Once you go to the police, it ends up all over the newspapers and on TV. Besides, I don't want every thief within a ten-hour drive thinking my house is an ideal target."

Cricket raised her eyebrows and tilted her head, looking at me as though she'd heard that song before and couldn't do a thing about it.

"C'mon, Sophie. What do you think?"

I thought he ought to hire a retired cop or a security expert of some kind. But, to be polite, I mused aloud. "Looks like there are three ways to enter the room — through the house, through the window, and the back door. Assuming the thief wasn't already inside the house . . ."

I looked at the doorknob. It seemed perfectly fine to me. Aged brass, I guessed. It showed the blemishes of time, but no fresh scratches.

How many people had touched it since they discovered the print was gone? I didn't carry gloves with me like Wolf did. Spotting a box of tissues, I snagged one and opened the door to examine the other side, probably wiping off fingerprints in the process.

The knob on the exterior was a slightly darker color, not surprising since it was subject to snow and rain. Again, there were no new scratches or indications that someone had tampered with it.

I checked the door jamb. "I'm no expert, but if this door wasn't bolted, it might have been easy to unlock it with a credit card. Do you remember if it was bolted?"

Every single one of them stared at me as though I'd shocked them.

Roscoe burst out laughing. "Why, Sophie! I always thought you were such a proper woman. How would you know about such a thing?"

Before I could answer, a stern voice said, "The door is bolted every night."

I jerked in surprise when I realized that Violet was in the room. Her drab brown dress helped her blend in against the dark paneled walls, but that only caused her pale face to seem ghostly, like it was floating on its own.

I walked over to the window. It was a standard sash-type window with a screen on the outside of the lower half that hooked in the middle. I didn't touch it, just in case Roscoe changed his mind about calling the cops.

"It's unlocked." I turned to Violet. "Is it

usually unlocked?"

"No. Never."

There wasn't much more I could do. I went outside to examine it and returned to the group in the cool house. "Unless there's a trick I don't know, the burglar would have had to cut the screen to get inside. My guess is that he came in through another entrance or he had a key."

"That was amazing!" gushed Cricket. "You're like Sherlock Holmes or something."

"Hardly. All I did was use a little bit of logic. There's nothing remarkable about that. It would be helpful, though, if you could remember whether the door was bolted after the print was stolen. If a stranger without a key left through the back door, he wouldn't have been able to bolt it behind him."

"Was the print here after the party?" asked Mars.

"I couldn't say. I don't know about that bolt, either. I've been in and out of that door." Roscoe looked at Violet. "Did you notice or hear anything?"

"I am not a Doberman pinscher." Her deep tone left no mistake that she was angry. I couldn't help comparing her to Mrs. Danvers, a thought no doubt planted by Nina two days before.

"Who was here after the party?" asked Mars.

"Just Mindy and me. And Violet, of course." Roscoe frowned at him. "What are you saying? That one of us did it?"

Violet spoke again. Clear, crisp, no nonsense. "Other . . . people . . . have . . . keys."

He needed to report the theft to the police! I played dumb to convince him. "Will you be able to make an insurance claim if there's no police report?"

Roscoe snorted. "I won't need insurance once I find out who stabbed me in the back by stealing my mallards."

"I told you this would happen. You never should have allowed anyone in here during the party." Mrs. Danvers, er, Violet made a point of staring at me.

"Exactly when do you think the print went missing?" I asked.

"This morning," grumbled Roscoe.

"You mean you only noticed it this morning." The corners of Violet's mouth turned down.

Was she mad at Roscoe? Her black eyes reminded me of an angry hawk. I bet nothing happened in Roscoe's house that she didn't know about. Which made me wonder what she knew about a certain missing print.

"Did anything unusual happen between the party and now? Anything out of the ordinary? Open doors, sounds in the night?" I asked.

"Good morning, all," Mindy trilled from the doorway. "Don't tell me Roscoe is still going on about that print of his."

Roscoe pecked her on the lips. "You look positively glamorous. Are you joining us for lunch?"

"Gracious, no. I have a hair appointment, and after that I thought I'd better buy some new hats for our trip. You can fill me in later."

I was overdue for a haircut, so I was in no position to criticize someone whose every hair was in place, but it seemed to me that her silk dress and pearls might not be the best choices for a beauty salon appointment. Hair spray wreaked havoc on real pearls. Then again, maybe the double strand around her neck was costume jewelry.

Mindy adjusted a flashy gold bracelet on her right wrist and rubbed her arm. "Nice seeing everybody." She wiggled her fingers at us. "Don't let him bore you any more about those mallards." She walked from the room in the awkward jolting stride of a woman wearing four-inch heels.

Cricket smiled at us as though she was

the lady of the manor. "Mindy is right, Roscoe. The mallards aren't their problem. Do you want to reschedule lunch?"

Roscoe flicked his hand. "Aw, everybody's already here."

"Is lunch ready, Violet?" asked Cricket.

We all looked around, but Violet had vanished.

In a hushed voice, Cricket added, "That woman drives me crazy. How does she do that? She appears and disappears like she's walking through walls. Makes me nuts. I'd better go see if she's ready to serve lunch." Cricket strode through the doorway that led to the living room.

Mars shook his head. "Wow. Mindy doesn't mind that you have a drop-dead gorgeous assistant?"

Fortunately, Roscoe chuckled. "Down, boy. My Audie's got dibs on Cricket. They haven't set the date yet, but I don't think they'll wait long to be married. She's been with the company for quite a while. Don't know what I would do without her. Don't let the wrapping fool you — that girl's got brains, too. Audie couldn't have done much better this time around. What I want is a bourbon. Mars, I know you like my brand. Sophie? Care to join us?" Roscoe raised a cut-crystal decanter. "Blast that Audie. He and Cricket must have done some damage during the picnic. They didn't leave a drop."

He ambled to an aged globe on a wooden stand and lifted the lid. Pulling a bottle from the center, he said, "Having a second wife is quite a change. This thing was a wedding gift. Mindy keeps her scotch stash in here. Olive never touched the hard stuff unless it was so diluted with fruit juices that it turned pink. I'm not much of a scotch drinker, but in a pinch, when there's no bourbon . . ."

He poured the golden liquid into crystal whiskey glasses engraved with stags. Mars gladly accepted one, but I passed. It was too early in the day for me.

"How many times has Audie been married?" Mars asked.

"Lord, who hasn't that boy married? First it was the cheerleader. You'd have thought the queen herself was getting married from the production her momma put on. That one lasted less than a year. Then he ran off and married a stripper."

He guffawed and eased into a cushy leather chair with a deep rounded back. "Yep, you heard me right. I thought my wife might have a stroke over that one. But she turned out to be a real nice girl. We were sorry to see her go. After that, there was a tall blonde from Denmark who baked like nobody's business! I still miss her Danish apple cake."

Roscoe pulled at the collar of his shirt. "Is it hot in here?" He didn't wait for a response and slugged back his scotch. I thought the temperature was fine.

"Knowing Audie's propensity for marriage, I warned him about taking up with any of our employees. Did he listen? Clearly not. But he picked a winner this time. She worked her way up to being my personal assistant. Cricket is already like family."

Cricket must have overheard, because she smiled broadly when she appeared in the doorway to announce, "Lunch is served!"

We followed her to a decidedly understated dining room. A simple, boxy eight-leg sideboard with hammered copper hardware didn't shout money, but the horizontal plate rack that ran along the back cued me in that it was a pricy Gustav Stickley. The table also appeared deceptively simple. Long enough to seat ten people easily, it wasn't very wide. Someone, probably Violet, had set it with lacy white place mats so that the dings and dents of age showed through. A shining silver colonial candelabra shone over the table. Everything in the room appeared laid-back and restrained, almost upscale rustic, but none of it was inexpensive. Even the Harcourt goblets on the table followed that theme. Although they had classic lines without engraving or fancy patterns, they were definitely Baccarat.

A door slammed shut, and through the window, we saw Violet running through the side yard crazy as a bumblebee, waving her arms over her head, her tidy bun coming undone and flopping with each step.

Cricket looked up at the ceiling and sighed. "We're not at our best today. You'll have to excuse us. I'll bring in our lunch."

I followed her to help. We could see Violet through the kitchen window. She continued to zigzag through the yard like she'd lost her mind. "Um, is she okay?"

"She didn't even plate anything. Good grief. Yeah, she's fine. She does this when she sees animals in the garden. She thinks a fat calico is lying in wait for birds, and she has it out for him. But she does the same thing for raccoons and possums. Who knows what she'll poison next."

Oh no! "Poison? I hope you're kidding."

"Nope. She protects those birds like they're her children."

I was itching to know what the deal was with Violet. "She's awfully grim."

"Isn't she?" Cricket placed pieces of fried fish on each plate. "You'd think she had gone through some kind of horrible trauma, but that's just how she is. I don't know how Roscoe can stand it. It's not like she's family. He could get rid of her. For some strange reason, Audie loves the old crow, so I guess we're stuck with her."

"I hear congratulations are in order. You're marrying Audie?"

She held out her left hand. "No ring yet." She lowered her voice to a whisper. "Princess Mindy threw a hissy fit when she found out we wanted to marry. Apparently, she was afraid we might steal her limelight. Can you imagine? Roscoe asked us to wait a few months before we make the engagement official, but I've already bought the dress! All I need is a date and I'm there!"

"Is this catfish?" I asked.

"One of Roscoe's favorites."

I might as well be nosy, since Cricket seemed forthcoming. "I gather Violet lives here?"

"She's been with them for years. The story goes that she's a family friend who fell on hard times, so they took her in, and she never left."

I glanced out the window at Violet. She hunched ever so slightly, like an animal about to launch an attack.

Cricket looked out at her before adding

164

spoon bread to the plates. "I hope she doesn't catch that cat."

The sun hit Cricket's hair through the kitchen window and reminded me of the way Wolf had looked at her gleaming tresses when we saw Cricket on the street. "I think we might have a friend in common. Wolf —"

She sucked in a little bit of air. "How is Wolf? I haven't seen him in forever, well, not since Anne . . . vanished."

I wasn't quite sure what to say. It felt somehow disloyal to rattle off the details of my discovery of Anne's handbag. I went with the truth. "He's well." Maybe it wasn't the complete truth. He'd been better. Then her words sunk in. "You knew Anne?"

Cricket piled biscuits into a basket lined with a rustic tan cloth embroidered with chickens. "She was my best friend. Not a day goes by that I don't think about her. She would have been the maid of honor in my wedding to Audie."

I carried two plates laden with food into the dining room and set them in front of Mars and Roscoe.

When I returned to the kitchen, Cricket said, "Thanks for helping, especially since you're a guest."

"My pleasure." I didn't add that I was

thrilled to have a few moments alone with her. "What was Anne like?"

She paused and leaned against the tiled kitchen counter. "In a word — sweet. The opposite of me in a lot of ways. Maybe that's why we were friends. I'm sort of bold and brassy, while Anne was timid and quiet. She was stunningly beautiful but didn't think so. You know the type?"

I did. I usually liked that kind of person.

Cricket picked up the basket of biscuits and a bowl of kale dotted with bits of bacon.

"Just a sec," I said. "What do you think happened to her?"

Chapter Fifteen

Dear Sophie,
I hate weeding. Love my garden, but those pesky weeds keep coming back. We eat organic, and I don't like herbicides because of the kids. How do I kill the weeds without poisoning the earth?
— Flower Lover in Weed Patch,
California

Dear Flower Lover,
Heat kills weeds. Try spraying your weeds with vinegar. This works best on hot, dry days to burn the leaves. Or you can pour boiling water on the weeds. Both plans will need to be used repeatedly until the weeds die. Take care not to kill surrounding plants!
— Sophie

"Now there's the million-dollar question." She handed me the biscuits. "After we've eaten, we'll take a walk in the garden."

Forget the lunch! I wanted to grab her by the hand and run out into the garden with looney Violet. But I minded my manners and tried to focus on Roscoe for the next hour.

Worried that I might stick my foot in my mouth, I tried to phrase my concern about Violet gently. "I understand there's a calico cat hanging around your garden."

Roscoe swallowed a bite of crispy catfish. "Pretty thing. Size of a Jack Russell dog."

"Does it belong to a neighbor?"

"I doubt it. Fur's matted. It comes and goes."

How could I bring the poison into the conversation without offending anyone? "Cricket says the cat is disturbing the birds. I'm sure Nina Reid Norwood could catch it in a humane trap. Would you mind if she brought one out here?"

Roscoe bellowed, "Now why didn't we ever think of that, Cricket? I'll call Nina soon as we finish up lunch."

Violet returned as abruptly as she'd left, even grumpier than before, but her hair had been pinned in place again. When she poured coffee and served blackberry cobbler, warm from the oven, Roscoe said, "Sophie, I have got a whopping problem.

My ex-wife, Olive, didn't care too much for parties. Give her a hoe and a sun hat and she was happy. But my new wife, Mindy, has a hankering to be a little bit more social, so we're going to be putting on the glitz for a couple of Mars's clients."

Pretty much what I'd expected.

Roscoe leaned back in his chair. "Mindy, bless her, wants to do it all herself. But if there's one thing I learned from our wedding, Mindy doesn't understand the word *budget*. Not that I want to be cheap, now, but good lord, the woman bought herself a diamond crown. A crown! I could have bought a racehorse for that money."

He stopped talking and ate three bites of cobbler. "What I need is someone who can keep Mindy happy while staying on a budget and putting on a good event."

Since Mindy had been absorbed with the details of her wedding, I hadn't dealt with her much on Roscoe's annual picnic, but I had a hunch she might not be easy to work with. I'd met my share of opinionated people, though. Mindy didn't scare me. I gazed across the table at Cricket. In that way, we were somewhat similar. I didn't think anyone would call me brassy, but I could hold my own.

Mars and Roscoe launched into a discussion about an up-and-coming politician. Cricket cocked her head at me and muttered something about showing me the garden. We slipped through the kitchen, under Violet's ever-watchful eyes, and out the door.

Cricket took a deep breath. "This is such a beautiful garden, but the stench does spoil it. The heat just amplifies that smell. Mindy still insists she didn't order the manure. But . . ." Cricket laughed. "Sometimes she's a real ditz."

I wanted to move over to the subject of Anne. "I hear Anne was a big gardener."

"She was. Just like Audie, so passionate about gardening. He putters around out here once in a while since his house doesn't have much of a yard, and what he does have is mostly concrete. I live in an apartment with no balcony, so everything is in pots. Anne loved plants. She would do silly little things like plant a cactus in the cut-off bottom of a milk carton. But they always thrived!"

We walked under the trees, keeping to the shade.

"I like Wolf." She closed her eyes briefly, as if there might be some pain behind her words. "I really do, but I just can't get past the notion that he had something to do with

170

her disappearance. They were fighting. Wolf doesn't like to admit it, but they had some issues. Her mother and I both heard about them. Frankly, I think Anne may have admitted more to me than to her mom because, well, there are some things you just can't talk about with your mom."

"Do you remember what sort of things they argued about?" I steered clear of mentioning the handbag so I wouldn't plant that idea in her mind.

"Anne hated her job. She just loathed it. She never should have been an accountant. It stifled her. Have you ever had a job you hated? The kind when you don't want to get up in the morning because you think you can't face another day of it? That's how Anne felt. She wanted to quit, but money was an issue. Plus, Wolf wanted to have kids. That was a huge problem between them. Anne wasn't ready, and she said she couldn't handle the demands of work *and* motherhood. Wolf had irregular hours, so she knew she would be doing the bulk of the parenting. She was already completely stressed about work, and she couldn't see adding a baby to the mix."

The air felt a little bit cooler as we strolled near the pond.

Cricket hadn't mentioned the handbag or

arguments about money. "Did she say anything about leaving Wolf?"

"She had certainly considered it. If you know Wolf, I guess you know he has a temper."

Why did people keep saying that? Not the Wolf whom I knew. The only flash of temper I'd seen was about Roscoe.

"But then, if she left him," I said, "wouldn't she have contacted her parents?" If Anne feared Wolf's big bad temper, she might have gone into hiding from him, but surely not from her parents.

"Exactly." Cricket plucked a daisy from the garden. "I've never quite been able to wrap my brain around it. If she were alive, she would have called me, texted me, sent me a postcard!"

"So, the last time you saw her — was she despondent or anything?"

"A little bit, I guess. She was very upset with Wolf. It was a Friday night. To cheer her up, after work we went shopping and out to dinner. It got a little later than we'd intended because we wound up having drinks in a bar. I remember Anne worrying that Wolf would be angry with her for coming home so late." Cricket pulled a leaf off the stem.

"When Mars and I were married —"

"You were married to Mars? The Mars with whom we just had lunch?"

"Yes." We shared a last name. Why was this a surprise to her?

"He says such nice things about you. You don't act like a divorced couple."

I laughed. "No one ever gave us the manual on how divorced people are supposed to behave. We're still friends."

"I thought all divorced couples fought like crazy. Olive and Roscoe sure do! Did Mars get mad when you came home late?"

"Are you kidding? Both of us were always out late because of work. Political advisors and event planners have to expect that kind of hours. I can understand Anne's situation at work, though. I love my job, but sometimes it absorbs every waking minute."

Mars shouted to us from the house. Lousy timing. I wanted to pump more information from Cricket. She turned to head back, so I hurried to zing her with two questions.

"Do you think Anne could have taken her own life?"

Her forehead wrinkled, and I thought she might tear up. "No way. The cops asked me about that way back when. She wanted to change her life, not end it."

"So, I guess you were the last person to see her alive?"

Cricket bobbed her head. "Except for Wolf."

"Wolf? I thought she wasn't home when he arrived that night."

"That's easy to claim, isn't it? Only two people know for sure, and one of them isn't around to tell us."

Those ominous words hung in my head, but the sound of a motor drawing closer distracted me.

The putter of a machine engine grew into full-fledged thunder as a backhoe rolled through the grass toward the impressive gardens. It turned around and aimed its bucket at a colorful bed of delphiniums.

Cricket gasped and tried to run toward it, waving her hands and stumbling in impractical heels. She shouted to the driver. He let the engine idle, but I couldn't hear their conversation. Roscoe huffed his way out to the machine, and a little exchange took place between the three of them.

The driver cut the engine. Roscoe pulled a money clip from his pocket, peeled off bills, and handed them to the man, who tucked the money into his shirt pocket, started the backhoe again, and drove it out the way it came in. The grass was crushed, but I didn't see any irreparable damage.

What on earth? It looked as though Roscoe paid the man to leave. I wished I could have heard what had transpired. Not that it was any of my business, but I was curious. I hoped Mars might ask. It had certainly been peculiar. Hadn't Mindy said that she wanted to dig up the garden and pour concrete?

Roscoe followed the backhoe, while Cricket stopped at the terrace and chatted with Mars. I scoped out the garden in search of the cat, no doubt extremely alarmed by the noise. Two days had passed, but no one had come to spread the mulch over the stinky manure. Bits of leaves had been scattered in the garden beds, like someone had weed-whacked bushy plants nearby, so someone *had* worked in the garden.

Even though I was concerned for the cat, my thoughts came back to Cricket and Wolf. She'd said what I didn't want to hear — that she, too, could only come to the sad conclusion that Wolf had murdered his wife.

Neither Mars nor Cricket faced me, but I realized with a start that Mars was rubbing his jaw with his index finger and middle finger. I hadn't seen him do that in years. It was an old gesture from our married days that meant *rescue me.* Surely gorgeous Cricket hadn't managed to intimidate him?

I stifled a giggle and returned to the terrace.

Minutes later, we'd thanked everyone and said our good-byes. Mars and I walked out to our cars.

"Thanks for getting me this gig," I said.

"Hey, if you can deal with Natasha, you can handle Mindy."

"Wasn't that weird with the backhoe?" I asked. "What was that about? Did Cricket tell you?"

"Mindy and Roscoe are having a little spat. Mindy wants to sell the family homestead, but Roscoe won't hear of it. She hates the garden, hates gardening, and hates that it represents Olive, so she hired someone to dig it up. Seems she's planning to pour concrete over the entire thing and make it some kind of fancy architectural thing worthy of Versailles."

"And what was this about back there with Cricket?" I mimicked the way he'd rubbed his jaw.

We stopped at Wolf's car. Mars's eyes widened. "She was playing footsie with me under the table at lunch!"

This time I laughed aloud. "Oh please! You flatter yourself."

"I'm not joking. She was rubbing my foot with hers."

"Yeah, right. I hate to tell you this, sweetheart, but she's out of your league. Beside, she's engaged to Audie. You probably hit her with your foot." I cackled at the thought. "You better hope she doesn't tell Roscoe. We'll both lose him as a client."

"Hah! This old guy still has it going on. Something you might take note of."

I unlocked the door. "You wish."

"Did something happen to your car?"

"I lent it to Wolf."

Mars cocked his head at me. "What's going on?"

I explained as briefly as possible.

"Brilliant, Sophie! So your car was Wolf's getaway car."

"He's not on the lam from anyone but the press." At least I hoped not. "Stop talking like that."

"How do you get into these things? You never had problems like this when we were married."

"I had a bigger problem — you!"

"At least no one ever accused me of murder," he muttered and walked on to his car.

It was a teasing exchange, yet it brought me right back to the uppermost issue on my mind — Wolf. During the short drive home, I thought about him and the things

Cricket had told me. As usual, there were no empty parking spots near my house, but as I drove by, I saw my car neatly parked in front of it.

I slammed the brakes. Was Wolf at my house?

CHAPTER SIXTEEN

Dear Natasha,
My husband insisted we buy a two-acre property for privacy. Turns out I have more privacy than I expected because he wastes his spare time at the golf course, while I take care of trimming, mowing, seeding, and deadheading two acres of land. How do I convince him to spend more time on the garden with me?
— Golf Widow in Garden City, New York

Dear Golf Widow,
Golf clubs make cute plant stakes. Design a theme garden by creating an adorable planter out of his golf bag. Petunias spilling out of the top and pockets will make a striking focal point.
— Natasha

I tore around the corner, parked, and walked back to my house as fast as I could in the heat and sandals.

Nina dashed across the street looking totally cool and rather chic in a broad-brimmed straw sunhat. I recognized her white sandals as the type that supposedly tighten one's thighs without special exercise. "I've been waiting for you to come home. Do you think Wolf is here? That the whole thing was just subterfuge for the press, and he's holing up at your place?"

I hoped so. I stabbed the key into the lock of my front door and rushed inside. Daisy danced happily in circles, and Mochie strolled in to investigate the excitement. I picked him up and petted Daisy. "Wolf?"

Nina and I checked the kitchen.

"There's not even a note," she said.

I set Mochie on a chair and raced back to the foyer. He hadn't left my keys on the console, either. "Wolf?" I shouted up the stairwell.

I returned to the kitchen. "I don't think he's here."

The kitchen door opened, and Natasha waltzed in, all smiles. "I'm so glad you're finally home. I'm supposed to take you shopping for repurp items."

"Repurp?"

"Repurpose! Learn the lingo, Sophie. They're things that were used for something

180

else and have been discarded. We're supposed to come up with brilliant new garden uses for them. Put on some decent shoes and let's go."

I smelled Troy trying to get rid of Natasha for the rest of the day.

"Gee, I'm really sorry," said Nina, "but Sophie promised to help me set up a trap for a cat."

I tried to disguise my surprise. Roscoe must have phoned Nina the second we left.

"I'm sure that can wait. Troy is on a tight schedule. It's not as though we can repurp next week."

"Someone is trying to poison the cat, and the trap won't fit in my car, so Sophie is my only hope."

When did Nina learn to fib so well?

Natasha threw her hands in the air in dramatic dismay. Her sunrise-red nails were far too well manicured to repurp anything. I had a bad feeling I knew who would be doing the repurping.

Happily, Nina's potential poisoning won the my-need-is-more-pressing-than-yours contest. In truth, all I wanted was to find Wolf and talk to Kenner to find out what had happened since morning. Kenner probably wouldn't talk to me, though. He'd never been a chatty sort of guy, and he certainly wouldn't bend the rules and tell me the real scoop.

"Sophie!" Nina snapped her fingers at me. "We'd better go before it's too late for that poor kitty."

I crumbled leftover turkey burger into Mochie's bowl and gave a bite to Daisy as a treat. "We should be back soon," I assured them.

I brought Wolf's car around to Nina's house so she could load the Havahart trap. When we were on our way, I asked, "What are you using for bait?"

"Canned people tuna."

I chuckled. That didn't sound right, but I knew what she meant. Minutes later, I walked up to the front porch of Roscoe's house again and rang the bell. No one answered this time. I hoped Violet wasn't out back poisoning the cat.

"Roscoe asked me to come over as soon as possible," said Nina. "I'm sure he wouldn't mind if we set the trap."

I agreed and picked up the trap. "It's not like we need access to the house anyway." Nina and I crept around the side of the house to the backyard.

"Wow. It's even more beautiful when it's not full of children trying to push each other into cow pies. No wonder a cat wants to live here."

"Where's the best spot for it?" I asked.

"Too bad Mrs. Danvers isn't around to tell us where she sees the cat."

"You're so bad," I scolded. "Stop calling her that or you'll have me doing it, too. Violet, her name is Violet."

"I see the cat. She's huge!"

"Where? And how do you know it's a she?

"She's fishing at the pond. Most calicos are female. It's a genetic thing. Look at the size of that girl. She must be a Maine coon with all that long fur."

How could I have missed her? Nina was right, the cat was easily twice the size of my Mochie. The long fur only served to make her appear even larger.

"I'm glad to see she likes fish," whispered Nina.

We inched toward her. The cat continued to focus on the fish, but as we drew near, one ear rotated in our direction, proving that she was aware of our presence.

Like a flash, her paw swooped through the water and a red and white koi flipped onto a rock. She seized it in her mouth and scampered for the woods.

Nina blew air into her cheeks and released it. "This one might be hard to catch. She's obviously smart."

"Now we know why she's hanging around here. I hope Violet doesn't have the same attachment to koi that she has to birds."

"I'm trying to figure out where to put the trap. If she's hungry for fish, maybe she'll go for the easy tuna."

"She knows the fish are in the pond, so maybe you should place it on the other side of the pond, close to the woods."

Nina carried the trap around the pond and set it on the grass, near the site where the calico had been fishing. She adjusted the door to swing shut when the cat stepped on the trip plate that would hold food. Easing her arm inside, she positioned tuna on the trip plate and dropped tiny bits of it in a trail to lure the calico all the way in. "And for good measure," she said, "I'll leave a few teeny tuna chunks right here on the outside so she'll realize how yummy it is."

She paused before laying a burlap type cloth over the trap. "Just in case she knows about traps, we'll cover it up."

"Like that's enough to change her mind about it?"

Nina tsked at me. "Haven't you ever heard that curiosity killed the cat? They love to butt in where they don't belong, and they like confined spaces, too."

"You're the expert." Two birds landed on

184

a flat stone the perfect depth for bird bathing. They fluttered their wings, splashing water like crazy. Without party noise, Roscoe's garden was a beautiful, if odiferous, refuge. Birds twittered happily in the trees, and butterflies chased around bushes and flowers. A little hummingbird zoomed by us on its way to a vivid pink foxglove plant. The trumpet-shaped flowers seemed custom made for the hummingbird's long beak. The garden reminded me of a nature preserve. "This is a huge property. I can't even see neighboring houses. Who takes care of it now that Olive has moved out?"

"Audie said it's a couple of acres, but Olive left a lot of it natural. She cut paths through the trees for walking, but liked the forest effect. They hired a yard company to keep it up when she left, though Cricket told me at the party that Audie likes to putter around in it. Apparently, it's his way of relaxing."

"Olive must have been sick to leave this place after the enormous effort she put into creating this garden."

"According to Francie, Olive and Roscoe's divorce was all-out war. Very ugly. Olive says it was partly her fault because she never wanted to get involved with the catalog business."

"That doesn't make sense."

"Mindy was Roscoe's assistant. Olive said if she had realized what was going on, she would have insisted he hire Violet as his assistant. There wouldn't have been any hanky panky with her."

"What else did Olive say?" I asked.

"That Mindy married Roscoe for his money."

"She said as much to me. Think she's right?"

"I think Mrs. Danvers is watching us."

I twisted around and scanned the house. Sure enough, Mrs. Danvers . . . Violet . . . observed us through a window on the second floor.

"Man, but she's spooky." Nina shuddered. "We'd better get out of here."

We walked through the lush grass, but Nina kept her eyes on Violet. "You don't think she'll put poison in the trap, do you?"

"That beautiful cat! I can't bear the thought of it."

"Maybe Roscoe knows what kind of poison she uses. He could hide it," said Nina.

"Hello? She doesn't even have to go to the store for poison. Look around this yard. It's like a pharmacy. Foxglove, hydrangea, yew, delphinium, holly, cardinal flowers — there's poison everywhere!"

"I have some of those plants in my back-yard, but I don't have the first notion how to make them into a poisonous stew."

"Tea. You steep them like tea."

"Then we're in luck. Cats are carnivorous. I don't think they drink much tea."

"She could mix the tea with tuna."

We scooted around the side of the house and out to the front.

"Are you going to call Roscoe about the poison?" I asked.

"Absolutely. What are we going to do about Wolf?"

"Good question. I have this nagging feeling that something happened when Anne left that we don't know about. Wolf won't talk."

"Maybe *I* should talk to Wolf."

"Good luck finding him."

"Are you worried about another woman?"

"No. Wolf must have tons of friends. Cop friends whom we probably don't even know. Or maybe he went to a hotel."

"Maybe he did kill her."

"Nina!"

"Right, act appalled as though that thought hasn't crossed your mind. He's so private. He could keep murder a secret."

"I wish we knew who Anne's friends were. Think we could ask Cricket? She must have known Anne's other friends."

Nina squealed.

I slammed the brakes, and we lurched forward. "What is it?" I looked frantically for an animal in the road.

"We're doing exactly what Mona wanted us to do."

Chapter Seventeen

Dear Sophie,
Every year I plant all kinds of bright, colorful flowering plants, but they never look like much. What am I doing wrong?
— Pansy in Daisy, Kentucky

Dear Pansy,
To make an impact, plant one type of flower in masses. It's easier than it sounds if you do it with perennials, because they'll come back every year. Or try massing impatiens. They pack a punch of color!
— Sophie

"Don't do that! I thought I hit something." Nina had a point, though. "We're not doing it *because* of Mona."

"Really? What if Mona planted the purse there to revive interest in Anne's disappearance?"

"There's no way she could have known I planned to dig in his garden."

"She could have planted the handbag and the knife there years ago."

"Why would she have Anne's wallet?" I pulled Wolf's car into a parking space in front of Francie's house.

Nina gulped. "You don't think Mona could have had anything to do with Anne's death?"

"I *sooo* do not want to think that. Her own mother? No! Besides, if that were the case, why would she have come around to stir things up? She would have let Anne's mysterious disappearance quietly slip away. I think we can safely eliminate her as a suspect."

My own words clarified my thoughts. I'd known it all along, but somehow, everything had happened so fast that I hadn't honed in on it until now. I stepped out of the car and locked it. When Nina and I were on the sidewalk, I said, "If we believe that Wolf didn't kill Anne, then we need to find the person who did."

Nina followed me into the house. Daisy ran to us but didn't wait to be petted. She turned and loped to the kitchen door. Troy's voice blared. It was so loud that I suspected he was making a call from the service alley that ran along my side doors. Evidently he didn't realize how well we could hear him. He must have thought it a private place for making calls.

"Heath! This is your last warning. If you don't call me in five minutes, you're toast. Don't bother coming to my hotel room tonight with your tail between your legs to tell me how much you need this job. I'm done with you."

A few seconds of silence followed.

I pulled walnut pesto and prosciutto out of the refrigerator to make crostini appetizers.

"Harry! Drive over to the hotel and get Heath. I don't have time to mess with him. Tell him if he doesn't show up in the next half hour, he's out. I can't deal with people who don't come to work. He knows better than to do this."

Nina and I rushed to the sunroom.

Troy strode into our view, shaking his head. Within seconds, the cameras were on him.

"Good grief, he's even sexy when he's mad." Nina leaned forward for a better look. "I hope Heath isn't getting the boot. He looked like he rode in from wrangling cattle. Had that steamy rough-and-tumble bad-boy appearance."

"Think they arranged his 'absence' to add spice to the show?" I couldn't take my eyes off the garage, which had magically been framed during the day. "They work fast."

"Told you so. What's the rest of that concrete for?"

The pad of concrete extended beyond the back of the garage toward my house. "I have no idea. It's too big for a walkway."

We retreated to my kitchen, frazzled from the heat and the drama with Wolf.

Nina mixed cosmopolitans and poured them into martini glasses that were hand-painted with colorful flowers. The pink drinks were just what we needed.

We settled in the kitchen, our shoes off and feet propped up on chairs, munching on savory goat cheese, prosciutto, and walnut-pesto crostinis topped with halved cherry tomatoes.

Nina sipped her cosmopolitan. "Ahh. Much better. Come with me tomorrow morning to see if we caught the cat?"

"Sure, as long as it's not at the crack of dawn. I'd like to sleep in a little now that I'm not working."

"So if Wolf didn't kill Anne, who did?"

"Could have been Audie if he had an affair with her."

Nina choked. "You caught that, too? Olive

thought she was being so discreet, but she practically told us that Anne had been involved with Audie."

"I wish I had known Anne. How will we ever figure out who else might have wanted to kill her?"

"According to Mona, she worked around here somewhere. Think Wolf or Mona would tell us where?" asked Nina.

"We can ask. Cricket might tell us. I wonder if her mother knows that Audie was the other man in Anne's life."

"We don't know that he was."

"Nina! Surely you don't think it was Roscoe."

Troy rapped on the kitchen door and entered. "We're about done for the day."

"Care for a cosmopolitan?" I asked.

"A little too pink for my taste. The boys and I will clean up and head out to a bar for some brews. Any recommendations?"

"The Laughing Hound." Nina and I said it together.

"Then that's where we'll go. Has Natasha come back yet?"

"We haven't seen her," I answered.

He grimaced. "I sent her out to get estimates on fencing material. I thought she'd be back by now."

"That won't give you much time to order

it." I didn't want any delays.

"Not a problem. We don't need it." He winked at me and left.

By the time darkness fell, I had broken my diet twenty-nine ways and phoned Wolf four times. His home phone and his cell phone rolled over to voice mail.

I was eating softened chocolate ice cream right out of the tub when Daisy whined at the door. I stuck the container in the freezer, grabbed a leash in case I needed it, and let her out. She ran to the backyard, and I trailed along in the dark. The moon lit an unfamiliar world of eerie new posts and structures that didn't look like my yard at all.

At least the garage hadn't overpowered my lot or taken up too much space. I still wasn't sure about the other posts that rose from the ground along the fence that I shared with Francie. How could she let that go without calling me and making a fuss? Of course — Troy. That man could sweet-talk bees into giving up their honey.

"Soph?" I recognized Wolf's voice. He said my name softly.

I looked around. He had kneeled to play with Daisy.

If I had been watching a movie, at this

point I would have been yelling at the starlet to run into the house and lock the door. Things just weren't like that in real life. Wolf had surprised me, and his appearance in the dark was a little bit disturbing, but I had no real reason to fear him. To be honest, I was happy to know that he was still speaking to me.

"Hi." Well, that was stupid. I should have said something more welcoming. Should have let him know how glad I was to see him.

"Thanks for helping me this morning. I wasn't sure how I would get out of there without the press following me."

"No problem."

He rose and drifted toward me. "Do you mind if I keep your car for a while? They asked me to come down to the police station this afternoon, and it was easier to go in a car no one followed."

"Sure. What did they want?"

"Same old stuff about Anne. I'm officially on leave."

Given the circumstances, that wasn't terribly surprising. "I'm sorry. If I hadn't dug up the purse, none of this would have happened. Where are you staying?"

"With a friend. Only one person knows

and that's the friend. I'd rather keep it that way."

I was a little bit stunned. He could trust me to get him out of his house without being followed but he couldn't trust me enough to tell me where he was staying?

"You understand, don't you?" he said.

"No."

"I can't stay here. Mars, Francie, and Nina were spying on us last night. Don't bother denying it. They love you, Soph, and they would have flipped out if I had stayed with you. Nina and Mars would have insisted on moving in, too, just to be sure I didn't go nutso with the kitchen knives. The press would have figured it out in two seconds flat. It would have been awful."

He was right. He wouldn't have been hidden at my house. Everyone would have known he was there.

"You could at least tell me where you're staying."

He shook his head. "It's better this way. Don't look so hurt. I . . . I need some time alone."

"I can't even reach you by phone."

"Sophie," he sighed my name. "Everything I do will be watched and analyzed. I left my cell phone in my house on purpose."

"Don't you think it's time you told me

what happened that night?"

"I've always been completely up front with you about that. Anne took some of her things and left."

"Did she leave after an argument?"

"No! I don't know — maybe. Couples argue sometimes. You must have had disagreements with Mars. She wasn't there when I came home from work. I thought she was still out with her friend."

I wanted to confirm that it was Cricket, but he was finally talking, and I didn't want to ask anything that might make him clam up.

"The next day, I realized she'd taken a bag and probably wasn't coming back. Sophie, I had to answer all these questions for the cops. I'm not going through them again with you."

"Wolf, it doesn't make sense. What kind of stuff did she take?"

"Clothes, a little carry-on bag."

"But she buried her purse and ID?"

He spoke slowly, his tone reflecting his growing agitation. "That's why I thought she was alive. It appeared that she took her purse with her."

"Don't get upset with me. I'm trying to understand the circumstances."

He clutched me to him. For a few long

moments, we stood in an embrace, my head leaning against his chest.

He finally released me. "I don't want you involved in this."

"But I want to help. And you need all the help you can get."

"No! Do not go sticking your nose into it. There are things you don't know about, things you don't understand."

I took a wild stab. "You mean about her lover?"

"Oh no! No, no, no. Where did you hear that?"

"It doesn't matter."

"She didn't have a lover." He spoke through clenched teeth. "That's just an irresponsible rumor that sullies Anne's memory. There's no way she was seeing anyone else."

"How can you be so sure?"

"You wouldn't get it. She wasn't like you. Anne was delicate . . . fragile."

Why did I suddenly feel like a big galumphing oaf? "I would have a secret lover?" Memories of that spark-filled moment between Mars and me came flooding back. I thanked my lucky stars that it was dark out, and he couldn't see the blaze that I could feel flooding my face.

"That's not what I meant. Anne . . . if you

had known her, you would have realized that she would never do that. She did everything she could to avoid conflict. You have moxie."

I guess he could see my face better than I thought because he immediately tried to backtrack. "I'm not saying you would cheat, just that you have spunk. You're tenacious. Anne didn't have your courage."

"Falling for someone else doesn't take guts. Sometimes it just happens. Maybe it was the road of least resistance."

Wolf groaned like a wounded bear. "Stay out of it, Sophie. I mean it." He stalked away from me and vanished into the night.

Daisy and I returned to the house. I dug around in the freezer until I found a package of brownies I had stashed away. I might not be as sweet or delicate as Anne, but I could be stressed out as much as anyone. I had my own ways of dealing with it. I boiled water for a large mug of hot tea, cut one brownie, thought better of it and cut a second brownie — the one I would have given Wolf. I carried the fudgy, thawing brownies and my tea into the cool confines of my tiny den and plopped down in front of the computer. Mochie jumped onto the desk and sat like an Egyptian cat, watching me. Daisy curled up at my feet underneath the desk.

By three in the morning, I was dragging, and the sleep sofa had become alluring. I had searched Anne Fleishman's name every way I could imagine, trying key words like *accounting, horticulture,* and *garden.* If she ran away, she probably would have changed her name. Still, it had become a compulsion to see if I could find any information on her. The only thing of interest that turned up was her association with a local accounting firm, most likely her previous employer.

Too tired to give it more thought, I trudged upstairs to bed.

I woke to the sound of hammering and . . . humming. I rubbed my eyes and sat up.

Someone was in my closet.

CHAPTER EIGHTEEN

Dear Natasha,
I'm sure your house must be full of your stunning flower arrangements all the time. What do you do to make them last longer?
— Long-Stemmed Gal in Rose, Kansas

Dear Long-Stemmed Gal,
I like to add a few drops of vodka and one teaspoon of sugar to the water. Remember to change the water every few days.
— Natasha

Frantic, I searched my bedroom for a weapon. I picked up a crystal vase, not bothering to dump the water or the black-eyed Susans. Holding it over my head, ready to slam someone, I peered into my walk-in closet.

Mona was standing there, pawing through my dresses. "My Anne used to have pretty clothes like these. Not nearly as many

evening gowns. You must go to a lot of parties."

"What are you doing here?" I beckoned
her out of the closet and set the vase on a
nightstand. How did she get into my house?

Daisy appeared to accept Mona's presence, and Mochie sniffed her shoes. I
glanced at the clock on the nightstand. Nine
in the morning. At least I'd gotten a little
sleep.

"Natasha let me in. Such a nice girl. A lot
like my Anne. Or what Anne should have
been — gorgeous, confident, successful.
Don't you envy their long, slim legs? I do.
I'm surprised that Wolf dated you and not
Natasha."

"Excuse me, but this is my bedroom."

"It's very nice, dear. Perfect, really. Except
the walls should be blue and those drapes
are all wrong."

Was the woman deranged? Dark demi-
moons hung under her eyes, surely from
lack of sleep.

I wondered if she could turn on me.
Suspecting I would do better with her if I
pretended to be sweet, I said, "I need coffee. I bet you'd like some, too."

"I would!"

I had lucked out on my first try. She accompanied me down the stairs. Coffee

already brewed in the kitchen. Natasha must have put it on. From the enticing aroma, I guessed it might be Equal Exchange's Love Buzz. I poured it into two Portmeirion Botanic Garden breakfast mugs, with floral motifs painted on them, and offered Mona sugar and cream, fully intending to get rid of her as soon as possible. What had Natasha been thinking?

Nina rapped on the kitchen door. It was only a formality — she let herself in. "Mona!" Raising her eyebrows, Nina didn't have to say a word to express her surprise at Mona's presence. She helped herself to a white breakfast mug with pansies on it, poured in coffee, and settled at my table.

Mona added a tiny splash of cream to her coffee. "It's funny. I used to scold Anne because she preferred to wear overalls and jeans. Isn't it strange the little things you regret when someone is gone? At the time it seemed so important that she dress like a career woman. She did at work, of course."

I winced. Mona's trickery had gotten the better of me. I kept forgetting that she had lost her beloved daughter, and when she said something like that, I felt sorry for her all over again.

"I'm sorry, Mona," said Nina.

Immediately changing my mind about getting rid of Mona, I freshened everyone's coffee and pulled out the waffle iron to heat. While Mona talked, I whisked together large eggs, tangy buttermilk, and melted butter for Belgian waffles.

A jagged, suffering sigh escaped Mona's lips. "My husband can't take it. He won't talk about her anymore. He's at home, pretending like nothing ever happened. We all deal with grief in our own ways, I suppose. I won't rest until I find her. I can't. It would be like abandoning her." She wiped her eyes with the back of her hand and sniffled. "You girls be good to the people you love. Once they're gone, you'll wish you had taken more time for them, had been kinder."

I poured the thick batter into the waffle iron and closed the top. Instead of whipped cream or syrup, I sliced strawberries and washed blueberries for a fruit topping.

Nina reached out to Mona and patted her hand. "I'm sure Anne knew how much you loved her."

"You're very sweet, Nina Reid Norwood. My sister had two children. I was always comparing Anne to them. Can't you get straight As like your cousins? Why aren't you in the school play like your cousins? You know why?" She looked at us, nodding

204

her head. "She wanted to sew the costumes! I forced her to do everything they did. Ballet — she had no coordination, voice lessons — that was a joke, field hockey — she hated that, violin — poor child had a tin ear." A little smile appeared. "My husband said if we went deaf, it would be because of that violin screeching off-key when she practiced."

A heavenly scent floated from the waffle maker. I removed the first waffle to a square Portmeirion plate with leaves that trailed all the way around the edge, then added more batter to the waffle iron. A dollop of vanilla yogurt went on top of the plated waffle, topped by a generous helping of sweet strawberries and juicy blueberries mixed together with just a breeze of sugar and the tiniest squeeze of lemon. I placed it in front of Mona.

"Thank you, dear!" Mona searched her purse for a tissue and blew her nose. "We gave her every opportunity to excel, and all she wanted to do was stay home. She was meek. Always happiest puttering in the dirt or embroidering. It wasn't until she was gone that I understood what I had done. It was all about me. *My* competitive nature, *my* competition with my sister, *my* desire to wear tailored suits and be a professional. I was trying to make her into what I had wanted for myself."

I delivered the second waffle to Nina.

"Thanks, Soph. This smells delish! Mona, honey, I don't think you should be so hard on yourself. Don't all parents try to help their children be all they can be?"

"You know what my husband tells me?" Mona lowered her voice to mimic a man. " 'Mona, you tortured that girl when she was alive. Why don't you finally let her rest in peace?' " Her voice broke. "And now she'll never know that she didn't have to be a modern do-it-all businesswoman. I loved her for the kind, gentle person she was, but now I'll never have the chance to tell her!"

After preparing my waffle, I patted Mona's shoulder and wished I could do or say something to comfort her. I sat down at the table between Nina and Mona. "Did they find anything else at Wolf's yesterday?"

"No. They're going to dig more today. It's so tedious." Mona sipped her coffee. "I think I'm too old to stand around and watch. But I'm going over there as soon as I'm done here. Thank you so much for this lovely breakfast. I haven't eaten a bite since they found the bloody knife."

I stopped eating. It was that kind of thing that bugged me about her. The discoloration could just as easily be rust. "So what brought you here?" *To my bedroom!* I stopped short of saying it. "What did you want in my closet?"

Mona had the decency to blush. "Clues. You didn't have anything of Anne's that I could see. Did Wolf tell you anything more?" Mona asked.

Did she really think I would tell her if he had? "I'm sorry, Mona. You probably know much more than I do. And I have nothing that belonged to your daughter!"

She patted my hand. "I believe you, sweetheart. It's just . . . Well, I don't think he would have buried her in their yard. True, if *I* had murdered someone, I would think the most logical place to hide the body would be in my own private yard, where no one would see me doing it, and where I would know no one else would dig." Her mouth twitched into a grin. "You sort of blew that for him."

"But since Anne's" — I stopped short of saying *killer* and rephrased my point, after all, this was her *mother* — "purse was buried there, wouldn't the person have also buried her there?"

Mona finished her waffle. "That was wonderful, thank you. You can say his name, you know — Wolf. Since Wolf buried her purse there, wouldn't Wolf have also hidden her body there? No. Wolf is a cop. He would have buried things in different locations to throw everyone off."

She was testing my patience with her insistence that Wolf had killed Anne. "Mona, isn't it possible that someone else killed her? Like her lover?"

Mona gasped and clutched the white beads around her neck. "There was no lover! If there had been, Wolf would have been the first to point it out to throw suspicion on someone else." A gurgle rose through her throat and she hacked. "Unless he killed her *because* of the lover!" She wrung her hands. "Where did you hear about this? Did Wolf admit it to you? I knew you had information."

My little attempt at eliciting information from her backfired on me big time. How would I get out of this? As calmly and casually as I possibly could, I said, "Wolf insists there was never another man in Anne's life."

Nina's head swiveled toward me, her eyes huge. She must have figured out that I had spoken to Wolf after we left his house yesterday. Thankfully, she didn't spill the beans to Mona.

Mona fixed me with a squinty stare. "Then why did you mention it?"

"To see if Wolf was lying to me." *Ohhhh! Why did I say that?* It sounded like I didn't trust him, which wasn't what I meant at all.

Placing her hand over mine, she asked, "Where is Wolf?"

I leaned toward her, like I was going to confide something. "I don't know."

"You can tell me," she whispered. "I'm only trying to protect you from the same fate as my Anne."

"I still don't know."

Her lips pursed, and she stared at Nina. "I suppose you don't know, either?"

"Don't have the first clue," said Nina.

Mona placed her hands on the table and rose from her chair, stiff and slow. "You're a nice girl, Sophie, I'm glad that Wolf hasn't murdered you — yet. Don't fight me, darling. We're stronger when we work together."

I saw her to the front door and watched as she toddled away. I had no allegiance to her, and I was still boiling mad that she had putzed around my house while I slept, yet I couldn't help feeling just sick for her. If I were in her position, I would probably be every bit as frantic. Who knew what strange things I might do for the tiniest lead if I were in her shoes?

When I returned to the kitchen, Nina asked, "What was she doing here? And why didn't you tell me you saw Wolf?"

"I haven't had a chance. Mona was in my closet when I woke up! She said Natasha let her in."

"Don't underestimate Mona."

I was pouring myself a mug of coffee when Natasha opened the door and flounced into my kitchen. She wore a large robin's-egg-blue hat with netting over her face that she lifted.

"What are you doing?" She seized the coffeepot. "That's not for you!"

"Let's see . . . my house, my kitchen, my coffee."

"Don't be ridiculous. It's for Troy."

I held out my hand. "I would like my keys back, please."

She pulled them from a ruffled pocket in her blue and white toile apron and readily gave them to me.

It was too easy. "You have copies, don't you?"

"Mars likes to have a set on hand." She must have noticed my expression of disbelief. "To collect Daisy."

"Mars isn't the one who let a stranger in my house this morning while I was asleep."

She gasped. "That's horrible. Who would do a thing like that?"

Nina burst into laughter.

"Apparently you would," I said.

"I have no idea what you're talking about."

"Did you, or did you not, allow a little old lady to enter my home this morning?"

"Mona. Of course, but she's not a stranger. She's family."

That was news to me. "You're related to Mona?"

"Sometimes you're so dense, Sophie. She said she was Wolf's mother-in-law and a friend of yours. She was looking for Wolf and wanted to know if he was here. I was busy with Troy, so I told her to go ahead and look for Wolf."

So that was it. Mona thought Wolf was taking refuge in my house and wanted to see for herself. How convenient for her that Natasha had simply let her in. That didn't explain her presence in my closet, unless she told the truth about snooping for Anne's belongings. Did she think I was hiding Anne in there?

"You just accepted what she said? She could have been anyone."

Natasha flipped her hand at me like I was an annoying mosquito. "Are you saying she's not Wolf's mother-in-law?"

Oh brother. Now Natasha had caught me. Not my best day. Nevertheless, it wasn't unreasonable of me to be put out with her.

"You had no idea who that woman was. She could have stolen things or stabbed me while I slept."

"Everything turned out fine. You have such a penchant for drama."

Nina sat back, clutching her coffee mug in both hands. "So what exactly is that you're wearing, Natasha?"

"Aren't they darling? I just had to get them on camera so the people at the network could see what I can do with merchandising. I was up all night working on them. Isn't this the most stunning gardening hat you've ever seen? It's big, to keep the sun off your eyes and shoulders, and it has this netting in case the bugs are being annoying. I have another one to wear tomorrow with little packets of seeds on it. The apron will be for sale, too. I'm thinking of calling the line 'Natasha's Garden Couture.' "

Nina and I stared at her. I didn't think she was joking.

"Too many people dress like you, Sophie," she added. "An old T-shirt and shorts or, heaven forbid, sweats, which are simply ghastly. There's no reason we can't be beautiful when we garden."

She'd said two words that resonated with me — *the network*. "That's what this is all about? You think when the people at the network see you, they'll give you the national show you've always wanted? That's why you set up this whole backyard garage business with Troy?" I knew she had an ulterior motive!

"Why are you upset? You *do* need a garage. If I happen to come to the attention of a network executive in the process, then it's all good."

"So I'm right. That's why you lied to Troy and said I was a little old lady!"

"I would never call you that, Sophie. But you are short and you're not getting any younger."

Nina checked her watch. "We need to get going to check on the cat, Soph. If it's in the trap, I don't want it to overheat."

I dashed up the stairs to change, smirking over the fact that I didn't have a ruffly, sequined cat-catching outfit and would have to wear skorts and a top that would surely horrify Natasha.

A sleeveless white V-neck seemed crisp and cool for the blistering day ahead. I paired it with navy-blue skorts and white thong sandals. Sweeping my hair up off my neck in a modified French twist to stay cool, I pinned it with a big clip and then added navy and white enameled earrings. I passed on necklaces and bracelets, since I wasn't sure what cat chasing might entail.

Nina drove this time.

When we stepped out of the car at Roscoe's house, Nina paused and searched the windows. "I don't see Mrs. Danvers. Bet she sees us, though."

We walked around the side of the house.

"Psst." Nina nudged me. "What did I tell you? Mrs. Danvers is watching us."

She floated from room to room like an apparition, peering out windows and keeping track of us. I shuddered. "Why is she so creepy?"

In the backyard, Mars and Roscoe strolled along under the arcing limbs of trees at the rear of the property. The heat hadn't set in yet, but the sun had shone long enough to do away with the dew. Mars waved at us, but Roscoe appeared to be deep in thought.

"Is it my imagination or does the manure smell worse today?" asked Nina.

The stench impressed me as worse than it was the day of the party. It appeared that at least some of the mulch had been spread, but the odor was still extremely powerful.

I scanned the yard for any sign of the calico cat. "I don't see the cat. Maybe she's in the trap!"

We walked toward the pond, passing the host of summery white daisies with huge heads. Once again, I admired the bed of delphiniums on my way. But today, some of them had been bent back and broken. Had Violet chased the cat through them?

Beyond the bed was one of the sprawling piles of mulch that waited to be spread. Someone had worked with it recently. The mulch on the top and right side was darker and appeared somewhat moister, as if recently uncovered. My gaze drifted down to the plants that had been destroyed. At the very bottom of the pile of mulch, a hand reached out toward the flowers.

CHAPTER NINETEEN

Dear Sophie,
My husband and I would like to buy a garden bench. The faux wood and wrought-iron ones are much more expensive than the wooden benches. Are they worth the money, or do they all rot?
— In It for the Long Haul in
Onion Creek, Texas

Dear In It for the Long Haul,
Wood benches require repeated painting with an outdoor paint, but they can last for years. Wrought-iron benches also require maintenance, since they can rust. They're very durable, though. If you want a long-lasting bench that doesn't need much maintenance, buy a concrete garden bench.
— Sophie

I screamed and jumped back. A chill ran

through me before it dawned on me that it might be a gag.

"What is it?" Nina searched the grass around us in a panic. "Is it the cat? Was it poisoned?

My scream caught the attention of Mars and Roscoe.

Mars called across the lawn. "Are you all right? Is it a snake?"

He knew my weaknesses. I loved the outdoors but didn't deal well with snakes, and my former husband knew that. I shook my head and stepped around the bed of delphiniums to see better. My hands quivered.

"Damaged flowers?" asked Nina — just before screaming like a victim in a horror movie. "Please tell me that's not what I think it is."

Nina's scream brought Mars running. Roscoe lumbered behind him, unable to keep up.

I leaned over for a closer look, my heart pounding.

"It's plastic, right? Please tell me it's fake!" Nina grasped Mars's arm.

Another wave of chills rippled through me. They could do amazing things with plastic, but the hand was definitely real. I stood up straight and tried to speak calmly.

"Better call 911."

Roscoe joined us, pale and gasping for breath. "Call 911? Something bite you?"

Mars pointed toward the hand.

I felt as queasy as Roscoe appeared. It seemed only minutes ago that I'd felt comfortable in the morning air, but I'd broken into a sweat, and the sun had begun to bake us.

"Bottom of the mulch pile, Roscoe," said Mars.

Roscoe leaned forward, swaying a bit. His eyes widened when he spotted the hand. "Audie! Where's Audie? I haven't seen him today!"

I took one look at his drawn face and said, "I think you'd better sit down." I returned, skirting the flower bed to avoid contaminating a crime scene. Mars grasped one of Roscoe's arms, and even though the sight of the hand had zapped my strength, I grabbed the other. We helped him to a cast-iron bench in the shade by the delphiniums.

Mrs. Danvers must have been watching because she came running, her long black skirt whipping around her legs. "What have you done to him?"

Mars slid his iPhone out of a pocket and called 911.

Mrs. Danvers looked at him in horror.

"He doesn't need an ambulance!"

When Mars spoke into the phone and said he thought we had found a body, Mrs. Danvers howled and slung the back of her wrist against his phone, knocking it out of Mars's hand. It flew through the air over the flower bed and landed next to the hand, as though the hand were reaching for it.

Mars and I exchanged a look. "I'm not going back there to get it," he said.

"You couldn't pay me enough to retrieve it," said Nina.

"The rescue people can retrieve it," I said. "That way we won't disturb the evidence."

"What is wrong with you people? Roscoe isn't dead, and he doesn't need an ambulance. You!" Mrs. Danvers pointed at Mars. "Go get the wheelbarrow from the garden shed and bring it here." Muttering to Roscoe, she added, "Nobody has any brains anymore. Did you forget to take your medicine again? There's nothing wrong with you except heat exhaustion. What were you thinking coming out here to walk around? Mad dogs and Englishmen, but you're neither."

Mars dutifully brought the wheelbarrow, sweat beading on his forehead from jogging.

Mrs. Danvers ripped it away from him and positioned it near Roscoe, who raised one hand and waved it weakly. "Stop fussing over me, Violet. Is it Audie? Can you tell?"

"Hush, you old fool."

There was no way we could swing him into the wheelbarrow. "I don't think —"

"That's the trouble these days. Nobody thinks. You lift his right arm, and you" — she pointed at Mars again — "you lift from the left. Cat woman!" She wiggled a gnarly hand at Nina. "You hold the wheelbarrow steady."

This was going to be a nightmare. With any luck at all, we would succeed in simply lowering Roscoe to the grass. I said a little prayer that we wouldn't drop or hurt him.

Mrs. Danvers walked to the rear of the wheelbarrow.

"Violet, tell me," begged Roscoe in a breathy voice. "Is it Audie under the mulch?"

She paused and turned her dark eyes toward the base of the mulch pile. She flinched with the slightest flicker of shock. She glanced at me, then at Mars, as though assessing whether we had noticed the hand. In a voice so calm that it sounded fake, she said, "On the count of three."

I did my best to get a good grip on Roscoe. There was no doubt he needed to be moved into the house, and he certainly wasn't in any shape to walk back on his own. The guest house looked to be as far away as the main house.

But on the count of one, he passed out and fell forward. I didn't think we could hold his weight, and I was right. Mars and I lowered him to the ground.

Mrs. Danvers fell to her knees and leaned over Roscoe, stroking his cheeks. "No! No! Don't you die on me, you old goat!"

Fortunately, the siren of an ambulance drew near. Leaving Mars and Nina with Roscoe and Mrs. Danvers, I ran for the house. I felt certain Mrs. Danvers wouldn't approve of me letting myself in and dashing through the cool house to the front door, but it was too hot and too far to run around the side of the house.

The ambulance arrived at the same time as Roscoe's wife, Mindy. I motioned to them all to follow me. When we reached the terrace, they spotted Roscoe and took off, leaving me behind. Mindy ran across the grass in high heels, calling "Roscoe! Roscoe, darling!"

The doorbell rang. Assuming that no one else was in the house, I returned to the front door and opened it, only to find Detective Kenner.

"You have to be kidding me," he said.

"Isn't it enough that you found the incriminating evidence in the murder of Wolf's wife? Don't tell me there's another murder."

"I don't know that there is." *Actually, I was fairly sure. No one would intentionally crawl under mulch. Was that even possible?* "Follow me. The emergency medical technicians are here for Roscoe, who collapsed in the heat. But there's a hand sticking out from under the mulch pile." I led him through the yard.

Mars and Kenner nodded at each other.

"Where is it, Sophie?" asked Kenner. "I don't see it."

"Who are you?" demanded Mrs. Danvers.

Kenner flashed his police badge.

"We don't need the police." She stood rigidly, as though she thought she could stop him by simply appearing forbidding.

I scooted around the gurney the rescue squad had set up for Roscoe. "It's right th —" Where had it gone? "It was about here. Mars saw it, too. So did Mrs. Danv . . ." — I swallowed the rest of the name — "Violet."

She circled around Roscoe, muttering. She was only in the way of the rescue squad. Had she covered the hand so the rescue squad wouldn't notice?

I took out my cell phone and dialed Mars's number. When his iPhone played musical notes from under the mulch, Mrs. Danvers glared at me with fury.

"The hand is holding a phone?" asked Kenner.

"Mars's phone accidentally landed near it," I explained.

The rescue squad lifted Roscoe onto the gurney and rolled it across the lawn. Mindy and Mars walked alongside it, but Mrs. Danvers seemed torn. She wavered, watching Kenner bend over to brush away mulch. He uncovered the phone and seconds later, the hand.

He stood up straight. "Looks like a man's hand." He pulled out his phone and made a call.

Mrs. Danvers's breathing was so labored, I feared she might be the next one to keel over. Her back straight as a board, she walked across the grass to the guest house, opened the door, and disappeared inside.

When she exited moments later, her back was still ramrod straight, but her head sagged like she'd lost her best friend. Unless I missed my guess, she already knew who was buried under the mulch. Her behavior had certainly been peculiar. Covering up the hand and trying to get rid of the police had been futile gestures at best. I couldn't help thinking that she was trying to protect someone. Given her actions and Roscoe's questions, I feared Audie was buried under the mulch.

The sun had shifted, and we no longer had the benefit of any shade. I fanned myself. "Unless you need us for something, I guess Nina and I will go."

Kenner shook his head. "Afraid not. I need statements from you. I'd appreciate it if you walked to the house on that little path with me."

"She's the one you need to talk to." Nina pointed in Mrs. Danvers's direction. "She doesn't miss a single thing that happens around here. Do you think we should dig him out of there? Is there any chance he could be alive? It looks like someone raked or shoveled it on top him."

"That would be something. I don't think anyone could breathe under mulch. Sophie, could I have a word?" asked Kenner.

We stopped to talk.

"Hey! I have to check the cat trap." Nina pointed to it. "The tuna will go bad."

I explained about the cat and the reason for our presence.

Kenner squinted at Nina. "Stay on the patio. I'll take the tuna to the trap." He addressed me. "Why would Roscoe and Mars be out here talking in this heat?"

"It was still cool when we arrived. But Roscoe didn't look well." That didn't actually answer his question. "I can only think of two reasons. Either Roscoe wanted to show something to Mars, or they didn't want anyone to overhear them. Nina's right about the housekeeper. She's up to her eyeballs in this. She must have been desperate to imagine that covering the hand would make the situation go away."

"Why do you think she's the one who covered it up?"

"Roscoe had fainted, and Mars was so creeped out that he didn't want to retrieve his own phone. Nina wouldn't have gone back there unless the cat was sitting on top of the hand. That leaves Mrs. Danvers."

Kenner's lips turned up in the barest hint of a smile, and the skin around his eyes crinkled. "You'd have made a good cop." He pulled out a pad and pen. "Do you know her first name?"

How embarrassing. "Mrs. Danvers is the name of the dreadful housekeeper in *Rebecca*. Remember the book? Alfred Hitchcock made it into a movie."

"Yeah, I watch a lot of chick flicks." His tone dripped sarcasm.

"Roscoe and Mindy call her Violet. I don't know her last name."

Two crime scene investigators arrived. Kenner spoke with them briefly, then motioned to Nina.

They retreated to the house, while I waited outside in the shade of old trees, watching the cops work from a distance.

In a matter of minutes, Mars called me. I met him, Kenner, and Nina on the terrace in the blistering sun.

"Roscoe thinks the walls have ears," said Mars. "That's why we were talking outside this morning. He's been feeling poorly for the past few months. The doctors think it's his heart."

Kenner made some notes on his pad. "Mars, what's your connection to Roscoe?"

"He's backing some of my clients in their bids for political office."

"His family doesn't know about his heart problems?" I asked. "Why would he keep that from them? Why confide in you?"

Mars shrugged. "Maybe he thinks they'll push him into retirement. Yesterday he mentioned a couple of times that his son, Audie, was eager to take over the company."

"How dare you. Audie would never hurt Roscoe."

The voice caught me by surprise. From the shocked looks on their faces, no one else had realized that Mrs. Danvers had positioned herself upstairs near an open window to listen.

One of the cops shouted to Kenner. He cast a critical gaze at us. "I'm going to need someone to identify the body. Single file on the little path, please."

We returned to the mulch pile, Mrs. Danvers close behind us.

The body had been uncovered. If Roscoe had heart problems, would he survive if this was the death of his only child?

Bracing myself for a gruesome sight, I swallowed hard, looked at the corpse, and gasped.

Heath, from Troy's crew, lay on the ground. He was grimy from the mulch, but there was no mistaking the attractive guy I met two days ago. Toned muscles strained at the sleeves of his T-shirt. Bits of mulch and twigs stuck in his sandy hair. I guessed him to be in his late forties. What struck me the most was the lack of blood or obvious injury. If he hadn't been grubby from the mulch, he would have looked like he had died of natural causes.

"Any of you know this guy?" asked Kenner.

Mrs. Danvers didn't say a word.

I nodded. "I only met him once, but I'm pretty sure it's Heath. He was supposed to be working with the crew in my backyard, but he didn't show up for work yesterday."

"Heath?" Kenner frowned at me.

Nina removed her hands from her mouth. "I concur. It's Heath."

"Dad!" Audie raced over to us from the house, Cricket followed more slowly, tottering on high heels again.

"Is it Dad? Is he okay? I got a call . . ." Audie stopped talking, and his forehead wrinkled when he saw the body. "I don't understand. That's Heath Blankenship. What's he doing here?"

CHAPTER TWENTY

Dear Natasha,
My mom claims she had a geranium that lived for ten years. She brought it indoors every winter and took it out again in the summer. I don't believe her. What do you think?

— Skeptical in Tulip, Indiana

Dear Skeptical,
My outdoor plants thrive indoors. The trouble with bringing annual plants indoors is that they take up so much room. Some plants are very happy to go dormant in the winter, but if you have a window that gets good light, you can enjoy flowers year-round.

— Natasha

"Who is Heath Blankenship?" Kenner asked Audie, but he couldn't take his eyes off of Cricket, who was busy trying to dislodge a heel from the soil. Carrying her shoes, she ran to join us.

"Violet called Audie. We came right away," said Cricket.

I assumed she was used to men acting like fools around her, but she appeared startled to see Kenner. Her voice soft, she said, "Tommy Lee?"

Tommy Lee? So what if Kenner wasn't my favorite person? *I* was a terrible and insensitive human being — I never once wondered what his first name might be.

She stretched out her arms and hugged Kenner. "I can't believe it's you!"

There was no mistaking the sadness in his eyes. "Good to see you, Cricket."

When Cricket finally turned her attention to the man on the ground, she squealed and flipped her fingers over her mouth. "Heath! I never thought I'd see him again, much less like this! What happened?"

Audie stared at Heath. "I can't imagine what he's doing here. He worked for our company a few years back. He's a little older, I guess, but it's him."

I'd seen him in the woods during the party. If he worked for the company once, he must have seen friends there. Maybe he mingled. "Do you think someone invited him to the party?" As soon as the words left

230

my mouth, I realized that I should have left the questioning to the cops.

Audie grunted cynically. "Not a chance. Where's Dad?"

Violet's jaw tightened. She glowered at Mars, Nina, and me as though we had caused their troubles. "They took him to the hospital. There's not a thing wrong with him except heat exhaustion." She stalked away, toward the house.

"Keep to the path!" yelled Kenner.

Violet ignored him. Audie jogged after her, pelting her with questions about Roscoe.

Cricket lingered, her attention on Kenner. "You haven't changed a bit." She tossed her copper hair back self-consciously.

He actually smiled. I didn't think he was capable. "You're as beautiful as ever."

I was beginning to feel like the rest of us were intruding on something private.

She tilted her head a bit. "You old flatterer. I'm so glad that you're on this case."

"Cricket!" Audie shouted to her from the terrace.

"I have to go. We'll catch up later. Okay?" She touched his elbow in a familiar way, then took off at a jog, keeping to the little path, her high heels still in her hands.

In a low voice, Kenner said, "You three

can go now, too. I know where to find you."

Mars, Nina, and I had been dismissed.

Mars held out his hand. "Could I have my phone back, please?"

"Nope." Kenner didn't even bother to look at him. "It's part of the crime scene."

"No it's not," protested Mars. "It didn't land there until Violet knocked it out of my hand."

"No can do, Mars. It was part of the crime scene when I arrived. How do I know the victim didn't grab it off you when you were attacking him?"

I had never seen Mars at a loss for words before. He blinked at Kenner. "Aw, that's funny. Okay, give me the phone."

"Get out of here." Kenner clearly meant to dispatch us.

"But it has all my contacts on it. It's my life!"

"Give it up, Mars. You're not getting it back." Kenner reached out and grabbed my elbow, pulling me aside. "It appears that Wolf's past has finally caught up with him. Thanks for turning in Anne's handbag."

"I didn't. Wolf reported it himself."

Kenner turned his face up to the cloudless blue sky. "Don't let him deceive you. Anne is dead, and I don't want the same to happen to you. He thought he got away with it, but he's about to pay the piper." He looked me in the eyes. "Are you in touch with him?"

"No. I don't know where he is."

"Huh." He obviously didn't believe me. "Did he stay with you last night?"

"That's none of your business."

"It's police business. How about the night before?"

Why did I feel like no matter how I answered that question, somehow I was going to sink Wolf deeper into trouble? Even though I understood the implications of the handbag, I felt compelled to defend Wolf. "You have never liked him. I don't know what your problem is, but I assume you're professional enough not to let your personal feelings intrude on the investigation."

He blinked at me a couple of times and then looked in the direction Cricket had gone. "There are things you don't know."

Why did everyone keep saying that? "Then tell me!"

"Maybe someday. Not here, not now. But thanks to you digging up that purse, I think I've got him this time." He walked back toward Heath.

Mars and Nina waited for me by her car.

"What did Kenner want?" asked Mars.

"He asked where Wolf was last night and

233

had to tell me how much trouble Wolf is in. Like I didn't already know that. And that it's my fault — for uncovering Anne's handbag. I'm just sick about it. People keep telling me there are things about Wolf that I don't know, but they won't tell me what. It's like he has some big secret."

An expression of pure delight came over Nina's face. "Ohhh, I love ferreting out a good secret. Must have something to do with Anne. Maybe he had a fight with her lover? Think we could coax Olive to tell us?"

Mars's eyes narrowed. "I'll ask around. Wolf is a decent enough guy, even if he does insist on dating my ex-wife. I have trouble imagining him killing anyone."

"You're the one with reason to kill your" — Nina stopped short — "whatever Natasha is. She'd drive anyone to murder."

Mars didn't flinch. "Has Wolf ever been violent toward you?"

"Never. He got a little hot under the collar the other day about my meeting with Roscoe. Evidently they had a run-in sometime."

"Olive!" Nina almost shouted her name. "Do you think anyone bothered to tell her about Roscoe? Maybe we should call her."

Was that butting into their lives or being helpful? When did life get so complicated?

234

"They're divorced. Maybe we should leave it to Audie to tell his mom."

"I would want to know if *you* were taken to the hospital." Mars raised his eyebrows at me.

I wouldn't have admitted it at that moment for the world because I didn't want to lead Mars on — I had enough problems as it was — but I would want to know if Mars was sick or injured. Audie had to be in his forties, so Olive had undoubtedly spent at least forty or more years married to Roscoe. In spite of the divorce, she probably still had a soft spot for him — unless she was still so angry she couldn't stand him.

Nina punched keys on her phone. "Rats! I can't find her number. I think we should drive over there. It's not far."

Mars nodded in agreement. "I'm headed to the hospital. I'll call you with an update on Roscoe."

We drove away in opposite directions.

"You want to pump Olive about Wolf," I accused.

"I'm shocked that you would even suggest such a thing. We're doing Olive a favor, and if she should happen to tell us something that might be helpful to Wolf in the process, then that would be a fortunate coincidence."

"So you don't think he killed Anne?"

235

She paused before answering. "Sophie, please don't hate me, but I don't know what to think. The Wolf I know and love would never hurt anyone. But everyone has a temper. Everyone! It's possible that they argued and there was an accident. Maybe she fell and hit her head." She glanced at me as if to gauge my level of annoyance. "Some people have two sides to their personalities. Maybe there's another Wolf that lurks underneath. He's not the type who tells all."

"If he has a violent streak, he's hidden it very well. We've spent a lot of time together, and I've never seen it." I had to suppose an accident was possible. "Would he have tried to cover up if she fell and hit her head and was dead? Don't you think he would have called an ambulance?"

"I'm very sorry to say I know from personal experience that you can't predict how someone will act in the heat of the moment. Wolf is as capable of panic as everyone else. Just because he's the strong, silent type doesn't mean he can't make a bad call in the horror of the moment."

We passed a dozen cars parked on the street near Wolf's house. Nina pulled into Olive's driveway. We stepped out and could hear the roar of a backhoe.

"Sounds like they're still digging at Wolf's." I hadn't paid much attention to Olive's house the day before. Azaleas that must have been gorgeous in the spring lined the front of the yellow Cape Cod. Scented lavender and golden black-eyed Susans bloomed profusely on both sides of the white steps that led to the front door. Pink petunias overflowed their pots and cluttered the little stoop.

Nina rang the bell. We waited in silence but never heard footsteps on the other side of the door.

"Maybe she's not home." Nina rang the bell again. "Audie might have called her. She could be on her way to the hospital already."

"Or she could be out back, doing what she loves."

We cut around the side of the house, which turned out to be larger than it looked in the front. Olive toiled in the back of her lot near the woods. She wore a sleeveless denim shirt and golf shorts, revealing bronzed arms and legs, wiry from working in the garden. A broad-brimmed straw hat kept the sun off her face. I noted with amusement that it had no veil or seed packets attached to it.

She saw us coming and waved a trowel. "I'm so glad to see you. I've been dying to hear an update on Wolf, and Francie doesn't know anything." She pulled off gardening gloves. "Watch your step. There's a patch of poison ivy over there behind you."

"Has Audie called you?" I asked.

"Audie?" She adjusted the hat. "Is something wrong?"

We explained what had happened to Roscoe. Olive took the news surprisingly well, but tension showed in the tightness of her mouth. "Excuse me while I place a phone call to my thoughtless son." She marched across the lawn with us and stopped mid-stride. "Is an ex-wife still considered family? Will the hospital let me see him?"

I shrugged. "I don't see why not. You've known Roscoe a lot longer than Mindy has."

"Excellent observation." She lifted her chin and stoically proceeded to her house.

We accompanied her into an older eat-in kitchen with country charm and comfort. The cabinets had been washed with white paint so that an earlier green paint showed through just a hair. Pots of herbs sat on a windowsill above an old-fashioned double ceramic sink with a floral cloth hiding the plumbing underneath. Pots hung from a black rack adorned with chickens. Olive hadn't bothered to hang curtains on the huge windows overlooking the property. Wall-mounted pieces of old mantels and headboards held a collection of vintage teapots, all in floral and herb patterns. A basket of pickling cucumbers rested on the table.

Although the kitchen was mostly white, flowers bloomed in a riot of colors in pots on the floor, the counters, and among the teapots.

I was still taking in the details of the kitchen when she screeched. "No!"

She said good-bye and hung up her phone, breathing hard. Placing her hands on the edge of the sink, she looked out into the yard, her back to us. A full minute ticked by.

"Is Roscoe . . ." I was afraid to ask if he'd died.

"I need a drink!" Olive opened the refrigerator and pulled out a pitcher. "Iced tea?"

After hours in the heat, Nina and I eagerly accepted her offer. She poured it into chunky hand-blown glasses with green rims and tiny bubbles. Mexican, if I had to guess. We sat at her kitchen table, as roughly hewn as her old dining room table at Roscoe's house.

Slapping the hat into an empty chair, Olive smoothed her forehead with a trembling hand. "I was planning to make pickles today. Roscoe always loved my three-day crock pickles."

Pickles! Either she was rambling or this was how she coped with stress. "Is Roscoe all right?" I couldn't stand not knowing.

"Audie says he will be fine. I could hear Roscoe bellowing about going home. But you didn't tell me about the murder! What is going on over there?"

"I suppose you heard about the stolen Audubon print," I offered.

Olive snorted. "I never like to hear of anything bad happening to an Audubon. I wouldn't have named my son Audubon if I weren't a huge fan, but in this case, I am just a teensy bit amused. Schadenfreude they call it. Amusement at someone else's misfortune. It's about as low as a person can get to feel happy about another person's bad luck, but after the way Roscoe replaced me with Mindy, I can't help being just a tad gleeful about the missing Audubon."

"So is Roscoe going home?" asked Nina.

"They're keeping him for a bit, for observation and tests. Can you imagine — Audie said that I shouldn't come to the hospital. He thinks I'll cause a ruckus and upset the new lady of the manor." She checked the time on a vintage wall clock featuring a cow's head. "I'll clean up and go over there in a couple of hours. Roscoe will need me. By then his hustler will have grown weary and gone home." She took a deep breath. "So tell me about Wolf. Did the press find him? I gather they still haven't located Anne's body? It's a shame what they've done to his yard. It looks like they don't plan to leave a bit of soil unturned."

"Olive," — Nina rested her elbows on the table and leaned toward her — "we need your help."

How very clever of Nina. Poor Olive felt discarded and unwanted. Nina honed right in on that by making her feel needed.

"As you know, Sophie has been dating Wolf."

Ack! Where was Nina going with that?

"All of Sophie's friends are worried about her relationship with him. She thinks he's a nice guy who would never murder anyone, but there seems to be some big secret about him."

Olive bent forward toward us, nodding her head. "What can I do to help?"

Nina gave a little jolt as though surprised. "Tell us the secret!"

Olive sat up straight. "Well Lord, honey, how would I know? You two are far better acquainted with Wolf than I am."

Nina frowned at me when her plan didn't work.

I tried not to sound accusatory. "Isn't there some conflict between Wolf and Roscoe?"

"They just had a disagreement is all. You know how it is when two stubborn men lock horns." She made two fists and slammed them together at the knuckles to make her point.

"May I ask what they argued about?" I said.

Olive tsked. "I don't want to hurt you by saying this, Sophie, but I believe Wolf put Anne on a pedestal. I'm not sure that she was the delicate angel he wanted to think she was."

"Go on." Nina crunched on a piece of ice.

"It wasn't a big deal. Wolf obviously loved Anne very much and refused to face the truth about her. He got angry when Roscoe didn't buy it and spoke his mind. Wolf would have defended that girl with his dying breath." Olive snorted. "I wish Roscoe had felt as protective of me."

I never expected to have so many conflicting emotions at one time. I wasn't hurt. After all, wasn't it commendable that Wolf had defended his wife? I had to admit that I was a tiny bit jealous, but in the end, wasn't

that what we wanted from a spouse? Someone who would stand by us through thick
and thin? "He told me she never had a
lover."

"That's a perfect example," said Olive. "It
was so obvious . . ." Her forehead wrinkled
and she twirled her glass on the table.

"Is something wrong?" I asked.

"It's just that . . . It's rather curious that
Anne's lover would show up right now, just
when you've discovered her handbag."

CHAPTER TWENTY-ONE

Dear Natasha,
My wife caught your show the other day and said you grew cucumbers that were the shapes of hearts and stars when you sliced them. How did you do that?"
— Stumped in Cucumber, West Virginia

Dear Stumped,
With plastic molds! They're very popular in Japan. You slip one over the cucumber when it's tiny, and it grows in the shape of the mold. Japanese gardeners do the same thing to achieve square watermelons.
— Natasha

"Show up? Who is he?" I asked.

"I thought you were there today — at my house. Well, Roscoe's house now. Didn't you see him?"

Who was she talking about? I wracked my

brain to remember. "Not Roscoe, surely not Mars or Detective Kenner. Audie?"

"Heath. He disappeared at the same time she did."

"Heath who worked for Roscoe's company?"

"That's the one. I'm afraid your Wolf was in denial about it."

The news knocked me for a loop. Wolf could not have been more insistent that Anne had never been involved with another man. Unfortunately, in an odd way, his adamant protests supported exactly what Olive had just said. "That would explain why he always thought she would return. Maybe he didn't want to admit it, but deep down he thought or hoped she had run off with Heath."

Nina jumped to her feet. "Thanks for the tea, Olive. We need to get going so you can check on Roscoe."

In a flurry of thanks and good-byes, we were out the door and in Nina's car in two minutes flat. She backed out of the driveway fast.

"What's going on? Why the hasty departure?" I asked.

"That was fascinating."

"Then why were you in such a hurry to leave?"

"Because she's in it up to her sweet southern highballs."

"You've lost me, Nina."

"Ah, my dear Sophie, you're overlooking something important. We have no reason to believe that Roscoe or Olive are related to Wolf or Anne. Correct?"

"Right."

"Olive admitted that we know Wolf better than she does. Wolf is a cop and Anne was an accountant, and we know they didn't work for Roscoe's company — which begs the question — why exactly do they know so much about Wolf and Anne? Why would Wolf and Roscoe have *ever* discussed something as personal as Anne's infidelity?"

Her logic took me by surprise, but it made sense. "You think she's lying to us?"

"At the very least, she's not telling us everything."

"Mona didn't know about an affair, either. Of course, she might be the kind of mother whose children don't confide in her — and for good reason. And honestly, how many people would tell their parents about their affairs anyway? Still, so far Olive is the only one who knows about this alleged affair."

"Isn't it convenient that Anne's affair happens to have been with a dead man? Now there's no way to verify it. Unless Cricket knows. They were best friends, right? You would tell me if you were having an affair." She glanced at me coyly. "Wouldn't you?"

"*I'm* such a dolt that I've been seeing a married man right out in the open. I'm not cut out for this, Nina. It was *awful* yesterday in Anne's bedroom — seeing her embroidery and decorating taste. She was never real to me before. Now I feel incredibly guilty about dating Wolf."

"I'm famished. You don't mind grabbing lunch at Bernie's do you?"

"Not a bit. The second I go home, Natasha will try to foist some project on me that I'll have to accomplish in a hat with a veil."

Nina parallel parked her car in a rare opening on King Street.

We walked into deliciously cooled air at The Laughing Hound, an upscale restaurant located in an old town house with dining areas on many levels. Our friend Bernie happened to be in the foyer with a blonde attached to his lips. Nina and I stopped in our tracks and watched.

The perky blonde giggled. "I'll see you tonight." On her way out, she waved at us. "Hi, Sophie! Hi, Nina!"

I knew that delicate face and the sophisticated haircut that framed it perfectly. "Was that Jesse's mom?"

Bernie blushed. The best man at my wedding, he was still Mars's best friend and lived in an apartment over top of Natasha and Mars's garage. A vagabond for years, he'd traveled the world taking odd jobs in exotic places. In an unexpected move, he'd become the manager of The Laughing Hound for an absentee owner. The goofy guy with a kink in his nose and unruly hair had turned it into one of the most successful restaurants in town.

In his charming British accent, he said, "Dana. You remember her — from the haunted house."

Nina spluttered, "Of course we remember her. We just had no idea that you had hooked up with her."

"A gentleman doesn't broadcast these things. I'm about to grab a bite. Care to join me?" He led us through the garden room to a small private dining room one level up. Glass enclosed, it looked out on quaint Old Town houses and the outdoor dining space below.

"Your regular sandwiches?" Bernie asked. "Sorry — forgot that you and Wolf have been watching your diets, Sophie. How about the vegginini Wolf orders?"

"Vegginini?"

"A vegetarian panini. Some of our guests nicknamed it the vegginini."

"Sounds good."

Nina stuck out the tip of her tongue. "I need meat. Steak sandwich, please, with your delicious fries. Those count as veggies."

Bernie left, and I leaned back in my chair. "At this point, I'm so confused and frustrated about Wolf, not to mention stressed from the nightmare in my backyard, and now finding Heath's corpse, I think I'm entitled to chocolate. A triple hot fudge sundae at the very least."

"You and me, both. Part of me wants to defend Wolf and get him out of this mess, and the other part is afraid of what we might find. What if he really killed her?"

Bernie returned just in time to hear Nina's question. A waitress followed him to place icy pitchers of water and tea on the table.

"Would either of you care for a drink?" she asked.

Nina rolled her head around, loosening her neck muscles. "Yes! A scotch, please, neat."

I knew I shouldn't indulge because of the calories, but the way things were going, I thought I deserved a splurge or two — or three. "I'll have a lemon slush, please."

When the waitress left, Bernie poured

water for each of us. "Were you talking about Wolf?"

"It's all so muddled," said Nina.

Bernie took a seat. "I'd like to help him. I find it hard to believe a decent bloke like Wolf killed his wife."

"So you think she's alive?" I asked.

Bernie rubbed his eyes as though he'd had a long morning, too. "She's probably dead, but not at Wolf's hands."

The waitress carried a huge tray into the room and set sandwiches and drinks before us.

Wolf's vegginini turned out to be a whole wheat English muffin, spread with a light, savory sauce and loaded with crunchy shredded carrots, creamy avocado slices, sprouts, and julienned cucumber and heated in a panini maker.

Bernie waited until the waitress closed the door. "What do we know so far?"

I swallowed a bite and put my sandwich down. "Not much. Wolf told me Anne took a little suitcase with some things of hers. She was gone when he came home. Of course, now we know her handbag and wallet were buried in Wolf's backyard. The only real lead we have is a claim that Anne was having an affair with a guy named Heath, who most conveniently turned up dead today under a mulch pile at Roscoe Green's house. And —"

"Hold it!" Bernie reached a hand toward me. "There's a dead guy at Roscoe's house?"

Nina quickly filled him in on the details.

Bernie frowned. "Seems highly unlikely that a person would happen to die of natural causes *under* a pile of mulch. Not unless it fell on him, which doesn't seem to be the case."

"Exactly!" said Nina. "And isn't it curious that he had a connection to Anne?"

"Crikey!" Bernie leaned back in his chair and ran a hand through his hair that left it even more tousled. "I'm still gobsmacked that a guy was likely murdered. Surely you don't think there's any connection to Wolf?"

I didn't want to think there was. "Wolf and Roscoe had some kind of falling out, supposedly over Anne's character."

"Have you asked Wolf about the problem with Roscoe?" Bernie sipped beer from a pilsner glass.

"He won't tell me anything. He just says to leave it alone. That he doesn't want me involved."

Nina snarfed a french fry. "You're his safe haven."

"What's that?"

"I've read about it. Shrinks see it a lot in little kids who have violence in their lives. There's a person, usually a grandparent, or an aunt, or a neighbor, who becomes a safety zone. Someone who shelters them from the turbulence and makes life bearable and normal when they're together. Don't you see? Wolf doesn't want you involved because you're the one he goes to when he can't take it anymore."

"Nice theory, but I'm not buying it," I growled.

Nina bit into her steak sandwich and groaned with pleasure. She swallowed and said, "I think Olive is lying about Anne having an affair with Heath. She's covering up for the real person Anne was involved with, like Audie, maybe. What if Anne was having an affair with Audie, and he's the one who killed her?"

"Want a taste of my soft-shell crab sandwich, Sophie?" asked Bernie. When I shook my head, he continued. "So you're thinking Anne met Audie and had an affair but then broke it off or said she wouldn't leave Wolf, so Audie murdered her, took some of her belongings, and buried her handbag in the backyard to implicate Wolf?"

"Wow," said Nina. "When you put it that way, it really sounds plausible."

"Who would know more?" I thought out loud. "Audie, Olive, and Roscoe aren't going to admit anything. Cricket said she was Anne's best friend, but she's almost part of Roscoe's family. She might repeat their standard line."

"I seriously doubt that she knows Audie was involved," said Bernie. "Surely she wouldn't be engaged to him if she knew he had killed someone. Perhaps they gave her the same song and dance about Heath to protect Audie."

"Heath was watching from the woods the day of the party. Do you think Olive brought him? What if Olive brought Heath back on purpose to upset Roscoe's new marriage? Wait!" I nearly spilled my lemon slush in my excitement. "Is it possible that Heath had something going with Mindy? I saw her being rather cozy with Audie the day of the party. Maybe Audie killed Heath to keep him away from Mindy."

"Heath and Mindy?" said Nina. "I don't see it. He's good looking, but in that macho I-split-wood-and-wear-flannel-shirts kind of way. Mindy's such a priss."

Bernie laughed. "Don't be so sure. You'd be amazed by some of the odd matches that come in here."

Nina gasped. "What about Mrs. Danvers?"

"Who's that?" asked Bernie.

"Violet, the housekeeper. She tried to cover up Heath's hand even though we'd already seen it."

"And she knocked the phone out of Mars's hand. She would do anything to protect Audie and Roscoe. Evidently, that includes covering up a murder."

"Hah! I don't trust that woman," said Nina. "She probably killed Anne *and* Heath."

She'd said it in a light tone, joking really, but the sad truth was that her jest wasn't out of the realm of possibility.

"I wish we knew what kind of connection Wolf had with Roscoe and Olive," she griped.

"We do know one person who knows them well and never minces words — Francie!"

In a rare move, Nina and I skipped dessert in our eagerness to speak to Francie. While Nina parked her car, I bolted into my house, fed and nuzzled Mochie, and snapped a leash on Daisy. Ordinarily, I would have left my purse at home, but I didn't want to alert Natasha to my presence in the neighborhood. Slinging it over my shoulder, I dashed out before she could know I was home.

I met up with Nina at Francie's front door, but before we knocked, I saw Mars helping someone out of his car. "Is that . . . Roscoe?"

Without a word, Nina and I hurried along the sidewalk and across the street to Mars and Natasha's house, on the corner. Mars and Roscoe had already disappeared inside the house.

We dashed up the stairs. Nina knocked on the door, and Mars opened it so fast that he must have been standing on the other side. He scanned the street. "This isn't a good time."

Roscoe bellowed, "Is that Sophie? Bring her in here."

Nina, Daisy, and I stepped inside.

"What's going on?" I whispered to Mars.

He motioned us into the dining room.

Roscoe sat at the end of the table.

It seemed only minutes ago that we had been at Olive's house, talking about Roscoe being in the hospital. In reality, a couple of hours had probably passed. Enough time for him to get here at any rate.

"How're you holding up, Roscoe?" asked Mars, taking a seat across from him.

"I've been better." He gripped the arms

of the chair.

Roscoe's color had improved, but I had never seen him so angry. The open, friendly face had turned sour. Nina and I hastily slid into chairs next to each other. Mars took off Daisy's leash, and she settled under the table.

Mars shoved his chair back and crossed an ankle over his knee. "Now what's this all about?"

Roscoe's complexion turned the color of beets. "Somebody in my family is trying to kill me."

CHAPTER TWENTY-TWO

Dear Sophie,
My elderly neighbor has the most beautiful garden. I was complaining about the price of plants, and she told me to look for a plant exchange. What is that?
　　— Crazy for Flowers in Raspberry,
Arkansas

Dear Crazy for Flowers,
Some plants need to be divided regularly, and others sometimes grow a little bit too well, providing the gardener with extras. Plant exchanges provide a place for people to meet and swap plants. There are even some online.
　　— Sophie

What? Roscoe had our full attention.

"Now don't you go telling Francie, either. She'd blab to Olive, who would spill the beans to Audie and Violet. Then Audie would tell Cricket, and before I knew it, the whole family would know. That's what I wanted to tell Mars about this morning when Sophie found Heath."

"Is that why you ended up in the hospital?" I asked.

Mars cleared his throat. "Let's get this straight. Roscoe checked himself out of the hospital against doctor's orders."

Roscoe bellowed with laughter. "Hah! That idiot doctor even made me sign something to keep him out of trouble if I drop dead."

"What was the diagnosis?" asked Nina.

"They always say the same thing — heart problems. There's nothing wrong with my old ticker. I'm telling you, somebody's been slipping something into my food. I don't know what I did to make somebody so mad at me, but someone has it out for me. It's no coincidence that my precious mallard print was stolen, too."

Was he delusional? Surely medical tests would distinguish between a heart problem and poison. I exchanged a look with Mars.

"Don't go making that face, Mars," said Roscoe. "What you don't know is that I had a doctor friend of mine take a blood sample a few days ago. He called me early this morning and broke the bad news that there's digoxin in my blood — only I'm not taking the digitalis my doctor prescribed. It shouldn't be there."

"Roscoe!" Mars's mouth dropped open. "Did you tell the doctor that today?"

"No sirree!" He scratched the back of his neck. "Everybody that can talk warned me about marrying Mindy. 'Roscoe,' they said, 'an old rooster like you has no business chasing a pretty young hen.' And now they're all going to say, 'We told him so, but he wouldn't listen.' And the loudest one will be Olive."

"You think Mindy is putting your digitalis medicine in your food?" I didn't know much about her, but I was surprised that he jumped to that conclusion.

"She must be getting it somewhere else. I flushed my medicine down the toilet. I don't want it to be Mindy, but who else would want to be rid of me?"

Nina slapped the arm of her chair and leaned forward. "Do you think that Mindy accidentally murdered Heath instead of you?"

"I have to admit that thought occurred to me while I was lying in the hospital bed with my family buzzing around me like flies."

"But why?" asked Mars.

"I don't know. It about kills me that I

think it's someone in my own family. But no one else is around me that much."

"Maybe the digoxin is residual," suggested Nina. "Or what if you're getting it from another source? What is digoxin anyway? Could it be in chicken or peanuts or something?"

Roscoe shook his head. "You're a smart cookie. I asked the same thing. It comes from the foxglove plant. It's not the kind of thing that can be in your system unless you ingest it. The medicine digitalis is actually made from the foxglove plant. It slows your heartbeat, but if it's not monitored, it can slow it too much or make it irregular."

I shuddered. Poor Roscoe! "What about the day of the picnic?" I asked. "Matt and his crew cooked that meal. Did you feel sick then?"

"Not sick as much as tired and slow. My vision wasn't quite right. I saw halos, and things that were green looked sort of yellow to me."

"Did someone bring you your food or did you get it for yourself?" Mars focused on Roscoe.

"That's the idiocy of it. I went through the buffet line just like everyone else."

"How about the day I was there for lunch?" I asked. "Violet cooked the food, and I was in the kitchen with Cricket when she dished it out. It all came out of the same pots. I saw it." I had left for a second to carry two of the plates to the dining room, but unless Cricket was unbelievably skilled at poisoning food, I doubted that she could have done it so fast.

"You know, *I* felt a little bit queasy after that meal." Mars wrinkled his nose.

"Mars!" I chided.

"I'm not being impolite, Sophie, just honest. This is no time for holding back the truth out of some misguided notion of polite obligation."

"That makes no sense at all." I rolled my eyes at Mars. "It would have been impossible for Violet to poison half the food, and since Cricket dished it up, she wouldn't have any way of knowing which portion was poisoned."

"Where was Mindy?" asked Nina.

Roscoe snapped his fingers. "Well now. I believe that lets my Mindy off the hook because she wasn't even there."

Nina kicked my foot and hissed, "Mrs. Danvers."

"The iced tea." I mused aloud. "I forgot about the iced tea. It was already at the table. I presume you always sit in the same chair, Roscoe?"

"I do."

"So someone could easily have poisoned your tea if the glasses were already on the table."

"What about me?" asked Mars. He sounded like a little boy left out of a fun game.

I chuckled at him. "Maybe the person with the poison just finds you annoying."

That innocent little moment of teasing eased the tension in the room. Even though I'd had a little fun tweaking Mars, if he had really felt sick, it might lead us to the culprit. "Seriously, did you have indigestion, Mars?"

"Not so much stomach issues. That evening, I thought I'd go for a run down by the park, but I didn't have my usual stamina. I thought . . . Well, I thought maybe I was getting too old to drink booze in the middle of the day."

"I feel better already! It couldn't be my Mindy because she wasn't there for our lunch."

Just because Mindy skipped out on lunch didn't mean she couldn't have poisoned Roscoe's tea before she left. And she would have been an idiot to poison him on their honeymoon when it was just the two of them. "Roscoe, be careful. I think it might be too soon to eliminate anyone. Don't let your guard down."

I wasn't sure Roscoe heard anything I said.

"How do you like that?" He scrambled to his feet. "Now remember, not a word about this to anyone else. I'm going to set a trap for this culprit." He shook his forefinger in the air. "It's not that easy to get rid of Roscoe Greene!"

When we walked home, I considered going to Nina's house just to avoid Natasha, but Francie was leaving her house in a fishing hat, complete with hooks in it, and a leash in her hands. "I'm going to walk Duke. Wanna come with?"

"Isn't it too hot for the dogs?" The dogs would love a walk, but the heat might be too much for elderly Francie.

She saw right through me. "Eh. I have a hat. We can walk down to the waterfront. Maybe there's a breeze along the river."

"Okay. Anything to dodge Natasha. Have you seen my backyard today? Is it awful?"

"It's weird. I can't figure out what they're doing."

Swell. I stroked Daisy's head while Francie locked her house. Daisy and Francie's Golden Retriever, Duke, sensed an adventure and walked ahead of us instead of heel-ing. We didn't bother correcting them.

Olive had called Francie to tell her about Roscoe's illness and the discovery of Heath's body. The subject soon turned to Wolf and Anne.

I tried to sound casual. "How did Olive meet Wolf and Anne?"

"I have no idea. Didn't Wolf say Anne liked to garden? Maybe they met through a local plant exchange or in a class."

Sounded reasonable. "A garden club, maybe?"

"Could be. But a real one, not the kind where the women wear fancy hats."

I glanced at her sideways. "Was that a crack aimed at Natasha?"

"Yes! I saw those stupid hats she made with the veils. Hey! I should volunteer to model one for her and actually work in the garden. Do you know what that veil would look like in ten minutes?" She cackled with glee but quit abruptly and stopped walking. "That's Audie's house across the street."

I nudged her toward a large tree so a group of people on a walking tour of Old Town could pass by. They clustered next to us. The guide launched into the history of the eighteenth-century homes, noting the cobblestone street and architecture.

Audie's Federal-style redbrick town house,

typical for Old Town, seemed somewhat simple in comparison to some of its neighbors. An American flag waved at the front of the house. By the door, pink begonias thrived in a large terra-cotta pot, and vinca vines trailed over the edges.

A woman in a raincoat hurried along the sidewalk. Platinum-blond curls peeked out from under a baseball cap. She unlocked Audie's door and disappeared inside.

"Was that Mindy?" I asked.

"Sure looked like it to me."

I gazed up at the clear blue sky. "Are we expecting rain?"

"Not that I know of."

"I'm sure she has a good reason for being there."

"I'm not."

"Francie! What you're suggesting is repulsive. Come on. We can't stay here all day." It did bother me that Mindy had wrapped up as though she intended to disguise herself. And I *had* seen Audie embracing her after the picnic . . . "No! I'm sure you're wrong about this. Let's go."

She whipped her hand out to stop me. "Well, well, well."

A black Corvette convertible pulled into a parking space. Audie eased out of it like an old man, trudged to his house, unlocked the door, and let himself in.

"He looks awful," I whispered.

"He's had a hard day what with a dead man at Roscoe's and his dad in the hospital. Look at that — second floor."

Audie drew the curtains closed. I felt myself sag. The moment between Audie and Mindy in the garden hadn't been as innocent as I'd hoped. "Eww. I don't even want to know about this. It's wrong. It's disgusting! Go, go, go!"

We walked on to the river, Francie laughing at me.

"I had no idea you were so sensitive, Sophie. You know Audie and Mindy are about the same age."

"I don't care. Mindy is married to his father. That's revolting."

"I'll admit that it boggles the mind a little." Francie snickered. "Wait until Olive hears about this!"

"Won't she let the cat out of the bag?"

"So what if she does? Somebody ought to tell Roscoe."

Somebody ought to, and I *knew* I didn't want it to be me. Of course, neither Francie nor Olive realized that someone wanted Roscoe dead. I sighed. Audie and Mindy had just taken first place in that competition. Roscoe had to be told.

CHAPTER TWENTY-THREE

Dear Sophie,
I would love to get my kids involved in gardening. So far they like flowers, but they're mostly bored with the whole process. How can I make it fun?
— Garden Mom in Basil, Kansas

Dear Garden Mom,
Plant a pizza garden! They can make a pizza shape in the soil and divide it into wedges. Plant onions, tomatoes, red and green peppers, basil, and parsley. Plan a little celebration when you harvest enough ingredients to make your pizza. They'll check the garden every day!
— Sophie

I thought Roscoe should hear the news about Audie and Mindy from Mars. The two of them had developed a bond, and Mars would understand how important it was for Roscoe to be aware of the connection between Mindy and Audie. Unfortunately, Mars's iPhone had landed in the possession of the police, so I had no alternative but to call his house.

It was ten o'clock at night when he rapped on my kitchen door and opened it. Daisy whined and danced around his legs. Mochie stretched a paw at him, begging for attention.

"Why do I think this is bad news?"

"You and Roscoe seem very chummy these days. I'm beginning to think Roscoe might be planning to run for office."

Mars grinned. "Roscoe prefers the role of puppeteer behind the scenes. I've grown very fond of the old guy. He trusts me, and right now he needs someone outside his family circle whom he can trust."

I filled him in about what Francie and I had seen.

"Ugh! Roscoe will flip out if I tell him that."

"It's ugly all right. It could get even uglier if you *don't* tell him, and they manage to do him in."

Mars groaned. "Wait a minute. If Audie is involved with Mindy, why is he engaged to Cricket?"

"Good question. I don't understand it.

Cricket is like a goddess. Who would choose Mindy over her?"

"Mindy is sort of stiff," said Mars. "I keep waiting for her to loosen up. She's friendly enough, but there's something formal and priggish about her. Are you absolutely certain it was Mindy you saw?"

"Francie saw her, too, if you want to verify the sighting."

"Okay, okay, I believe you. Do you think I can wait until morning to break the news to Roscoe?"

Who was he kidding? "Well gee, if someone was trying to poison me, I think I'd like to know as soon as possible!"

He stroked Daisy and sighed. "Think about it, Soph. I can't exactly tell him over the phone because someone at his house might be listening in. And I can't exactly drive over there and knock on the door, because then Mindy will know something's up. What am I supposed to do, stand on his lawn and throw rocks at the window? Lurk outside his den waiting for him?" He checked his watch. "It's very late. He knows someone is trying to poison him, so he's already being cautious, and it's unlikely that he'll eat anything before breakfast anyway. I'll go over there early tomorrow morning."

Mars had a point. After all, Roscoe was

the one who figured out that he was being poisoned. The only new development was that it might be his wife doing the dirty deed. Besides, as concerned as I was, I couldn't think of a way to let him know that wouldn't alert Mindy or Violet. "We'll just have to hope for the best then."

He left by the front door. I scooped up Mochie so he wouldn't run out and felt the soft caress of the warm summer night. Since my backyard had been ripped apart, I considered taking Daisy for another walk, just to enjoy summertime.

I was about to close the door, when a movement on the other side of the street caught my eye. Wolf stepped out of the shadows. I couldn't see him well, but he bowed his head and walked away like he was thinking about something.

Still holding Mochie in my arms, I rushed outside. "Wolf!" I hissed.

He turned around.

"What are you doing?"

He glanced up and down the street before sprinting over to peck me on the cheek and pet Mochie. "I'm sorry that I've been so hard on you lately. It's not a good excuse, but I've been sort of self-absorbed."

"You don't need to apologize. I can't imagine what you're going through. Want to come in for a nightcap?"

A ragged sigh escaped his lips. "Sure it won't upset Mars?"

Did I detect a note of jealousy? We walked inside my house, and I set Mochie on the floor. "Quite sure."

I didn't bother asking what he would like. I pulled a couple of footed hurricane glasses from my cabinet and filled them with crushed ice. Using a jigger to measure, I poured sweet peach schnapps, vodka, cranberry juice, and orange juice into each. The orange and red colors melted into each other, no doubt the origin of the name, Sunset Boulevard.

It was all I could do to keep from blurting the uppermost thing on my mind — did they find any other evidence today? Handing Wolf a drink, I sank into a chair that faced him. "Are you hungry? I could whip up —"

"I'm good." He sipped the Sunset Boulevard. "This is perfect. So, did Mars's late-night call have anything to do with Roscoe's visit to his house earlier today?"

Whoa! I hadn't expected that. How could he possibly know? The shock on my face was surely giving me away. I bolted from my chair and sought a task.

I opened the refrigerator door. "I haven't

271

had dinner. I'm starved." I spotted a gorgeous, light-purple eggplant that I'd harvested from the garden before Troy arrived. If memory served, I had picked up a ready-made six-grain pizza crust. I found it and slid it out of the package.

Wolf watched me slice onions and toss them into a pan to caramelize. I busied myself with the eggplant and bright red peppers.

He rose, washed his hands, and opened the fridge. The next thing I knew, he was grating mozzarella. "What do you think about a little bit of fresh arugula on top for a zing? Basil, too?"

For the millionth time, I thought that there was no way Wolf killed his wife. What kind of murderer pitched in to make a white pizza — with arugula no less?

As though he could read my thoughts, he eased behind me, placed his hands gently on my shoulders, and turned me around. "We'll get through this. I don't know how it will all play out. But I know one thing. I did not kill Anne. Over the last couple of days, I have had to face the horrifying truth that someone did kill her. But it wasn't me."

An eight-inch chef's knife was still in my hand when I hugged him. "I wish you would let me help you."

He let go of me and returned to the cheese. "I know you do, Sophie, and if I think of anything at all that you or Nina can do, I promise to let you know."

I was willing to let the door close on this topic fast, before he could say to keep my nose out of it.

The kitchen door slammed open. "I knew I smelled pizza!" Nina sipped from my glass. "Sunset Boulevards without me?"

I made one for her as fast as I could. When I handed it to her, I whispered, "Ixnay on Anne."

Happily, the rest of the evening seemed like old times before I dug up that stupid purse. While the pizza baked, we snuck out to the backyard to see what changes had taken place. Windows had been installed on the side of the garage, and they had begun the process of laying brick on the walls. A door and another window opened to the rear.

Pallets of stone were clustered near the back of the garage.

Wolf hefted a stone. "I bet they're building a path to the gate."

As a rule, I liked stonework. "Maybe this will turn out all right in spite of Natasha."

Unfortunately, Natasha and Mars woke me

at six in the morning. They let themselves in and shouted up the stairs to me.

I clomped downstairs. "Give me my key," I growled. "Why won't anyone let me sleep in this week?"

"Don't mind her, Nat. It takes Soph a while to wake up." Mars grabbed Daisy's leash.

"She doesn't have time this morning." Natasha shoved papers under my nose. "Here are your lines. See if you can get them right this time."

I ignored her and asked Mars, "Where are you taking Daisy?"

"She never gets to run when she stays with you."

"She walks!" I protested. "Besides, shouldn't you . . ." I stopped mid-question. Natasha probably didn't know what was up with Roscoe.

Mars tilted his head and held his palms up, communicating that I wasn't getting it.

Aha — he was using Daisy as an excuse to go to Roscoe's house.

Natasha bustled into my kitchen. I could hear her starting coffee. "Right," I whispered to Mars. "Like Mindy and Violet are really going to think you ran all the way over to their neighborhood?"

"I need an excuse to go there early, and

chances are pretty good that they don't know where I live. Daisy, want to go for a ride?"

They ran out the door, sticking me with Natasha.

"Sophie," she trilled. "Better shower and do your hair." She hurried into the foyer. "Should I pick out something for you to wear?"

"That won't be necessary." I grumbled. "What are we supposed to be doing?"

She handed me a mug of coffee and pumped her fists on her waist. "Honestly, Sophie, if you would read the script I gave you, you wouldn't have to ask. Now hurry! You're on camera with Troy in half an hour, and you're a mess."

I returned wearing a summery pink dress that I particularly liked because of the slimming vertical pin tucks all the way around it. The skirt flared out ever so slightly. I'd added a handmade necklace featuring a large pink druzy stone. The tiny, rough quartz crystals on the top shimmered when I moved. I wasn't going the four-inch-heel route, though, and wore comfortable strappy sandals with low heels.

"I knew I should have picked out your wardrobe." She sighed like a ten-year-old drama queen and thrust papers in my hand. "You left your lines down here. Troy is waiting."

I glanced at the paper in my hand. Exclamation marks preceded and ended every single line. I gathered I was supposed to be excited.

They positioned me on the sidewalk in front of my house, and Troy asked a few questions. I answered with what I hoped was the proper blend of doubt and perkiness.

The best part of the whole thing was knowing that it would be over soon. At least I hoped it would. What if it rained? What if they didn't finish everything?

"Thanks, Sophie. We'll be wrapping up soon."

I looked up at Troy. "I'm so sorry about Heath."

"It came as a big shock. I'd been running around bad-mouthing him and leaving mean messages on his phone like I always do when he takes off — and this time, oh man, some woman must have finally caught up with him. Hey, you were there. Was he really buried under mulch?"

"Everything except his hand."

Troy gagged. "We're dedicating this episode to him. You know, he pushed and pushed to do this show, telling us how terrific Old Town is and that an opportunity like this was too good to pass up. He wanted to come back here, and look where it got him."

"Troy, did Heath have a girlfriend?"

"So, Heath was your type, huh? Women were all over him. Didn't matter where we went, Heath was never alone."

"I meant a special girlfriend. Someone he loved? Someone named . . . Anne?"

"He used to talk about some knockout. What was her name? A kind of bug, I think."

"Cricket?"

CHAPTER TWENTY-FOUR

Dear Natasha,
Every year, my wife plants annuals in containers. Then she makes me cart them around — to our pool for parties, to the driveway for the annual block party — and those things are heavy! There has to be a better way.
   — Pooped in Oak Bluffs, Massachusetts

Dear Pooped,
Fill the bottom of large pots with light material, like an upside-down plastic pot or crushed soda cans. Just be sure the water can still drain.
                              — Natasha

"That's it — Cricket! He described her like she was centerfold material."

Eww. What a compliment. My head spun. Heath and Cricket? There was an unlikely couple. Maybe he was infatuated and admired her from afar?

"Sophie? Sophie?" said Troy.

"Sooophie!" Natasha called from some-where.

I dashed into my house, fed Mochie, retrieved my purse, and left, bolting past everyone outside, walking as fast as I could. I had to get away from the commotion. I had to think.

On King Street, I stopped by my favorite bakery for a croissant and a tall cup of English Breakfast tea with milk and sugar. I took them to a bench overlooking the Potomac River, shared my breakfast with the seagulls, and thought about Heath.

He had worked for Roscoe, so it wasn't peculiar that he knew Cricket. But I still wasn't sure about his connection to Anne. I massaged my temples and forced myself to think about a possibility that I didn't want to consider. If Olive was correct about Heath and Anne having an affair — could Wolf have killed Heath? Surely not. Had they seen each other in my backyard that first day? I hadn't noticed any awkwardness, but then, I was a little blown away by it all when Troy arrived. There had to be some other explanation. Could it be that Olive lied about Anne's involvement with Heath to protect Audie? It seemed like every bit of information sent me in a circle. I wasn't making any progress at all.

I wished Wolf would tell me about his issues with Roscoe. That information might be key. Or maybe it just didn't matter. Most likely, whatever happened to Anne had nothing to do with Roscoe or his family. Who else had known Anne? Her boss at the accounting firm. Maybe he was still with the company. I pulled out my phone and found the address I'd seen on the Internet. At nine o'clock, I headed over.

The company where Anne had worked occupied a large town house just off King Street. I tapped the brass door knocker and opened the door slightly. A worn oriental carpet covered gleaming hardwood floors. I ventured inside. An umbrella stand and a simple table holding a basket of silk peonies were the only other items in the foyer. Stairs ran up on the left side. "Hello?" I called.

A woman's voice asked, "How can I help you?"

I finally saw her seated at a desk in a room to my right. "I was wondering if I might talk to someone who knew Anne Fleishman."

She took a deep breath, stood up, and walked into an adjoining room.

A man shouted, "I don't have all day to

talk to the police. You tell them that if they want any more information, they'll have to subpoena it. I'm not breaching client privilege. All this garbage should have ended years ago when she died. I rue the day Anne set foot in this office. I will not lose my business because of her."

I was ready to give up and crawl toward the door when I heard him say, "Oh, really?"

The woman returned. "Mr. Overton will see you now."

What could she possibly have said to change his mind? I entered his office, and Mr. Overton rose from his seat. Tall and gangly, his head seemed oddly proportioned — longer than it should have been. Either his eyes were recessed or his brow jutted out, I wasn't quite sure. Dark brown bangs had been cut too short in a straight line at the top of his forehead.

He shook my hand. "I had no idea that policewomen were so pretty these days."

I snatched my hand back and worked hard at making sure my smile didn't fade. He motioned to a chair and perched on his desk, looking down at me like a delighted vulture ready for lunch.

Echhhhh. "I didn't mean to mislead you. I'm not with the police." I hurried to stroke his ego, hoping he wouldn't throw me out immediately. "I'm just so thrilled that you could take a minute out of your busy day to talk to me about Anne."

"Of course. She was a dear. We certainly miss her."

"What kind of work did she do for you?"

"She was a corporate auditor. Have you ever considered that field?"

"What is that exactly?"

"They ensure a company's tax and accounting systems are working correctly. They look for mismanagement and fraud, make sure everything is accurate. It's a very exciting area."

I was clearly going to have to lie if I wanted information from him. "I have always been sorry that I didn't pursue that myself. Anne made the right choice."

"Actually, it was not the correct path for her, but you seem very bright."

"Anne wasn't smart?"

"Not when it came to men, obviously!" He cackled as though we were sharing a joke. I wasn't sure what he meant, but it gave me the opening I needed.

I forced a weak laugh. "They say she was having an affair."

He toyed with his suit jacket. "She certainly was beautiful. I cannot fathom what she saw in him. She was shortsighted in that regard. I see *you're* not wearing a wedding ring."

In him? Who did he mean? Wolf? Heath? "Not yet." Better set up any roadblocks that I could lest he get ideas. "I'm still working on my boyfriend." I took a chance. "Did you know Heath?"

Overton huffed. "I don't associate with embezzlers. You can imagine that his ilk are exactly what we are paid to guard against. Do you like Mexican food?"

Embezzler? Could Heath have been embezzling? I wished I could ask him straight out. "So, um, I heard that Anne ran into some problems at work because she wasn't all that bright."

His arms folded over his chest and the sick smile faded. "I can't talk about that, Miss . . . I'm sorry, what did you say your name was? Maybe you could give me your number?"

Out of an abundance of caution, I wrote down Natasha's name and number and hoped he would never call.

I left his office, certain his eyes were following me, and not in a nice way. I shook like a wet dog when I stepped onto the sidewalk, wishing I could wash off the ickiness Overton projected.

"Overton come on to you?"

I whipped around. Wolf leaned against the brick wall of Overton's office building, his arms crossed resolutely over his chest.

"Not exactly. He wanted my number, though. No wonder Anne hated her job."

Wolf rubbed his eyes. "What do I have to do to convince you to stay out of this? I've asked you, I've told you — Sophie, I'm begging you to knock it off."

I felt small, like a kid who'd made Dad angry. "Why couldn't you tell me about Anne's relationship with Heath? If you'd told me, I wouldn't have to ask other people. Did Anne get caught up in one of his embezzlement schemes?"

"Is that what he told you? That jerk!" Wolf flung open the door and stormed inside.

I ran after him.

He barged past the receptionist and into Overton's office. A door slammed shut somewhere.

I dashed into Overton's office, but it was empty except for Wolf, so I peered out the window in hopes of catching sight of Overton. I was in luck. In the back of the building, Overton looked over his shoulder, walking so fast that he stumbled over his own feet.

When I turned around, I expected Wolf to still be angry with me, but he had fixated on a picture on Overton's wall. I hadn't noticed it before because it was behind me when I spoke to Overton.

In it, Overton's arm looped around Anne's shoulders. Their heads tilted toward each other and they wore laughing smiles.

CHAPTER TWENTY-FIVE

Dear Sophie,
My wife and I love the flavor of home-grown tomatoes. We both work, and mornings are always a rush. We come home late and are too bushed to spend a lot of time watering plants. How can we make sure our tomato plants are getting the water they need?
— Tomato Sandwich Aficionado in
Strawberry Plains, Tennessee

Dear Tomato Sandwich Aficionado,
Cut the bottoms off of plastic one-gallon jugs. Empty vinegar jugs are perfect for this. Stick the small spout end in the ground by each tomato plant. Fill with water and allow it to soak in as needed.
— Sophie

Wolf ripped the photo off the wall. He opened the frame, and slid the picture out.

Leaving the empty frame on Overton's desk like a picked-over chicken carcass, he strode out as though he had forgotten all about me.

From the front door, I watched him blast down the street.

The receptionist stood beside me.

"I'm sorry about that," I said. "He's under a lot of stress."

"Are you kidding? It's fun to see that blowhard Overton get his comeuppance."

I took a harder look at her. Medium height, short curly hair, no makeup, wire-rimmed glasses. She wore a simple short-sleeved blouse and skirt that wouldn't win any fashion prizes. Birkenstock sandals adorned her feet.

"Did you know Anne?" I asked.

"No. I interviewed for my job on the day she didn't show up for work. What a mad-house! The tension was terrible." She smiled sadly. "I always thought I got the job be-cause they were in too much of a panic to give hiring much thought. Accountants are very precise people. Planners, you know? They don't take disruptions well."

"Can you tell me what happened?"

She shifted her feet uncomfortably. "I can't divulge anything about clients. That would be a big ethical breach. But between the two of us, I'll say this, I always wondered if Roscoe Greene didn't kill her."

Roscoe! "What did Anne have to do with Roscoe?"

"I can't say anything more, or I'll lose my job."

"There was a picture of Anne and Overton on his wall. There weren't any, um, rumors about them, were there?"

She cringed as if repulsed by the thought. "None that I ever heard. You must not have studied the other pictures. They're all of Overton with pretty women. I call it his fantasy wall. Here he comes. I didn't tell you anything, okay?"

"Not a word! How do you keep him from mauling you?"

She giggled. "I told him my father was a martial arts instructor, and that I knew five easy ways to kill him."

"And that worked?"

"Like a charm." She slipped inside and closed the door.

I hurried in the other direction, hoping Overton's long legs wouldn't help him catch up to me. I turned the first corner I came to and ducked inside a little store. Feigning an interest in baby clothes, I made my way to the show window and watched the street. I picked up a toddler's sundress with white ties on the shoulders. A teensy ladybug adorned each tie. They reminded me of Anne and the ladybug she embroidered on the pillow in Wolf's house. Wolf said she loved ladybugs and praying mantises. I examined the stitches. Flipping the strap over, I decided the outfit was machine embroidered. A person wouldn't achieve such tight, even stitches.

Would I think of Anne each time I saw a ladybug for the rest of my life? I looked up in time to spy Overton striding by on those long legs like Ichabod Crane.

No doubt disappointing the saleswoman who hovered nearby, I put down the dress and peered out the door. When I thought the coast was clear, I headed straight to Nina's house.

I slipped through the alley and snuck through her back gate so Natasha wouldn't see me and try to rope me into something that she hoped would impress TV executives.

I knocked on the kitchen door.

Nina opened it cautiously. "Nobody ever comes to this door. You scared me half to death."

"Ready to check on the cat?"

"You're going dressed like that?"

"I can't go home to change. I'll be so glad

when this backyard nightmare is over, and Natasha isn't at my house all the time. Come on. I want to ask Roscoe a few questions. I'll tell you all about it on the way over there."

Birds twittered and butterflies flitted between flowers in the garden Olive had created, but not a soul was in sight.

"I was afraid Kenner's men might still be camped out here," whispered Nina. "It's like a garden paradise. Are those humming-birds?"

"Looks like a fight over territory." They zoomed in circles, chasing each other. One flew away, and the other feasted at a plant. Beautiful to watch, but I had a feeling it was very serious business to them. The long, tubular flowers drooping in clusters on tall stems must seem like a buffet to hummingbirds.

"Those would be gorgeous in a tall vase. Think anyone would mind if I snipped a few to take home?" asked Nina.

"I don't think you want to — they're poisonous. In fact, those are foxglove. Roscoe said the medicine digitalis comes from foxglove plants. If memory serves, I think Agatha Christie used foxglove leaves to kill people in one of her stories." I studied the plants. "You know, whoever poisoned Roscoe didn't have to use medicine." I gestured toward the garden. "It's right here for free."

The pinkish blooms flared at the end like trumpets, revealing little dots of burgundy on the inside. Olive had planted them in large groups. Even with the other stunning plants in her garden, the foxglove stood out in size and brilliant color. The green leaves lower on the stalk resembled basil or young spinach leaves.

"Those cone-shaped things? How come the hummingbird isn't dead?"

I had no idea. We edged toward the foxglove cautiously, as though it might leap at us.

Nina sucked in air. "Look! Some of the foxglove plants have been cut."

I crouched to examine the stems. "Maybe they were deadheaded by the gardeners."

"Or by Audie."

A chill skittered over me at the thought of Audie poisoning his father with a foxglove planted by his mother.

A happy *woof* came from the direction of the house. Daisy hurtled toward us, acting as though she hadn't seen us in weeks.

"Mars must be here."

Daisy wriggled with glee and pawed the air.

I gave her a big puppy hug, then looked around for Mars.

Nina bent to her. "Sweetie, I'm trying to catch a kitty cat. Maybe your mom could take you back to the house?"

"No problem." I ruffled her fur. "Come on, Daisy."

She walked beside me, happily wagging her tail. As we neared the corner of Roscoe's home, I could hear hushed voices. Roscoe and Mars sat outside on the porch at a round table covered with a sunshine-yellow cloth. Vivid red geraniums bloomed in pots along the black wood floor, and someone had placed a cluster of the red blossoms in a white vase that matched the earthenware. Tall glasses of orange juice added more splashes of color.

Roscoe and Mars called to me and invited me to join them.

"I'm surprised you're willing to eat here," I said.

"We watched every single step of the preparation." Mars fed Daisy a piece of cantaloupe.

Through the window, I could see Violet hovering inside, no doubt listening to every word.

I pulled up a chair, ready to get down to business. "Roscoe, did Heath embezzle money from your company?"

He slapped his napkin on the table, horror on his face. Pointing a fleshy finger at Mars he said, "This is exactly what I'm talking about." He turned his attention to me. "Where'd you hear that?"

I didn't want to get anyone in trouble. "You and Wolf have some kind of beef, so I've been asking around, and I sort of put two and two together."

"Calm down, Roscoe." Mars glared at me. "I've called in the crisis team."

That brought back memories. When we were married, Mars had called the crisis team each time one of his politicians made a salacious blunder. They were public relations specialists who dictated a course to minimize the impact of a painfully public catastrophe. "Because Heath stole money? I'm not following."

"To handle the news of Heath's death on Roscoe's property."

Roscoe's jowls quivered. "There have to be consequences, Mars. Otherwise, people talk. There might not be anything we can do about the police and Heath, but can't we stop everybody from reviving that old stuff? It's water under the bridge."

I'd been surprised by Roscoe's reaction to my statement. Clearly, there had been some kind of issue involving Heath, Roscoe, and money. Maybe I should have backed off, but I was tired of getting the runaround and half-truths.

"Roscoe, I'm sorry to upset you, but this is important. Someone murdered Anne and Heath. I'm not the only one who will be asking questions."

He pounded his fist on the table, causing the dishes to jump and clatter.

Daisy shuffled backward in alarm.

"For pity's sake, how many times do I have to say it? It's over and done with."

Mars kicked me under the table.

"Do *you* know what happened?" I asked him.

"You'll have to excuse Sophie. She's been dating Wolf."

Roscoe leaned back in his chair and contemplated me, drumming the fingers of his right hand on the table. "I did not know that." He thought for a moment, the left side of his mouth pulling to the side in an irritated expression. "Anne Fleishman was not the angel Wolf thought she was. When Heath worked for me a few years back, he and Anne stole my money. Millions. Funneled it right out of my business accounts.

It was a perfect setup because Anne was supposed to audit the accounts. If it hadn't been for Cricket, we never would have known about it. She noticed a discrepancy and figured it out. Fortunately, Cricket managed to get the money back. That girl is a gem, got every last cent of my money. We didn't want any bad publicity, so we threw a blanket over the whole thing and never pressed charges. All's well that ends well, you know. If anything, Wolf ought to be thankful that I didn't put that precious wife of his in jail."

No wonder Wolf didn't want to tell me. He probably had trouble dealing with it himself. An embezzler! And with another man, which meant she probably *was* in a relationship with Heath. Wolf must have been mortified . . . and hurt. A double whammy. Anne had been a duplicitous, two-timing criminal. She betrayed Wolf in every way possible. She couldn't have been farther from the sweet innocent he or Mona had described.

I sat back. Cricket had been Anne's best friend. What would I have done if I'd discovered Nina was stealing from someone? Probably the same thing Cricket did. Report her, try to get the money back, and hope the consequences wouldn't be severe. Was that the real reason Anne was murdered? Did Heath murder her for taking him down with her? What about Overton? Had anyone considered him? He was a first-class sleazebag. I wouldn't put it past him to kill her for putting his firm in jeopardy. Or had she angered him by spurning his revolting overtures?

"What I want to know," Roscoe grumbled, "is how Heath had the nerve to show his face around here again."

I studied Roscoe. I thought I'd known him — not terribly well, but enough. Yet his words gave me an unexpected peek into his mind. Heath had gall to show up after trying to steal Roscoe's money, no question about that. But why was that Roscoe's main concern? Why wasn't he worried about the fact that someone had murdered Heath? Someone who was probably in Roscoe's inner circle.

I looked up to see Mrs. Danvers fixing me with a steely glare from a kitchen window. She'd tried to cover up Heath's hand after we had seen it. It had been laughable, really. Did she think she was protecting Roscoe? Audie? Had one of them killed Heath when he showed up again? Or had she done him in herself?

A scream broke the tense silence. Another

followed, and another.

We all jumped to our feet. Roscoe yelled, "Was that you, Violet?" He lumbered into the house.

Daisy had better hearing than the rest of us. She vaulted over the steps to the grass and shot toward the guest house.

Mars raced after her. I wasn't as fast, and my sandals slipped on the grass. I slid them off and ran across the lawn.

Mars and Daisy had gone inside. I flung open the door.

CHAPTER TWENTY-SIX

Dear Natasha,
My wife and I are having a disagreement about basil. She says we should only cut off the leaves that we need. I say we're supposed to harvest the leaves by cutting the stem so that only a few leaves remain. Who's right? Breakfast in bed is riding on this one.
— Vicious Pruner in Rosemary, Maine

Dear Vicious Pruner,
Get ready to enjoy a delicious breakfast in bed. Pruning the stem will produce fuller plants. Leaving the stem allows the plant to go to seed, making the leaves bitter.
— Natasha

Nina stood in the center of the guest house shaking, her hands over her nose and mouth. At the bottom of steep stairs, Mindy sprawled stomach down on the hardwood floor. Her head was turned to the side, her eyes closed.

Mars fell to his knees beside Mindy. "No pulse! Sophie, we're going to have to flip her!" He tried to tug Mindy away from the wall without much success.

"Nina! Call 911." I ran to Mindy and asked Mars, "What if she broke her neck? Maybe we shouldn't move her."

"We *have* to start CPR!"

He was right. I grabbed her shoulder and shoved.

We managed to scoot her out into the room far enough to maneuver behind her.

"On the count of three, we flip." Mars counted out loud. "One . . . two . . . three!"

We rolled her over onto her back, and I started hands only CPR immediately.

Daisy sniffed Mindy's head.

"Did you get 911?" I shouted to Nina.

"They're on their way. I told them we're in the guest house. What else can I do?"

The door banged open. Roscoe and Violet peered inside.

"What's going on?" Roscoe went pale. "Mindy," he whispered. He rushed at us and collapsed in a heap beside her.

Violet screamed. "Roscoe! Roscoe!"

Mars took over the CPR. A good thing,

because I was in no shape to keep it up for long.

Sirens wailed in the distance.

Nina and I helped Roscoe to a chair. "I'm fine," he breathed. "No need to fuss."

He didn't look well to me.

Two EMTs rushed inside and relieved Mars, whose face sweated like he'd raced in a competition. We waited silently, hoping for the best.

One of the EMTs asked questions about how Mindy fell. We had no answers. He hammered Roscoe with questions about Mindy. Roscoe appeared to be in a mild daze, and clearly not familiar with Mindy's medical history or possible drug allergies.

They stopped CPR, and I felt as though my own heart had stopped. Raising my voice, I asked, "Is she alive?"

"Barely."

They stabilized her neck with a brace, and rolled her out to the ambulance in a gurney. Mars followed them asking questions.

He returned quickly. "Roscoe, they need you to go to the hospital. I'll drive you."

I sidled over to him and whispered, "Maybe Roscoe should ride in the ambulance, too. I don't think he's well."

Roscoe reached up to grab Violet's hand.

"Call Olive. I need Olive."

Mrs. Danvers's dark eyes darted around, restless and fearful.

With Mars's help, Roscoe managed to stand, but he shuffled out as though he'd been zapped of all energy.

Violet raced up the stairs. She returned quickly, grabbed a mop, and set to work washing the floor. She moved rapidly, in crazy frenzied motions.

She glanced at the phone, then at Nina and me. Dropping the mop in the middle of the floor, she collected a pair of white high-heeled shoes with red soles that must have been on Mindy's feet and ran for the main house.

"What were you doing in here anyway?" I asked Nina. I'd never been inside Roscoe's guest house before. We were in a cozy room with a fireplace. A cobalt blue ceramic tile counter separated a tiny kitchen in the back. Books and floral pillows were everywhere. I wanted to brew a cup of tea and snuggle among the pillows with a book.

The steep stairs led up on the right side. I could see a railing upstairs. I guessed it was some kind of sleeping loft and maybe a bathroom.

"I wanted to find Violet's poison so she wouldn't kill the cat. Do you think it was an accident? That Mindy just slipped and fell?" Nina migrated toward the stairs, looking upward.

"Good question. Something weird is going on around here, that's for sure."

Nina started up the stairs. "Tell me if Mrs. Danvers comes back."

"What are you doing?"

"I'm snooping, if you must know."

"Nina!"

She looked over the railing at me. "You saw Mrs. Danvers. If there's any evidence in this place, it will be washed, bleached, or sterilized within the hour. Besides, it's not a crime scene."

"If someone pushed her, he might be hiding up there."

Nina swung around. "Daisy! Here, girl!"

Daisy galloped up the stairs, her heavy paws alerting anyone who might be in the loft.

"Daisy will let me know if someone is hiding."

"Well, hurry up!" I poked my head outside, searching for Violet. No sign of her.

"Sophie! Sophie! Come up here!"

We were going to get caught. Violet probably hadn't gone to call Olive. She was probably retrieving a gun. I tried to recall what had happened to Mrs. Danvers at the end of *Rebecca* but couldn't remember. Why did I have a bad feeling that she died? Reluctantly, I climbed the stairs. I knew one thing — Roscoe wasn't in the habit of going up to the loft. The stairs were treacherous. I paused to catch my breath at the top.

Nina and Daisy inspected an under-bed storage box on wheels. It held fourteen pairs of designer shoes, from an outrageous leopard print, to silver-gray sequins, to black suede with diamond starbursts on the five-inch heels.

Nina giggled. "I think Mindy has a shoe addiction."

"Please tell me those are rhinestones and not real diamonds."

Nina picked one up and slid it onto her foot. "They're like walking on stilts! Oof!" She took it off and replaced it. "They're all the latest designers."

I blew air out of my mouth. "At least it's not poison."

"No, but this little stash is worth about fifty grand. I bet she's hiding them from Roscoe."

"Please. No one would kill anyone over shoes."

Nina laughed. "Hello? Have you ever been to a major shoe sale?" Her tone dipped. "It's ugly."

"Put that back, and let's get out of here. This isn't any of our business."

Nina rolled the shoe box under the bed. "Maybe not, but she's not going to need those at the five-hundred-acre hunting and fishing bed-and-breakfast."

We trod carefully down the stairs.

"I forgot about that."

"Check for Mrs. Danvers, will you?"

"What are you doing now?"

"Looking in the kitchen for poison."

I followed her. "Who would keep poison in the kitchen?"

"Everyone. Maybe it has to be refrigerated." She opened a tiny pantry. "Someone has a thing for Italian dressing and olives."

Although it was sort of interesting to peek into their lives this way, I *did* feel guilty. On the other hand, Roscoe wasn't up to the task of searching his property for poison. I pulled open the fridge.

Nina peered over my shoulder. "Anything interesting?"

"Bottled water, more of the Italian dressing, roasted peppers in a jar, mozzarella —"

"Oh! I love those pralines. Think they would notice one missing?"

I shut the refrigerator. "How do you know they don't have poison in them?"

She made a face at me and opened the

trash can. "Violet must arrange flowers here."

I peered inside the metal trash bin. Tiny bits of leaves and flowers had been dumped inside, along with long stems.

"Let's go."

We turned to find Mrs. Danvers blocking the doorway. We were trapped.

"Did you find it?" Violet asked.

"You mean the po—"

I kicked backward. My heel made contact with Nina's calf.

"Ouch!"

Trying to smile, I asked in as sweet a voice as I could muster, "Did we find what?"

Violet pulled her chin back and studied us with cold, hawkish eyes. "The mallard print. Isn't that why you were snooping?"

"The mallard print! No, we didn't see it. I know Roscoe would feel much better if someone found it."

Honestly, the woman had such a sour expression that it was hard to tell if she was angry or upset. The corners of her mouth quivered, and she fell into a chair, limp as a rag doll.

"Could I get you a glass of water?"

She stared at the floor. "There's nothing anyone can do. I've done myself in."

Nina and I exchanged a wide-eyed look.

Could we get her to confess and tell us where the poison was?

"It can't be that bad." I tried to sound soothing.

"I'm afraid it is. I can't undo it. It's all my fault."

CHAPTER TWENTY-SEVEN

Dear Sophie,
I love my dog, I really do! But she's eating my cucumbers. She pulls them off the vine and eats them. How do I stop this behavior?
— Pooch Pop in Dogwood, Tennessee

Dear Pooch Pop,
It could be worse. Don't fight it. Plant extra for the pooch!
— Sophie

Good heavens! She hadn't taken poison, had she?

Nina beat me to it. She gripped Violet's shoulders and gently shook her. "Violet! Did you poison yourself?"

Violet shrank back. "No!"

"Maybe we could help. Where did you put it?" I asked, hoping Violet would tell me where she had stashed the poison.

"Upstairs in the loft. I hid it there during the party."

"Did you put any in the party food?" asked Nina. "There were children present!"

Violet lifted her dark eyes to meet mine. "Is she daft? Who could put a print in food?"

"Oh! You moved the mallard print from Roscoe's den to the loft?" I squatted to her level and nearly tipped over.

"For safekeeping, you see." Her head sagged. "I admit that I wanted to teach Roscoe a little lesson. But I didn't mean for it to be stolen! Not really!"

"So *you* stole the mallard print." Nina sounded annoyed, no doubt due to the "daft" remark.

Violet moaned. "Yes, yes, yes. Only I didn't think of it as stealing because I intended to put it back when Roscoe learned his lesson." Her voice grew thin. "But now it's gone."

"Someone took it from the loft." I stated it to be clear that I understood the situation. "Mindy, maybe?"

Her eyes narrowed, which did nothing to improve her menacing appearance. "She wants to be rid of me. I watch her, you know. I hear the nasty things she whispers to Roscoe about me. She told her friend that I'd better hope Roscoe lives a long time because when she inherits everything, I'll be the first thing she throws out. I know what goes on around here."

Could Violet have intended to poison Mindy but ended up poisoning Roscoe by mistake?

"Who killed Heath?" blurted Nina.

"How should I know?" Violet leaned toward me. "Is she your ward? Must be difficult for you."

I had to bite my upper lip to keep from cracking up. I nearly keeled over on my bottom. Fortunately, my legs were stiff from crouching, and my groan when I stood up disguised a chuckle. "Violet, we know you covered up Heath's hand. Why did you do that? Who were you protecting?"

Her eyes darted around frantically. "I don't know! I'm so afraid it's someone in the family."

"It might have been Mindy who murdered Heath," said Nina.

Violet focused on Nina. "That woman wouldn't touch mulch unless jewelry was hidden in it. Did you find the shoe collection upstairs? She hides them there so Roscoe won't know about them."

"Someone else might have covered him with the mulch to help her."

"The Greenes are a respectable family.

They're the salt of the earth. Good people. Always have been. I won't see Mindy sully the Greene name, even if she does throw me out of the house."

Violet rose and seized the mop, her mouth pinched. "Catch that cat and leave."

We flew out the door.

"Sheesh," said Nina. "I'm feeling sorry for Mindy. I'd want to kick Violet out, too."

At that moment, Cricket stepped out of the door to Roscoe's den onto the patio, carrying a trendy designer duffle bag. "There you are! I wondered why the door wasn't locked. Did you catch the cat?"

"Not yet," said Nina. "You do know about Mindy's, er, accident?"

"Isn't it awful? I warned her about those five-inch heels. They make your legs look terrific, but they're like walking on stilts."

I glanced at Cricket's feet. She wore running shoes and was using the top of one foot to rub the other calf.

"I couldn't wear them. I would fall for sure," said Nina. "Everyone else is at the hospital. The only one left here is Mrs. . . . Violet."

"Poor thing. I'm sure she's distressed." Cricket swung the bag off her shoulder and set it on the patio. "I just stopped by to see if she wants a ride to the hospital."

We told her we would let ourselves out and hurried through the house to the driveway.

Moments later, Nina clenched the steering wheel with both hands and glanced back at. "I hope Mrs. Danvers goes to the hospital with Cricket. I'm so afraid that she'll poison the cat." We turned the corner and merged into heavier traffic heading toward Old Town. "I'm starved. Do you mind stopping for lunch, Sophie?"

"Not at all." While Nina drove and talked about the cat, my mind was on Heath. According to Troy, Heath had wanted to return to Old Town. Why would an embezzler be eager to return to the scene of the crime? For money.

Roscoe said he'd gotten every penny back. Had Heath intended to burglarize Roscoe's home? Maybe he'd found the mallard print in the guest house and stolen it. Would he have known how valuable it was?

Or had he come to blackmail someone? Anne was dead, so he couldn't have been after her. Did he think he could blackmail Roscoe? Roscoe wasn't the type to go along with a scheme like that. Did he want to see Cricket? She caught him in the act of embezzling. According to Troy, Heath had spoken of her in lecherous terms. He certainly remembered Cricket; maybe he wanted revenge.

Even if he had come to Old Town for some completely different reason, he'd made a point of paying the Greenes a visit. Why?

Nina parked near the river. "The Dancing Crab across the street has an outdoor patio where dogs are permitted. And I'm craving their clam pasta. No, I'd rather eat the spiced shrimp. No, the pasta. Too bad I can't have both."

My phone rang as I opened the back hatch so Daisy could leap from the car. I glanced at the caller. "It's Olive!" I answered and said, "Hello?"

Mars's voice responded. "Where are you?"

"We're having lunch. Why are you using Olive's phone?"

"Kenner still has mine."

I told him where we were and hung up just as Daisy, who had been standing quietly by my legs, backed up and snarled. "What are you upset about, Daisy? It's okay . . ."

"That dog is going to bite somebody one of these days."

I swung around. Kenner approached us on the sidewalk.

Never would I have expected to be glad to

see him. "Hi! If I buy you some spiced —"

"Save your breath, Sophie. I can't tell you anything."

"Aw, come on. Nina and I are going to have lunch. Five minutes?"

He accompanied Nina, Daisy, and me across the street to an outdoor table in the shade but with a great view of King Street, Old Town's main drag.

We ordered three iced teas, their fabulous sweet Vidalia onion hush puppies and spiced shrimp for the table, and clam pasta for Nina. The waitress brought our tea immediately, along with a bowl of cold water for Daisy.

Kenner gulped half his tea. "Thanks. That hits the spot, but I still can't tell you anything."

"How do you know what I want to ask you?"

He groaned. "What was on the knife we found, and how did Heath die."

I made a buzzer sound, as though he had gotten the question wrong on a game show, even though I would have loved to hear the answers to those questions. "You seem to know Cricket pretty well. Is it possible she had an affair with Heath?"

He studied me for a moment, then burst out laughing. "You never stop surprising

313

me. Cricket? Not a chance." Kenner shook his head. "Poor Cricket, she's had this problem her whole life."

"What problem?"

"You've seen her. Men claim she's dating them when she's not. It's the curse of being so attractive. Guys lie about her, and it makes her sound like a loose woman."

"Did you date her?"

"No." He spoke softly. "We went through a lot together, Cricket and I. Eventually we lost touch. For a while there, we were the only ones who understood what the other one was going through. But we never dated. Listen, Sophie" — he scratched the back of his right hand — "you'd be doing everybody a big favor if you could get Wolf to tell you where Anne's body is. The stress of not knowing is about to do Mona in."

Now I was sorry I'd bought him iced tea! "Kenner, hasn't it ever crossed your mind that someone else might have killed her?"

"You don't know Wolf like I do."

"So tell me."

The waitress arrived with Chesapeake Bay spiced shrimp, warm hush puppies, and little tubs of creamy, unsalted butter. A cool breeze blew off the river, and it felt like the heavenly days of summer.

"A long time ago," said Kenner, "Wolf and

I went through the police academy together. We were friends. Back then, Wolf dated a knockout. A copper-haired woman with a body that never stopped."

"Cricket?" No wonder Wolf had looked at her that way when we saw her on the street.

"Exactly. Cricket had a friend, Anne. The four of us hung out together. I would have done anything for Anne. She was sweet . . . gentle . . . kind. I thought I would spend the rest of my life with her. I even bought the ring. Still have it."

"Let me get this straight," said Nina. "*You* dated Anne, and Wolf dated Cricket?"

"That's right. But I guess sparks were flying between Wolf and Anne, and before we knew it, she was wearing a ring on her finger, and it wasn't the one I had bought for her."

My head was reeling. "No wonder you hate Wolf."

"Let's just say that I don't trust him. Then, when Anne vanished overnight, I knew it had to be because of him." Kenner's hands had curled into angry fists. "I'll never forgive him for that. Wolf stole her from me twice. Once when he married her, and once when he killed her. I'm going to nail him for it, Sophie. This time I'm going to get him."

"Why didn't you tell me all this before?"

"Dirty laundry. I tried to warn you about Wolf." He shrugged. "The rest really didn't matter. I wish I had seen through him sooner. I could have warned Anne."

"Olive said Anne was having an affair with Heath. Do you know anything about that?"

A twisted grin spread across his face. "I hope she did. Wolf deserved to have her cheat on him."

Had he always been so bitter, or had his experience with Anne turned him into a morose and churlish man? "I'm sorry, Kenner. I truly am." His revelation stunned me, but it explained a lot about him and his behavior toward Wolf. And toward me, for that matter. His strange conduct had been an attempt to steal a woman, any woman, away from Wolf. Maybe he didn't have some peculiar attraction to me after all.

"I'd better get back to work." He rose from his chair.

"You're through looking for Anne at Wolf's?"

"Pretty much." He gazed out toward the river. "Unless the tests on that knife come back showing there's blood on it, we'll be back to square one. Sophie, call me any time. The smallest detail could lead us to Anne's body and bring closure for a lot of hurting people."

I nodded. What else could I do? "Wait!" He hadn't said a word about the embezzlement.

He stopped and looked down at me.

"When Anne disappeared, did you hear anything about money problems?"

"Like she forgot to pay the electric bill? Anne and Wolf weren't wealthy by a long shot, but I never heard them complain about their finances."

He strode away, leaving us to contemplate the bombshell about his love for Anne.

"Quite a story!" Nina applied a dab of butter to a hush puppy. "Don't look now. There's Audie! I thought he'd be at the hospital with the rest of his family."

I turned around in time to see him enter a store farther up the block.

Nina jumped to her feet. "We should follow him."

"We have Daisy with us. We can't go in there."

"I'll snoop and report back."

She popped the hush puppy into her mouth and jaywalked across the street, passing Mars.

He spied me and hurried over. "Finally, food that isn't poisoned!" He helped himself to spiced shrimp and signaled the waitress for more. "From now on, I'm not eating or drinking anything without a taste tester."

He chowed down on a hush puppy like he was starved and stole my iced tea. "The cops are questioning Roscoe. There's a real possibility that he'll be arrested for attempting to murder Mindy."

CHAPTER TWENTY-EIGHT

Dear Sophie,
My neighbor is excited because the circus is coming to town. He's taking his truck to get a load of elephant manure! He says it makes plants grow like nothing else. I can only imagine what it will smell like around here. How can I discourage him?
— Sensitive Sniffer in Lilac Park,
California

Dear Sensitive Sniffer,
You're in for a treat. Oddly enough, elephant manure does not have a strong odor. But it's great for plants. Maybe you should get some, too!
— Sophie

"What? That's turning the tables!"
"No kidding. You won't believe this. They found digoxin in her blood. She's not on

any meds, and Roscoe has a prescription for it, so they put two and two together . . ."

"But they know he was sick yesterday. They have the records!"

"I'm not a cop, Soph. All I know is that they're questioning him."

"I guess he can't prove that he flushed his digitalis. Did you tell him about Mindy and Audie's relationship this morning?"

"He . . . was . . . furious. I thought he might implode right then and there. His heart can't take much more of this. Mindy and Audie are everything to him. That was a colossal blow."

The waitress replenished the shrimp and brought Mars an iced tea, which I snagged, since he'd taken mine.

"Correction. Mindy and Audie are *almost* everything to Roscoe. Did you notice that it was Olive he wanted by his side this morning?"

"That was interesting! He called Olive the second we were in the car. It was as though he didn't know what to do without her."

"Yesterday, Roscoe said he was going to set a trap for his poisoner. Do you think he's just a horrible, vengeful man who suspected Mindy and tried to kill her?"

"And he lied about getting rid of the digitalis? Here's how I see it." Mars leaned his elbows against the table and spoke softly. "Roscoe *could* have tried to poison Mindy with his digitalis. Or Olive could have done it for revenge. I understand she was *not* happy about the divorce and placed all the blame on Mindy."

"There's foxglove growing in the garden," I said. "That's where digitalis comes from. Olive must have planted it. She tinkers around making her own herb teas and home remedies. She would know how to use foxglove to poison someone. It would have looked like a digitalis overdose. Maybe she tried to kill both of them!"

"Don't forget that Violet is a little bit off her rocker. We can't eliminate her. And although I hate to suggest this, it's not out of the realm of possibility that Audie is behind the poisoning. He's eager to take over the helm of the company."

I took a deep breath. "At least two good things came out of this mess. The police can test food in the house for digitalis and figure out who's behind it. And Roscoe's family will all be on notice to be careful about what they eat and drink."

"Is that Audie?" Mars squinted.

"Yeah. Nina is spying on him."

"He looks terrible."

Audie waited to cross the street at the light.

I lowered my sunglasses. "Don't tell me he's sick, too."

Nina weaved through traffic to join us. "Audie bought antacids, gingersnap cookies, and ginger tea."

Oh no. Ginger settles the stomach. "That man has a serious tummy ache."

Mars ate a shrimp. "I'm trying to remember the symptoms Roscoe complained about. Slow heart rate, seeing halos, trouble with yellow and green perception. I don't recall anything about a stomach ache. Maybe Audie just ate too much spicy food or something."

"Anybody else think it's interesting that he's not over at the hospital?" asked Nina. "What could that mean? I would go if a stepparent was admitted to the hospital."

Audie walked straight toward us. "Mars, I'm glad I saw you. I want to thank you for being so good to Dad. This has been a rough time for him."

"My pleasure, Audie. Have a seat."

"I suppose you heard about Mindy?" asked Nina.

The waitress refilled our glasses and brought another iced tea for Audie.

Audie closed his eyes briefly and massaged

his forehead, as though tired of all the drama. "I would never want to deny either of my parents any happiness, but it seems like everything has gone haywire since Dad married Mindy. It's all I can do to keep crazy rumors from flying all over the office." He opened the bag, took out a gigantic bottle of antacids, and unscrewed the top. "Can you imagine — Dad called me early this morning and accused *me* of having an affair with Mindy. Of all the crazy notions! No wonder I'm eating these things like candy." He wolfed two tablets and washed them down with tea.

Mars and Nina glared at me.

"You're not having an affair with Mindy?" asked Mars.

"I don't even like the woman. The mere notion is distasteful on so many levels. Ugh."

Mars and Nina raised their eyebrows at me like I had lied about Audie.

Fortunately, Audie didn't seem to notice. "It's such a peculiar sequence of events." He ticked them off on his fingers as he spoke. "First the mallard print went missing. Then Heath, who left our company under unpleasant circumstances, showed up dead under a mulch pile — of all the bizarre places. It's no wonder Dad's heart couldn't take it, especially with this heat we've been having. And now someone has poisoned Mindy? I feel like there has to be a connection, but nothing makes sense."

"You forgot the manure," said Nina.

Audie laughed. "That I know about. It was Mom's little joke on Mindy. My mom's a pistol. Pretty outrageous. I mean, really, *manure?*" He laughed heartily. "How many people could have come up with that? And placing the order in Mindy's name was a stroke of genius, because Dad wound up paying for it. Gotta love Mom!"

Audie's phone jingled. "Excuse me. With Dad's heart problems, I'm afraid to skip calls." He clicked it on and said, "Hi, babe." After a short silence, he added, "Send them to the house. I don't want them parading into the office, creating a stir and more speculation. Okay?"

He hung up. "The cops want to talk with me. I'd better get going. Good seeing everybody."

He tickled the top of Daisy's head and walked away, but not as fast as a man his age ought to.

"He doesn't appear to realize that Roscoe was poisoned," I observed.

"I wonder when Roscoe will admit it to his family," said Mars. "But I don't know about the thing between him and Mindy. I thought he was very convincing."

"Me, too!" Nina picked up a shrimp and peeled it.

"All I know is what I saw. Would you admit it if you were having an affair with your new stepmother?"

Mars and Nina were busy eating pasta but looked appropriately appalled by the thought.

I plucked a shrimp out of the bowl. "You know, when Audie was running through their recent disasters, all I could think was that Roscoe must have flipped out when he saw Heath. Can you imagine Roscoe's reaction if Heath tried to blackmail him? Then, when he learned Mindy was seeing Audie, he probably concluded she was poisoning him, and he pulled a fast one by putting digitalis in *her* food."

Mars put his fork down. "That's funny, because I was thinking the same thing — about Olive. If she sent the manure, how do we know *she* didn't murder Heath and poison Mindy?"

"I don't know," said Nina. "Playing a prank — and a very clever one at that, since everyone will always associate the manure with Mindy — is a far cry from killing."

■ ■ ■ ■

It was late afternoon by the time I went home. The moment I stepped foot on my property, Natasha swooped down on me like a screaming banshee. "You've been away all day! Sophie, this is it. I'm not taking no for an answer. We have to repurp!" Natasha's voice became shrill and frantic. "Please! Do this for me. I got you a free garage. You owe me! We have to come up with a brilliant repurp."

I had a bad feeling that the "free garage" phrase would pop up frequently in the future. More specifically, every time Natasha wanted a favor from me. "Okay, quit whining. Is first thing in the morning all right? I'm a little bushed."

"That's cutting it close, but it will have to do. Why are you so tired? You're on vacation, just dawdling about. *I'm* doing all the work." She rewarded me with a hug. "Now, there are strict rules tonight because you *have* to be surprised tomorrow when it's all revealed. And I don't mean phony surprised. You're not a great actress. Can I trust you?"

I said yes, but when she ran through her list, I nearly choked. Not only was the sunroom off limits, but the living room was, too, which really worried me. I hoped it meant they didn't want me to look out the window, but the huge plastic sheets they'd hung at the entrance to my dining room concerned me.

"And absolutely no going into your backyard whatsoever. Agreed?"

All I really wanted was to relax with my feet up in my own home. I would have agreed to nearly anything at that point.

Mochie met Daisy and me at the door, mewing like crazy. I had to think he was complaining about Natasha. When I cut up a couple of shrimp, his favorite treat, and offered them to him, he seemed to forgive me for leaving him to deal with her.

Troy knocked on the kitchen door and opened it. "Is Natasha here?" he whispered.

"You're safe."

"I've met a lot of people through this show. Some of them have been obnoxious, some have been worried, but up to now, no one has ever tried to write and direct the show."

"That's Natasha!"

"I think you're going to be happy with the results. I sure hope so." He fidgeted with a key chain. "Um, I just wondered — have you heard anything more about Heath's death? He doesn't have family here to look after him, so I talked to the cops. They said he probably asphyxiated under the mulch. That doesn't sound right to me. How could that happen unless he was unconscious?"

"Maybe he was. Did he drink a lot? Could he have passed out?"

"He drank more than anyone ought to. But he held his liquor very well. I never saw him weave or stumble. And even if he did pass out, someone had to cover him up with that mulch."

"I don't think there's any question that it was murder. Do you know anyone who would have wanted to kill him?"

Troy snorted. "The husbands and boyfriends of a dozen or so women."

"I know he was your friend, so I hope you won't think ill of me for asking you this, but do you think Heath could have killed someone?"

Chapter Twenty-Nine

Dear Sophie,
My mom and I garden together, but we have one major beef. I say plants should be watered at night. Mom says they should only be watered in the morning. Who's right?
— Night Owl in Drytown, California

Dear Night Owl,
You are. At the end of the day, plants are parched from the hot sun. Watering them in the evening refreshes them and gives the roots the benefit of the water throughout the cool night.
— Sophie

"Heath wasn't any better or any worse than the rest of us." Troy bowed his head. "My dad was a less-than-shining example of a human being. When I was a kid, and I was disappointed in him, my mom used to say,

'We all make mistakes. It's part of being human.' It took me a long time to understand that all of us are flawed. The worst people among us have some redeeming qualities. And the ones who seem like angels have made mistakes. And Heath was no angel."

It was a very gracious way of saying he thought Heath could have murdered someone. "You're a good friend, Troy."

"I've made some mistakes of my own. And this week, I was sorely tempted to commit murder." He winked at me and left.

The noise out back melted away, and I knew the production crew had shut down for the day. As tempting as it was to run outside and see what they'd done, I decided against it. After all, at this point, there wasn't a thing in the world I could do about it. I might as well go along with them and be surprised tomorrow. I had come to terms with the fact that they tore up my plants. Who knew? Maybe I would like it. I would try to keep an open mind.

I trotted up the stairs and into the bathroom to turn on the shower. Troy's crew had covered the window with plastic sheeting. They were taking this no-looking business very seriously. I turned on the water and took a long cool shower, delighted to be alone in my own home without any banging or engines in the yard — or Natasha.

Refreshed, I pulled on a cotton dress the shade of periwinkle flowers and blew my hair into a passable style. Finally doing the relaxing vacation thing of puttering around the house, I watered the herbs in pots outside my kitchen door. I refilled my water jug and opened the front door to water the geraniums in the front.

The smoky smell of someone cooking on a grill wafted to me. Mona toddled along the sidewalk and stopped to chat with Nina.

They crossed the street to me. Mona held out a little package, wrapped with a coral ribbon.

"What's this?" I asked, pulling the ribbon.

"A little thank-you. I appreciate all you and Nina have done for Anne."

I opened the box and found a sweet little vase.

"It's a rosebud vase. Just for a single flower," said Mona.

"She gave me one, too!" Nina smiled at Mona. "That really wasn't necessary."

"Thank you, Mona. You didn't need to do this." I felt a bit guilty. We'd been hoping to help Wolf.

Mona glanced at me, licking her lips. "I

still want to get inside Wolf's house."

"Sorry to disappoint you," I said. "I don't have a key."

She huffed. "Kenner won't go inside, either. He says he has to have a search warrant unless Wolf gives his permission — and we know that's not going to happen. Well, if you get any leads, let me know."

Nina and I watched her stroll away.

"I know she needs closure, but I wonder if it would be worse for her if Kenner found Anne's remains," said Nina.

"It's awful! Either way, there can't be a happy ending for her." We headed for my kitchen. "Want some dinner? I thought I'd make a salad with chicken tenders."

"After seeing all that Italian dressing, I have it on the brain. Can you make a Caesar salad with Italian dressing?"

"I don't think it would be called a Caesar salad, but we can make it any way we want." I picked up a paring knife and headed for the door.

"Where are you going?"

"To cut fresh herbs for the salad. At least Troy didn't disturb my pots of herbs." I stepped outside and cut sprigs of parsley, oregano, and thyme and tweaked a branch of leaves off a bushy basil plant. The spicy scents of oregano and basil floated from my little bouquet of herbs. When I returned to the kitchen, Nina was setting the table with a cheerful yellow and blue French tablecloth and round, peacock Fiestaware plates.

"Maybe we should have asked Mona to stay for dinner," I said.

"It's too bad that we didn't. I feel terrible for her. Imagine having to live like that. I go nutso when I know there's an animal missing or scrounging on the streets. If it were my daughter who was missing, I don't know if I could deal with it."

"I wish she weren't so determined that it was Wolf who killed Anne. I'm beginning to believe Heath must have murdered her. It probably had something to do with the embezzlement. Maybe an argument about giving back the money. But now that he's dead . . . We'll probably never know what happened to her."

I rinsed and dried the herbs. I bundled the basil into little rolls and sliced them into a chiffonade with a chef's knife, then went over them again to chop them into fine bits for the dressing. The fragrant smell of basil overtook the other scents.

Nina watched me pull tiny thyme leaves off the stems and chop them. She gasped and pointed at the chopped herbs at the same time that I said, "What does that remind you of?"

"Maybe the poison is in the Italian dressing!"

"It would be so easy to mince foxglove and add it to bottled dressing — I bet it wouldn't even taste very different. Most people probably wouldn't notice. Call Mars. He should tell the cops to test it." I finished chopping the oregano and parsley and put them aside. I whisked together white wine vinegar and olive oil, added salt, pepper, and the chopped herbs, and whisked again.

My phone rang exactly as Nina reached for it. "Wooooo. Spooky!" she said. "Hello? You're kidding! We'll be right there." She nearly jumped up and down. "We caught the cat! That was Francie calling from Roscoe's house to tell us."

I covered the dressing and shoved it into the refrigerator. "Wolf's car is closest." I grabbed the keys, locked the house, and the two of us raced to his car.

Traffic was light, so we made excellent time.

"It's too late to take the cat to the shelter tonight," mused Nina. "I'll have to take her home. Do you think she's feral or just skittish?"

"I don't think we'll know until you open the trap."

In minutes, we drove up to Roscoe's house. I counted six cars in the driveway. "Wonder what's up?"

A man wearing a clerical collar stepped out of one of the cars.

Nina and I looked at each other. "Roscoe!" We hurried to the door.

Happily, Violet had the courtesy to say "Good evening" to the minister. She pointed him toward the family room.

"Is something wrong with Roscoe?" I asked.

Violet hovered nervously, glaring at us with those frightening eyes. She wore a black dress with a lacy white collar that was eerily reminiscent of Mrs. Danvers.

"What's going on?" I asked.

She hissed at us like an angry black cat. "You will *not* betray me by revealing my indiscretion."

"Mum's the word," I said, although I suspected she would eventually be outed for removing the mallard print.

Nina and I sped through the empty family room and out to the patio, where a three-tiered wedding cake waited on a round table. Amazingly lifelike pink and white roses and lilies cascaded down the cake. We stopped short. Dom Pérignon champagne cooled in an ice bucket.

"Thanks for coming to get the kitty!"

We looked up. Cricket waved to us from the window. "Audie and I are getting married in a few minutes." She grinned, obviously deliriously happy.

A heart-wrenching yowl issued from the direction of the pond.

Nina and I rushed across the lawn and around the pond. Sure enough, a very unhappy calico cat looked out at us.

She was gorgeous, though, with long luxurious fur. A queen among cats. But she weighed a ton. Nina and I lifted the trap together, but it was slow going with one of us on each side of it.

The Greene family and Francie had gathered on the patio. As we neared the house, Audie walked toward us wearing a dark suit with a pink rose in his lapel.

"Is that the calico cat?" He peered in the trap. "Hi, Cupcake." He poked a finger into the cage. "Where are you taking her?"

"To my house tonight, then the shelter," said Nina. "Is she your cat?"

"Not really. She comes and rubs against my legs when I putter around the garden. She's my little Cupcake. Why are you taking her away?"

Violet hovered just behind him. "Because she's killing my birds."

I leaned toward him and whispered, "Violet was going to poison her."

"Violet! You wouldn't do that to a sweet kitty like this!" He wedged open the trap and pulled out the cat. She snuggled against his chest. Holding up one of her paws and waving it, he spoke in a little kid's voice. "Hi, Violet. I'm sorry I disturbed your birdies. I promise I won't ever do it again."

I couldn't help thinking Audie's behavior was slightly odd, but it worked.

Violet giggled. "Audie, you rascal!"

The austere, gloomy woman giggled! She clearly had a very special relationship with Audie. He brought out a completely hidden side of her.

He stroked Cupcake's luxurious fur. "Can I have her?" he asked Nina.

"Absolutely. She needs shots." She glanced at Violet. "It's probably unwise to leave her out here."

"Hey, Cupcake! How do you feel about being a bridesmaid?" He whispered, "We thought we better speed up the wedding, given Dad's health issues." Audie lifted Cupcake into the air and looked up at her. "We'll get you your shots first thing tom . . . tom . . ."

Nina ditched the trap and grabbed Cupcake as Audie clutched his stomach.

Olive hurried toward us. "Audie?"

"I'm okay, Mom. Just wedding jitters."

"You haven't eaten anything here, have you?" she asked.

"Don't worry so much. Cricket brought food from my house." He smiled at Nina and me. "I'm so sorry, ladies. Nina, why don't you put Cupcake in the guest house? She can stay there during the ceremony. Excuse me while I get a drink of water."

Olive took a deep breath. "This poisoning that's going on is very scary. Would you like to stay for the wedding? The cake came from my favorite Old Town bakery, so it's safe!"

I accepted for both of us, while Nina carried Cupcake to the guest house.

"How's Mindy?" I asked.

Olive's mouth twitched to the side. "I understand she's better now, but they're keeping her overnight to watch her heart."

"Oh?"

"Digitalis is powerful medicine. It slows the heart. Too much of it can kill you." Olive spoke unemotionally, as if she were a scientist merely relaying medical facts.

Nina returned as everyone gathered near the sprawling bed of daisies.

A woman played the wedding march on a violin, and Roscoe walked Cricket toward us on his arm. She wore a strapless wedding gown with a voluminous ball gown skirt and smiled like it was the happiest day of her life. Her stunning copper hair was pulled back off her face and cascaded down her back in loose curls.

Audie, on the other hand, had gone white as a ghost. He weaved, and instead of watching his gorgeous bride, he stared at the ground. I thought he might heave right then and there. He doubled over.

Olive gasped, but Audie waved everyone off and struggled to stand upright. "Continue, please."

The minister watched Audie as he recited, "Dearly beloved —"

"Gah!" Audie fell to the ground and writhed.

CHAPTER THIRTY

Dear Natasha,
My daughter and I garden together. She insists on watering plants in the evening, which I think is wrong. (I suspect it's because she likes to sleep in.) Who's right?
— Early Bird in Drytown, California

Dear Early Bird,
You are. The water evaporates on the hot soil and never reaches the roots. In cooler weather, watering late in the day promotes root rot.

— Natasha

"Water! He needs water!" shrieked Olive.

I ran to the guest house. Using the phone on the wall in the kitchen, I called 911 and told them what had happened while I filled two glasses with tap water. It spilled over my hands when I ran to Audie with them.

Olive seized the glasses and propped his head up. "Drink." She looked up at me. "More water."

I wasn't sure about the wisdom of giving Audie water, but Olive seemed to know what she was doing, so I fetched more water.

When I returned, Cricket leaned over Audie, screaming his name. "No! No! Not Audie!"

"Cricket, what did you bring for dinner?" I asked.

She looked at me like I had lost my mind.

"It could be important. What did he eat?"

"He hasn't been feeling well and didn't want anything heavy, so I brought some salad."

"With Italian dressing?"

She blinked at me. "Yes."

I grabbed her shoulders. "Where is it? Did anyone else eat any?"

"It's in the kitchen at the main house."

Audie didn't look good. He moaned and curled into a fetal position. I feared the person doing the poisoning might have gotten it right this time. I hoped not. Running as fast as I could, I headed for the house, through the family room to the kitchen. A siren grew louder in the distance.

Most of a salad had been tossed into a tall trash can. A fly landed on it right in front of me. The buzzing stopped immediately and the fly fell over. *Not a good sign.* I tied the flaps of the trash bag and looked for the dressing. It was in the fridge. Afraid to handle it, I used an oven mitt to stick it inside a plastic bag.

The EMTs had arrived when I dashed back outside. They fussed with Olive, but she stood her ground. "He has to keep drinking huge quantities of water."

"Ma'am, we don't know what's wrong with him."

"Two other people have been poisoned here over the last couple of days. What do you think is wrong with him? Drink, Audie, keep drinking!"

I handed an EMT the two bags. "I think the poison is in here."

"What is this?" he asked.

"A salad and dressing. I wouldn't touch either with bare hands if I were you."

He turned his attention to Olive, who coaxed Audie to drink. "Ma'am, we don't know what the poison is. Drinking water might be contraindicated."

"Well I do know — Audie, drink more — and I'm telling you that he needs to drink as much as he possibly can. Vast quantities of water."

Roscoe reached for his son's hand. "You'll

be all right, Audie. Do as your mother says."

I didn't think Audie would drink much more, since he seemed to be in a lot of pain.

The EMTs made quick work of loading him onto a gurney and placing him in the ambulance.

The Greene family, Cricket, and Francie dispersed quickly to follow the ambulance to the hospital. In minutes, only the minister, the violinist, Nina, and I were left.

Practical Nina said calmly, "I guess we'd better take Cupcake with us. I seriously doubt that it will occur to any of them to feed her tonight."

At nine o'clock, I paced the floor, a peculiar mixture of exhaustion and taut nerves that wouldn't let me sleep. Every few minutes, I stepped outside, looking for lights in Francie's house.

Unless there were several killers in the Greene family, someone had murdered Heath and tried to kill Roscoe, Mindy, and Audie. What did they have in common?

I could link Roscoe, Audie, and Heath due to Heath's attempt to embezzle from Roscoe's company, but Mindy was outside the loop.

I could link Mindy, Roscoe, and Audie, because Mindy's arrival in the family had

343

caused heartache, but then Heath didn't fit into the equation.

What were the facts? What did I know for sure?

Roscoe and Mindy were both poisoned by digoxin, yet that didn't seem to be the case for Audie, since he'd had different symptoms. Had the poisoner run out of digitalis and switched to something else? Had he changed to another drug because Mindy and Roscoe survived?

That was all useless speculation. I had to focus on the facts.

Audie and Cricket intended to marry. Mindy could have been jealous. No, that, too, was speculation. Who knew what Mindy felt? Why did everything lead back to unfounded theories?

Audie had been poisoned by food Cricket brought from his home. Now there was something concrete. It pointed a finger at Cricket. Who was I kidding? Olive, Roscoe, Violet — the whole family probably had access to keys to Audie's house, the same way Natasha kept taking my keys from Mars.

But Francie and I had seen Mindy go into Audie's house. If Audie wasn't having an affair with her, why had she been there? What if he didn't know she was in the house? Was that possible?

"Don't jump to conclusions, Sophie," I muttered to myself. There were bottles of the dressing stored in the guest house. That was a fact. It was also indisputable that Mindy had a key and let herself into Audie's home.

My pulse quickened.

She had easy and private access to bottles of dressing in the guest house, which she could have doctored. Francie and I could place Mindy at Audie's house, the scene of the crime. It would have been a snap for her to replace one of the bottles in Audie's house with a poisoned bottle. But what about Cricket? Why wasn't she sick? That blew my whole theory.

I walked outside again. There was a light on in Francie's house. I rushed to her door and banged the knocker. Nina must have been watching for Francie's lights, too, because she ran up behind me.

Francie opened the door. "I should have known." She walked back to her kitchen. I closed the door and followed Nina. Francie set three Waterford sherry glasses cut in the Colleen pattern on the table and retrieved a bottle of Hartley and Gibson's Cream Sherry.

I always enjoyed the ambience of Francie's kitchen. It struck me as part kitchen, part library. The stove and other kitchen appliances took up one corner in the back. The rest of the room was lined with cabinets topped by bookshelves. A chunky French farmhouse table occupied the center of the room.

She sat down, shoved the bottle toward me, and closed her eyes.

I poured some of the sweet amber liquid into each glass. "How's Audie?"

Francie sipped her sherry. "He's my godson, you know. I never thought I'd see a day like today. The police, namely that idiot, Kenner, think Olive tried to kill Audie."

"Olive?" Nina cried. "She loves Audie."

"That she does." Francie slowly swung her head from side to side. "The EMTs said she was acting like she knew what had poisoned him."

"She was, sort of." She had been adamant about that water.

Francie glared at me.

"She kept telling him to drink," I said. "In fact, I think she might have told them she knew he was poisoned."

Francie rested her elbows on the table. "Turns out all the water probably saved him."

"Did they test the dressing?"

Francie scratched her head. "See, that's

346

the weird thing. It was mostly dressing. The doctor said they spread some out, and it looked like someone had chopped up various plants and added them. Harmful ones, as well as bits of daisies and petunias."

"So what caused the problem?" I asked. "He was violently ill."

"Monkshood. One of the most poisonous plants in the English garden. You can be poisoned just by touching it. Olive suggested they test for it because she had planted some back near the pond. Fortunately, Audie must not have gotten much, and all that water Olive forced him to drink helped save him. It also made her the prime suspect."

"But that's crazy," said Nina. "If Olive had wanted to poison someone, she wouldn't have added all those nontoxic plants. She would have known what she was doing."

"It's absolute nonsense to place blame on Olive," said Francie, looking more alert. "She would never hurt Audie. Never! She was spitting mad about Mindy's plan to dig up those beautiful gardens and cover them with concrete, but Olive wouldn't kill anyone."

"Okay, I'm making a list," said Nina. "This is driving me crazy." She snatched a pad of paper and a pencil off a shelf. "It all began with Roscoe. Then Mindy fell. And now Audie."

"You forgot Heath," I reminded her. "He was really the first victim."

"Wow. Four victims." Nina added Heath to the top of the list.

Francie lowered her head into her hands. "It's as though someone wants to wipe out the entire Greene family. No wonder they suspect Olive."

"I'm making a suspect list on the right," said Nina. "Olive. Have to add Mrs. Danvers, er, Violet. She's looney."

I swiveled the liquid in my glass. "What I don't understand is why Cricket didn't get sick. Didn't she and Audie eat the same foods?"

"Hah!" spat Francie. "The doctor asked her that. Turns out she doesn't like Italian dressing. She's a ranch dressing girl all the way."

"Adding her to the list of suspects," said Nina, writing.

Francie set her glass on the table. "I love Olive like she's my sister, but I never understood her desire to plant monkshood. Audie was just plain lucky that he didn't get a bigger dose."

"Which begs another question," I said. "Why switch from digitalis to monkshood?

Roscoe and Mindy had digoxin in their systems, but Audie was poisoned by monkshood."

"It's faster." Francie twisted the stem of her glass around while she spoke. "Monkshood can kill a person in thirty to sixty minutes. Foxglove brings a slower death."

"It was Mindy," I pronounced.

They stared at me.

"Who had the most to gain from Audie's death? Mindy! If Roscoe's only child was out of the way, wouldn't Mindy think she would be in the best position to inherit Roscoe's entire estate?"

"But she was poisoned, too," said Nina. "Maybe she has the motive to kill Roscoe and Audie, but she hates the garden. She wouldn't know which plants were poisonous."

"You can look up anything on the Internet these days," said Francie. "You don't have to be a pro at gardening to poison someone."

"Nina, if you wanted to poison someone with plants, how would you do it?" I asked.

She cocked her head at me like I was being silly. "You already told me the easiest way is to make a tea."

"What would you put in the tea?"

"I'm not on trial here!"

"I'm not accusing you. I'm trying to make a point."

"I guess I'd put in foxglove and that monkshead stuff."

I grinned at her little distortion of the plant's name. "What does it look like?"

"I don't know," she wailed. "Was the foxglove pink or purple? But I'm not stupid. I'd look it up . . . ohhhh. I see what you mean. She couldn't research poisonous plants on her computer because the cops could track it to her. So she chopped up bits of plants, hoping she was getting some poisonous ones."

CHAPTER THIRTY-ONE

Dear Sophie,
I watched a local domestic diva on TV who insisted that gardens must be planned carefully on paper. She even recommended the use of a color wheel to make sure the flowers will coordinate, not clash. I was exhausted just watching her. Is it really awful just to shake out some seeds and hope they'll take?
— Lazy Gardener in Lantana, Florida

Dear Lazy Gardener,
Have fun with your garden and scatter seeds as you wish. You never know what wonderful things might happen! If you don't like what comes up, you can always move it.
— Sophie

Francie perked up, her eyes shining. "That's what we saw, Sophie! Audie didn't go home to meet Mindy. He probably didn't even know she was there. She snuck into his house to switch out the bottle of dressing."

I placed my finger on my nose like we were playing charades. "That's exactly what I think."

Francie rose and brought me her phone. "You have to call Kenner right away and tell him."

"Wait!" shouted Nina. "Why did Mindy poison herself?"

"That wicked minx," growled Francie. "She used plants so it would cast suspicion on Olive, the garden expert. I knew Mindy was trouble. Then, when Roscoe didn't die, I bet Mindy thought it was safe enough, so she took some of her own poison so no one would suspect her."

Mindy had opportunity and motive, not to mention that we had seen her entering Audie's house, but something was bothering me. "Why would she kill Roscoe first? Assuming her goal was to inherit everything, it would have been a huge risk to poison Roscoe before Audie died."

I thought Nina might spew her sherry.

Francie sat down, deflated. "Maybe she thought the digitalis would take longer to kill Roscoe. If she gave it to him in small doses, his eventual death would have been chalked up to a heart condition." She shook her head. "Poor old stupid Roscoe."

Nina snapped her fingers. "Then, when Roscoe went to the hospital, she became nervous. What if he died before Audie? So she had to hurry up a new batch of dressing and run it over to Audie's house!"

"That blows our theory entirely. If she chopped up plants because she didn't know which ones were poisonous, then how did she manage to avoid giving Roscoe monkshood? If he threw out his digitalis prescription like he said, and she didn't know one flower from the next, then how would she have poisoned him with foxglove?"

Francie sat back. "I'm exhausted. I don't know how you girls manage without sleep. Sophie, promise me you'll call Kenner and tell him about Mindy when you get home? He should know that we saw Mindy going into Audie's house."

"I must be getting older because I no longer bristle when someone calls me a girl." Nina kissed Francie on the cheek. "Get some sleep."

It was ten thirty when we left Francie's house. "Should I call Kenner now or wait until morning?"

"Mindy's in the hospital, so presumably she can't do much damage. On the other hand, maybe he should know now. He could be on the way to arrest Olive."

We went back to my house, and naturally, I couldn't find Kenner's number. When had he given it to me? At Wolf's house. I'd worn a sleeveless top that day with skorts and regretted it when the bushes scratched my arms. I ran upstairs and found Kenner's number stashed in the pocket of the skorts, along with the picture of Wolf and Anne on the beach that I'd swiped from Wolf's house. I pressed in the numbers on my cell phone to call Kenner and slid the photo into my purse for safekeeping. I wanted to return it in good condition. Except for memories, pictures were all Wolf had left of Anne.

Kenner answered immediately. I told him we had a theory about Mindy based on fact, but when I started to explain it, he said, "Are you at home? I'll be right there."

The door knocker banged before I reached the foyer. When I opened the door, Mars and Kenner waited outside, breathless.

"Were you standing out on the street?" I asked.

"Actually, we were. Natasha has some kind of weird project under way, and she's banging on metal," explained Mars. "We were trying to get away from the clanging."

They followed me to the kitchen. "Could

I get you a drink?"

"Nothing hard for me, thanks." Mars wrinkled his nose. "I think I'm off it for a while. I didn't like what that scotch did to me."

"Afraid of drinking and eating? How about a black cherry float?"

Kenner perked up. "Are you serious? I haven't had a float since I was a kid!"

Was it just me, or was Kenner becoming slightly more personable?

I took down soda fountain glasses that I had snagged at a yard sale for next to nothing.

While Nina explained our theory about Mindy chopping plants, putting them into Italian dressing, and delivering them to Audie's house on the sly, I pulled vanilla ice cream from the freezer.

Letting it soften for just a couple of minutes, I looked for old-fashioned black cherry soda in my pantry and brought several bottles to the island counter.

"I see another flaw in your theory." Mars ruffled the fur on Daisy's neck. "If Mindy didn't know anything about gardening, how did she know about foxglove and digitalis?"

"I've been thinking about that. Maybe she saw an article in a magazine, or someone happened to mention it to her." Nina suggested. "I'm always running across weird information."

I scooped creamy vanilla ice cream into the tall glasses and poured the soda over the ice cream. One long iced-tea spoon and a straw went into each. I brought them to the table with blue napkins on a little tray.

In all the time that I had known him, Kenner had never looked so happy.

Mars had a mouthful of ice cream but said, "Mmm. Perfect." He swallowed. "We should do this more often. Not the poison stuff, but the floats. I'll take this over Mindy's scotch any day. What's that?" He pointed at the paper Nina held.

"I made a list to help us figure all this out. The victims are on the left and the suspects are on the right." Nina shoved the list to the center of the table so they could read it.

"If you suspect Mindy, why isn't she on the suspect side?" asked Kenner.

Nina added Mindy's name to the other column.

"Heath is the odd man out here since he's not a Greene," mused Mars. "Shouldn't you add Anne Fleishman's name to the victim side? She was entangled with Heath in some way."

"What about Audie?" I asked. "He could

have killed Heath."

I watched as Nina wrote Anne's name, then added Wolf, Mona, and Audie to the suspects column. "I hardly think Wolf has been poisoning the Greenes."

"No one ever said there couldn't be two people trying to poison someone." Kenner's suggestion caught me by surprise.

"Of course! That would explain the two different poisons." I squinted at Kenner. How could I convince him to tell us more? Maybe if I said something outrageous. "Is Wolf a suspect in Heath's murder?"

Nina's entire body jolted. "I need a drink. The hard kind, scotch, not soda. Mars, can I get you one?"

"No thanks. I've been off scotch since the day I had some of Mindy's stash and felt so ragged afterward."

Mars and I said it at the same time. "The scotch."

"One of the poisons could be in the scotch. You didn't have any, right, Sophie?" asked Mars.

"I don't usually drink that early in the day. Well, maybe a Mimosa or something fruity. Nothing that strong anyway. Cricket didn't have a drink, either. It was just you and Roscoe. We didn't have any salad or dress-ing with lunch. Maybe you should call and warn Roscoe."

Kenner held out a hand. "It's okay. All kinds of things were taken from the house to be analyzed. I'm sure they're checking the liquor, too."

"They might not have known about it," I said. "It's in a globe."

Mars chimed in. "It looks like a piece of furniture." He picked up my telephone and dialed.

We listened to Mars explain the situation to Roscoe.

Mars placed his hand over the receiver. "Roscoe's on his way downstairs to remove the bottle so no one else will drink from it."

"Ask him if Mindy drank any of the scotch recently," I suggested.

We waited, eating the ice cream in our floats.

Kenner blew on the back of his wrist.

I recognized the blisters and bumps from my own encounters with a vicious weed. "Poison ivy?"

"I guess so. It itches like the devil."

"It's gone?" Mars shouted. "Yeah, good-night Roscoe." Mars hung up. "Mindy's scotch decanter is missing. Though he sounded more upset about the fact that Violet still hasn't refilled his bourbon decanter. And Mindy had a couple of drinks the night before she fell down the stairs."

"I knew it!" Nina waved her spoon. "Mrs. Danvers — er, Violet — is the poisoner. She probably poured out his bourbon on purpose to drive him to Mindy's bottle of scotch."

"I really drank poison?" Mars grabbed his throat with both hands and hacked.

It *was* frightening. Mars could have been seriously hurt. I knew his propensity to obsess over things, though. With the confident tone of a school nurse, I said, "You're fine. Maybe the cops found the scotch and took it to test."

Kenner remained silent.

"What are you thinking?" I asked him.

"Violet would be very clever if she had done that because it would appear that she had intended to kill Mindy, not Roscoe." Kenner's eyes narrowed, as though he was trying to figure something out.

"As cold and odd as Violet is, I think she truly loves Audie," I said. "I can't see her poisoning Roscoe or Audie. And since she does most of the cooking, she would surely realize that Cricket doesn't like Italian dressing."

"Good point," said Mars. "I'm in total agreement. We can cross Violet off the list of suspects." He frowned at Kenner. "I can tell you're up to something. Come on, tell us."

Nina aimed her pencil at Violet's name but didn't cross it off. "So you think we're right?" she asked Kenner. "Mindy tried to poison Audie?"

Kenner sucked the remainder of his soda through the straw. "I never said any such thing." He stood up and stretched. "Thanks. I'd better get going, it will be an early day tomorrow."

I walked him to the front door. "Overworked without Wolf?"

"Without him *and* because of him. Thanks for the soda. Wolf obviously has good taste in women. I just don't understand what they see in him."

He looked sort of wistful. I had thought the days of his romantic interest in me were over. Opening the door, I shuffled back, just in case he thought he was going to kiss me. I needn't have worried. Daisy had followed us from the kitchen and immediately growled at him.

He stepped out quickly to get away from her. "I don't know why you keep such a mean dog."

I closed the door and hugged my not-at-all-mean canine. When we returned to the kitchen, Nina and Mars were high-fiving. "I wouldn't be so fast to celebrate. We don't know that we're right."

"Hah!" said Nina. "We nailed Mindy. I know we did."

"Clearly the other person wants to eliminate Mindy," said Mars.

Nina gloated. "Pretty ironic, don't you think? There's Mindy chopping up plants from the garden to get rid of Audie, and meanwhile, someone is trying to kill *her*. My money is on Mrs. Danvers. Remember how upset she was about Mindy wanting to throw her out?"

"I don't know." I slurped the rest of my soda. "Olive is the one with expertise about plants and herbs. Mindy ruined Olive's life, practically pulled the rug right out from underneath her. I'd say Olive has the strongest motive."

"I've been spending a lot of time with the Greenes," said Mars. "It could be any one of them — Olive, Audie, Violet, even Roscoe. He was furious about the crown Mindy bought for herself."

Nina chuckled and wrote Roscoe's name in the right column. "Wait until he finds out about her shoe addiction."

Mars looked confused.

"She has a stash of expensive shoes hidden in the guest house," I explained.

"What is it with women and shoes? Natasha has an entire closet devoted to shoes and purses."

"Sorry, but I'm not buying it," I said. "If Roscoe wanted to be rid of Mindy, he could divorce her and be done with it. Erase his name, Nina. He might be a crafty old fellow, but I can't see him overdosing on his own meds just to make himself appear innocent. And if he had poisoned Mindy's scotch, he wouldn't have had a drink or offered it to us."

"Wouldn't it be even more ironic if Mindy were trying to kill Audie, and Audie were trying to kill Mindy?" asked Nina.

"Our speculation omits the fact that someone is trying to kill Roscoe and that Heath must fit into this equation somehow." Mars stood up. "It's late, and we've lost focus. I'm going home to bed. At least Mindy is safe from her poisoner in the hospital, and everyone else is safe from Mindy as long as she's there."

Nina accompanied him to the kitchen door and opened it. "Let's hope so. Who knows what else she might have poisoned?"

I walked out with them so Daisy could do her business. Mars and Nina headed to their respective homes. Daisy wagged her tail like crazy, and Wolf stepped out of the shadows.

CHAPTER THIRTY-TWO

Dear Natasha,

I'm all for reusing discarded items, but I guess I don't have much vision. My husband had four truckloads of broken concrete delivered. It's in unsightly piles in our yard, and I want to pay someone to haul them away, but my dear hubby won't hear of it. Help?

— Broken Up in Flower Grove, Texas

Dear Broken Up,

Chunks of broken concrete can be used to make wonderful walkways and driveways. They have a flat side, so they're also great for building fences and retaining walls. Set hubby to work using that stuff. Your unsightly piles will be gone, and you'll have a great new walk or wall.

— Natasha

"Wolf! You know, that's getting really creepy.

Why are you always hanging around outside my house?"

"I'm not sleeping well. It's not that I'm hanging around. I just happened to be walking by." Wolf crouched to pet Daisy, who apparently didn't feel creeped out at all because she licked his face. "Maybe it's a good thing. You're spending a lot of time with Mars."

I couldn't help myself. I had to say it. "There's a lot of stuff going on" — I stopped dead. I couldn't say Roscoe's name without Wolf making a stink — "that you don't know about."

"Like what?"

"Now you know how I feel when you say that to me."

He stood up and kicked a pebble into the street. "Sophie, I don't like to talk about Anne *at all* because it's so painful. Right now, it's even worse because all the old stuff is being dredged back up, and I'm reliving the nightmare again, over and over a million times a day trying to remember any little insignificant detail. And then there's the awkwardness of it all. Talking to you about Anne is like talking to my mom about sex. There's just something distasteful about it."

Distasteful or not, I wanted information.

"Wolf, I don't exactly know where we stand. I think chances are pretty good that we may never know what happened to Anne. It breaks my heart for you, and for her parents." I remembered Kenner's devotion to her and added, "For everyone who loved her. As much as I might want to, I can't change that. I know you're hurting, but if you mean to have a relationship with me, then you owe it to me to talk about Anne. I think I deserve that much."

Wolf looked away and said nothing.

I gave it a shot. "Kenner didn't seem to know anything about the embezzlement."

"Aw, Sophie!" he sputtered. "You told him about that?"

"I just asked if he knew anything about Anne having money problems."

Wolf huffed. "Roscoe never reported the embezzlement to the police. I couldn't get to his corporate records because it's a private company. Anne's employer was elated that Roscoe put a lid on the whole thing, because it would have damaged his reputation and put him out of business."

"So there's no way of knowing the truth. But Overton, her boss, didn't have any reason to lie."

"I still don't think Anne would ever have done that. But what was I supposed to do?

If I made it public, and she was alive, I might be putting her in jail. If I made it public, and she was dead, I was just besmirching her reputation. No one would give me access to the documents to prove anything. I will never believe that Anne embezzled from anyone." He gripped my wrist. "It was as out of character for her to embezzle as it would be for *you* to steal millions. I just can't prove it."

I didn't need to press him anymore. I'd managed to ferret out the thing he didn't want me to know about Anne. I could understand why he didn't believe it, especially since he wasn't privy to the records. In his shoes, I might have reacted the same way. He didn't want people thinking ill of Anne. Even now, he protected her in death as he had in life.

But there was one more thing I wanted to know. When he said good-night and strolled on, I hurried to lock my house, then Daisy and I followed him.

He walked toward Natasha and Mars's house, passed their front steps, and rounded the corner to the left. Daisy and I jogged to catch up. We stopped at the corner of Natasha and Mars's house and peered around it. Wolf ambled on down the sidewalk, evidently unaware that he was being tailed.

And then, in one second, he was gone. He vanished into thin air.

Daisy and I walked faster than I really wanted, but I hoped Daisy might wag her tail or bark if she smelled him hiding somewhere. Sniffing with her nose close to the sidewalk, she wanted to turn left into the alley. "No, Daisy," I hissed. Duke or some other dog had probably walked that way earlier.

And then a door shut with a little snap. Not a car door, a door in a house. The lights in Bernie's apartment over Natasha and Mars's garage went on — and I knew. I waited a moment, watching the window that faced the side street. Wolf drew the curtains closed. He was staying at Bernie's.

During the night, some kind of weather front moved in, shoving out the humidity and blistering heat. It left a glorious summer morning, the air slightly crisp but not cold. Energy coursed through me. Maybe we were right about Mindy. Maybe the Greene family's problems had come to an end. I threw on a khaki skirt and matching Keds, and found a sleeveless coral top that I'd forgotten I had. I took that as a good sign.

In the kitchen, I skipped coffee, but Mochie head-butted me just in case I'd forgotten about him. I hadn't. "Salmon and chicken, okay?" He purred. I spooned half a can of it into his bowl, grabbed Daisy's leash, and ran next door to Francie's house.

Her front door was open, and Duke was halfway out. Francie held his leash.

"Any word on Audie?" I asked.

"He had a good night. Did you talk to Kenner about Mindy?"

A car whipped by us, much too fast for Old Town.

Francie frowned. "Was that Mars? He knows better than to drive so fast around here."

We walked Daisy and Duke along our street, calling out "Good morning" to neighbors taking in their newspapers.

I filled her in on the details of our meeting with Kenner. "He intimated there could be two people trying to poison the Greenes."

"But they're such good, decent people!" Francie protested. "Who else would take in a grouch like Violet?"

"So what's the story there?"

"It's an old, familiar tale. I'm afraid it's not very exciting. Violet's husband emptied their bank accounts and ran off with another woman. Nothing new about that. It happens to a lot of people. She located him, but he'd wasted the money gambling on horse racing, so she found herself with nothing. Nowhere to go, nowhere to live, and not many skills to speak of. It was about a month after Audie was born, so she stayed with Roscoe and Olive to help out with the new baby and the house, and she became a fixture. She's part of the family."

I held Duke's leash while Francie bought coffees and caramel banana muffins at Big Daddy's Bakery. She handed me a muffin topped with banana slices and ooey-gooey caramel. "So it will blow your diet. You look fine to me."

If she only knew how many ways I'd blown my diet in the past week! I thanked her, hoping I wouldn't be like Daisy and start drooling before I could eat it. We drank our coffees and ate our sinfully delicious treats sitting by a fountain at Market Square, watching Old Town wake up. I was finally beginning to feel like I was on a little staycation.

We strolled back, stopping to window-shop in the cute stores.

Francie came to a halt outside of Café Olé. "Cricket?" said Francie.

Cricket raised her eyes from the grande coffee she carried out the door. "Francie, Sophie." She sniffed and hugged Francie.

"I'm devastated. It's all so horrible."

Blue rings under her eyes gave them a hollow appearance. Her makeup had smeared, and so had some of her glamour. She wore washed-out scrubs, white satin high heels, a pearl necklace, and dangling pearl earrings.

"I must look a mess. I'm dead on my feet. I stayed over at Audie's bedside last night. One of the nurses took pity on me in my wedding dress. Can you imagine what a scene that was? She scrounged up these scrubs for me."

"Let me buy you breakfast, dear," said Francie.

"That's so kind of you, but I have to go home and change and then get to the office. Audie insists that a Greene has to be there to break the news. I'm not a Greene yet, but I'm the only one who can do it!" She held her fingers over her mouth. "Have you talked to Olive? I know she must be distraught."

"Olive was planning to spend the day taking care of Audie," said Francie. "We just can't believe anyone would want to hurt poor, sweet Audie."

"I'm so glad he'll be okay," I said.

"He'll be fine, but —" An incredulous expression came over Cricket's weary face. "Oh my gosh! You haven't heard. Roscoe died at home last night."

The color washed out of Francie's complexion. I swung my arm around her lest she fall.

"I'm so sorry," said Cricket. "I thought you knew."

Francie seemed in a daze. Her chest heaved with each breath as though she couldn't inhale enough air. "Would you drive me over to Roscoe's, Sophie?"

"Of course. Why don't you wait in the cool bakery? You can sit at one of their tables. I'll take the dogs home and be back in a flash to pick you up."

She nodded. I took Duke's leash from her and watched to be sure she made it into the bakery safely. I knew the owner. He would look out for her.

Cricket stifled a yawn. "Sorry. I haven't pulled an all-nighter since college. I remember it being much easier then."

I said good-bye to Cricket and hurried home. Natasha wouldn't be pleased to see two dogs when she invaded my house, but I didn't care. Duke was a great fellow, a typically friendly Golden Retriever, and most importantly, he got along well with Mochie. Daisy and Duke settled on the kitchen floor, panting.

I scooped the other half of Mochie's food

371

into his bowl, checked to be sure the water bowl was full, and locked up. I drove Wolf's car to Big Daddy's Bakery. Naturally, there was no place to park. I was about to drive on, but Francie charged out of Big Daddy's yelling my name. Traffic waited behind me while she climbed into the car.

We wound through the morning traffic flooding into Old Town and headed to Roscoe's.

"Did you call Olive?" I asked.

"They have enough commotion on their hands without people adding to it by phoning. I need to help Olive, not make more work for her."

Mars's car was parked in the driveway when we arrived. No wonder he'd been driving so fast this morning.

Francie chugged up the porch steps. I reached out to ring the bell, but she turned the handle and walked right in.

The house lay still and cool. The faint sound of crying and a hushed voice drifted to us. Francie hustled through the living room to Roscoe's den, and I followed.

Olive slouched in the cushy leather chair, holding a tissue in her hand. Her eyes were closed tightly. She looked like she was having a tough time holding herself together.

Francie cried, "Olive!" and held out her arms.

Olive opened her eyes, rushed into Francie's arms, and sobbed hysterically.

Mars stood beside Roscoe's desk observing them.

I drifted over to him. "What happened?"

"Kenner arrived early this morning. When Violet brought him in here, they found Roscoe slumped over at his desk. She phoned me right away. He must have had a coronary. They think his heart went, since Roscoe refused to take his medication. They'll know more when they do a postmortem."

"But they'll check for poisoning, right?"

"Given the trouble with poisoning around here, I'm sure they'll run tests for foxglove and monkshood, just to be sure."

"Where's Violet?"

"On the side porch."

I left him with Olive and Francie and returned to the front porch. Tiptoeing around the side, I spotted Violet, rocking in a chair and looking darker and angrier than ever. Although I had a feeling she would only snap at me, I felt compelled to say something to her.

Walking softly, I approached her and kneeled next to the rocking chair. "Violet,

I'm so sorry. I know how much Roscoe meant to you."

Her thin lips trembled. She turned those dark eyes on me. "It was Mindy. She ruined everything. And now I'm old and . . ." She gripped the arm of the rocking chair. "Do you think Olive would take me in? I could keep house for her. She never liked to do housework."

"I'm sure she would love that." It was a lie because I had no idea how Olive felt and most certainly no business representing anything for her, but what else could I say? I felt sorry for Violet in spite of the fact that those frightening bird eyes made her look like she might take a bite out of me. "You obviously meant a lot to Roscoe. Maybe he provided for you in his will."

Her pathetic suffering expression changed to shock and then hopefulness. "Really?" she said. "You really think so?" She rose from the rocking chair, holding her chin high. "Roscoe always knew how to make an exit." She floated into the house a different woman.

I hoped I hadn't misled her.

Shouting in the back garden caught my attention. I hurried down the steps and into the backyard.

Chapter Thirty-Three

Dear Sophie,
I love to work in my yard, but I'm horribly allergic to poison ivy. Every year I end up with a miserable rash. I'm beginning to think I don't even have to touch it. It jumps on me when I go near it. Do you have a cure?
— Itching in Ivy Ridge, Delaware

Dear Itching,
Always wash thoroughly with soap and tepid water as soon as you're exposed. Never use hot water. There are several cooling gels on the market, but my favorite remedy is milk of magnesia. Apply it to the exposed area, and allow it to dry. It will stop the itching and dry up the rash.
— Sophie

Although she had just been in the house,

Olive was now outside, working in a frenzy beyond the pond, and Francie was running out to her. Two crazy old women in the sun. The temperatures were rising, and they'd both been through enough shocks in the past two days to kill an elephant. I sprinted to them, panting like Daisy by the time I reached the shade near the pond.

Olive wore heavy work gloves and mercilessly pulled plants out of the ground. She jammed them into a large trash bag.

Francie stood by, watching.

"What's going on?" I asked.

Olive paused, her face flushed the color of cherry peppers. "I'm pulling up the monkshood that nearly killed my boy. I won't have it happen to anyone else. When I planted the monkshood, I was so proud to have an unusual specimen in my garden, and look what it's brought us — nothing but heartache. Who could have done such a cruel thing to my poor Audie? I won't let them do it again."

I understood her desire to do away with the poisonous plant, but it was Roscoe who had died, not Audie. Digging up the monkshood wouldn't bring Roscoe back. Then again, maybe she just had to do *something*. People coped with grief in different ways. "Maybe you could rip out the monkshood in the evening when it's cooler? Or early tomorrow morning? It's getting pretty hot out here."

"No, it has to be done now." Olive kept at it. "Francie, watch out for the poison ivy on those hostas."

I looked around to be sure I didn't accidentally brush up against the poison ivy. The three-leaved plants were growing on trees ten feet away but none grew where we stood. "I don't see any poison ivy here."

Olive gestured toward our feet. "It's scattered through the flower beds. Those hostas one inch from Francie's feet are loaded with it."

I bent over for a closer view. Had she lost her mind? There was no poison ivy growing among the hostas. Clearly, Olive was grieving, and I didn't see the point in arguing with her about something as unimportant as poison ivy.

"Don't you think Audie has been through enough?" I asked. "He just lost his father. Do you want Francie to have to tell him that his mother keeled over and died, too?"

Olive swatted at a mosquito that buzzed near her ear. "You're not very tactful, are you?"

I had to suppress my desire to laugh. Olive wasn't very good at taking a hint.

"Honey," she said, "you are going to have poison ivy on your legs if you let those hosta leaves touch your calves."

"Olive, I'm not the expert gardener you are by a long shot, but I'm pretty sure hosta leaves can't cause a poison ivy rash."

"They can if somebody sprinkled them with poison ivy!"

"Sprinkled? What do you mean?"

Olive exchanged a desperate look with Francie. "I *mean* that if a person happened to chop up poison ivy leaves and vines and sprinkled them over plants, that a person dumb enough to rub up against those plants might get a rash from it."

I quickly scooted away from the hostas. Never in my life would I have imagined such a thing. "Why might someone sprinkle poison ivy on other plants?" It made no sense to me. As far as I knew, animals weren't sensitive to it. It wouldn't keep bunnies from eating plants.

"Well now, if a person thought her gardens were going to be brutally dug up and entombed under concrete, she might just try to make the garden assassin regret ever having stepped foot into that garden."

Francie giggled. "Did it work?"

Olive pointed a finger at me. "I'm trusting you not to give away my secret. They tell me that Princess Mindy has a raging rash on her right arm."

I gulped air. "That's what I saw on your plants. I thought someone had been weed whacking, but it was bits of poison ivy!"

Francie and Olive cackled like kooky witches.

"Exactly when did you do this?" I asked. "Not before the party, I hope. There were children playing back here."

"For heaven's sake! I would never want *children* to get poison ivy. I snuck back here early in the morning after the party and scattered it. Do you know how many of my friends called to tell me that the new shrew was going to ruin my gardens by pouring concrete over everything?" She gazed around. "It's all so beautiful and so defenseless. I just helped the garden get even with Mindy. But watch where you step — it will still cause a rash, even all dried up like it is now."

The garden had already attacked several people, and it might have placed them at the scene of a crime. I needed to talk to Kenner.

"You two go inside before you land in the hospital, too. You wouldn't want to end up sharing a room with Princess Mindy."

Olive tied the bag closed and heaved a

huge sigh. "I don't know what to do with myself. I'm at a loss without Roscoe. Heaven knows what Mindy will do to my beautiful gardens now that he's gone."

Francie held out an arm to her, and the two old friends slowly walked across the grass and disappeared around the side of the house.

I returned to the den. Mars was seated at Roscoe's desk talking on the phone, the doorbell was ringing, and I could see at least ten people talking quietly in the living room.

Mars covered the phone and said, "This place is going to be a madhouse soon. Both Mindy and Audie are being released from the hospital."

"So quickly?"

"Mindy's ready to come home. If I understand the doctor correctly, Audie is showing symptoms of being his father's son — he's demanding to come home against his doctor's advice."

"But we think Mindy might have poisoned Audie! Isn't Kenner going to arrest her?"

"Shh." Mars finished his phone conversation and turned to me. "What a pain. I can't have Mindy and Audie in the same car. I'm picking up Mindy. She'll be thrilled, I'm sure. Cricket is on her way to pick up Audie."

"Deftly done. We'll need food," I said. "I'll see if I can get a couple of people to help serve beverages and man a little buffet, then I'll go to Old Town and pick up some platters."

I pulled out my phone, but between the ringing of Roscoe's phone and the doorbell, it wasn't easy to hear. I cut through the living room, and perched on a rocking chair on the front porch. That didn't work out any better because people kept stopping to chat.

In spite of the midday sun, I strolled to the shade of the ancient tree towering in Roscoe's front yard. Happily, I managed to reach Bernie, who promised to deliver platters of assorted cheeses and fruit, a raspberry almond baked brie, a platter of bruschetta topped with pesto and yellow cherry tomatoes, and a large smoked salmon with cream cheese, onions, and bagels. He suggested he include turkey and ham sandwiches for family members who would need something substantial to eat and promised to bring along a couple of tea and coffee urns as well as jugs of sweetened iced tea.

My next call was to Big Daddy's Bakery. He said he could put together a tier of cupcakes if we were willing to take what he had on hand — classic coconut, raspberry with chocolate ganache, and lemon meringue. It sounded terrific to me. When he suggested bourbon vanilla, tears came to my eyes. Roscoe would have loved those.

In the driveway, Mars hopped into his car, no doubt on his way to pick up Mindy.

I leaned against the trunk of the old tree and buried my face in my hands. I'd kept it together until then, but when Big Daddy mentioned bourbon, the reality of Roscoe's death finally hit me, and tears cascaded down my cheeks.

I wiped my eyes and watched people mingle on Roscoe's front porch. Only a few days ago, he'd been bigger than life, enjoying his friends there.

Olive and Francie had joined the little crowd milling about the porch. Olive might not like parties and social functions, but it looked to me that she was very much in her element — back in her old home and surrounded by friends. I wondered what would happen when Mindy arrived.

Taking a deep breath, I braced myself to return to the house. I gazed up at the clear blue sky, hoping Roscoe was watching his friends celebrate his life.

A curtain moved in one of the dormer windows on the third floor, and suddenly I thought Roscoe might not be the only one watching us.

CHAPTER THIRTY-FOUR

Dear Natasha,
I'm into the repurposing movement. Do you have any suggestions for alternatives to store-bought trellises?
> — Wisteria Fan in Beans Cove,
> Pennsylvania

Dear Wisteria Fan,
Discarded wooden ladders are adorable for that cottage chic look. If you'd like something a little more space-age, look for an old TV antenna. The kind that stood on a roof. Or how about chairs without seats in them?
> — Natasha

I studied the dormer window where I thought I'd seen movement. Violet was prone to watching from windows. Had she retreated to her room?

Trying to act casual, which I felt I could

do, no matter what Natasha claimed about my acting abilities or lack thereof, I walked up the stairs to the porch, into the foyer, and glided up the stairs to the second floor as if I lived there. I paused for a moment before continuing to the attic floor, where the dormer windows were located. I caught my breath and listened. All the sounds gave the impression of coming from downstairs.

Glad that I had worn rubber-soled shoes that allowed me to sneak around, I started up the stairs, walking slowly. The third-floor landing wasn't much to speak of. A hallway branched off to the left and the right. By my calculations, I'd seen movement in a window to my right.

I passed an open door to a bathroom. Ahead, the doors on both sides of me were closed. I tiptoed to the first one, bowed my head, and jammed my ear against the door to listen.

A hand swung over my mouth, the door opened, and I was dragged into the room. I fought to open my mouth and bit down hard on the hand.

It fell away immediately. I turned to find I'd bitten none other than Tommy Lee Kenner.

He examined his hand and whispered angrily, "You bit me!"

"You mugged me!" I whispered back.

"I'm lucky you didn't draw blood!"

"Not that lucky. I haven't had my rabies shot."

I whirled around, painfully aware that someone had opened the door for Kenner.

And there, before my eyes stood Roscoe, back from the dead. A squeal almost escaped me, but Kenner clamped a hand over my mouth again. I kicked backward into his shin, and he grunted.

Roscoe grumbled, "You two cut it out. We have work to do."

I didn't know whether to smack him or hug him. "How could you do this to your family?" I hissed. I relented and hugged him.

"They'll get over it. Don't forget one of 'em is trying to do the rest of us in. I'm doing this *for* my family."

"We need a favor," said Kenner, massaging his hand. "To think I was worried about your *dog* biting me."

Roscoe rolled his eyes. "When Mindy gets here, you go downstairs and let people make a fuss about her for a little bit. Then we want you to make a production out of sending her to rest. Got that?"

"Okay. But I'm not following you. How's that going to help anything?"

Roscoe looked glum. He whispered, "Call me a stupid old man, but I don't want to think that my lovely Mindy tried to kill my only child. Marrying me for my money — I get that. She's younger and attractive. All I have going for me is money. But trying to murder my son? I don't think she did it."

Kenner sat down on a ladder-back chair. "Whoever poisoned Audie was very determined. We found the same assortment of chopped flowers in a bottle of salad dressing in the guest house. Bits and pieces were also in the trash can. As close as we can tell, the poisoned dressing was made in the guest house kitchen. We've replaced the tainted bottle of salad dressing with plain old salad dressing of the same brand. On the way home from the hospital, Mars is going to fill her in about Audie — with a few special details. He's going to say they don't know what poisoned Audie because Cricket took care to bring food from home. If Mindy is the one who tampered with the dressing, she'll want to dispose of the poisoned Italian dressing in the guest house."

"But everyone already knows that's what made Audie sick. She'd be a fool to do that," I protested.

"She doesn't know," said Roscoe.

"How is that possible?"

"She was already in the hospital when Audie was poisoned," said Kenner. "She knows he was sick, but she doesn't have any of the details. She didn't hear you ask what he ate or see you wrap up the trash. She hasn't heard your theory about her chopping up flowers randomly."

"Wait a minute. Are Olive and Francie in on this?" I asked.

"No one except you and Mars knows about this plan," said Roscoe.

I wanted to chew him out for putting Olive, Francie, and Violet through the anguish of believing he was dead. But they would surely do that themselves once the jig was up. I stared at Kenner. "Did you forget that Francie knows all about my theory? I'd be very surprised if she hadn't told Olive."

Roscoe hit his forehead with the palm of his hand. "I don't believe this."

Kenner settled his elbows on his knees and bowed his head. He lifted it after a minute. "Maybe it will still work. We just have to tell Mars to keep Olive and Francie away from Mindy."

"Good luck with that!" I had visions of Olive leaping through the living room with a dagger in her hand, accusing Mindy of trying to kill her baby.

"Could you call Mars and give him a heads-up about that?" I asked.

Kenner checked his watch. "Too late. He probably has Mindy in his car by now."

"One more little thing," I said.

"Aw, what now?" Roscoe slumped into a chair as if he couldn't take another problem.

I tapped my wrist. "You probably picked up that poison ivy when you were working around Heath's corpse. It seems that Olive was afraid Mindy would destroy her garden, so she chopped up poison ivy and sprinkled it through the flower beds."

Kenner shuddered. "I'm lucky I only have it in one spot."

"Exactly. But you're not the only one. Mindy must have picked it up on her arm when she was gathering plants for the poison."

"Interesting speculation," said Kenner. "By the way, the police are not in possession of Mindy's scotch decanter. Someone else must have taken it."

"There's another person who suffered the wrath of Olive's poison ivy — Cricket."

"Now don't you go bad-mouthing my almost daughter-in-law," said Roscoe.

"It's on her leg," I explained. "The day Mars and I had lunch with Roscoe and Cricket, Mars thought Cricket was playing

389

footsie with him under the table."

"Hah!" Roscoe clamped a hand over his mouth. "I hope nobody heard that," he whispered.

"Then, when Mindy fell down the stairs, Cricket came by to pick up Violet. She had a big bag slung over her shoulder, and she kept standing on one foot so she could scratch the back of her leg with her other foot."

"A big bag?" said Kenner.

"A quilted designer duffle bag. They're very popular."

"Big enough to hide a scotch decanter?" Kenner's eyebrows raised.

"Plenty big enough." For once, I thought I could see what he was thinking. "You mean she came by to pick up the evidence, thinking everyone was already at the hospital. She didn't count on Nina and me being here."

Kenner slid his hand along his jawline. "What would Cricket have done with it?"

"She might still have it." I had their full attention. "Think about it. She had Violet in her car, so she couldn't dispose of it on the way to the hospital. She called Audie a little bit later and said the police wanted to talk to him. Good grief! Then she put together a wedding in a big hurry. They had to get a marriage license and arrange for the minister and the violinist — she didn't have time to drive out in the country and drop it over a bridge like I would have."

Kenner squinted at me. "You scare me."

I bared my teeth like Daisy. "She didn't dump it last night because she spent the whole night at the hospital. I think it's a good bet that it's still in her car or apartment."

Kenner focused on Roscoe. "Is the car in her name or Audie's?"

"Audie's, I think."

Frustrated, I whispered, "Who cares?"

"I do," said Kenner. "If it's her car, I need a search warrant. If it's Audie's car, he might give us permission to look inside."

Kenner jumped up and strolled to the window.

"Better be careful," I cautioned. "That's how I knew you were up here."

Kenner turned to face us. "They're here. It's showtime."

CHAPTER THIRTY-FIVE

Dear Natasha,
My daughter will be having a tenth birthday party this summer. She's into being a princess, so that will be our theme. I wanted to plant special annuals in our flower beds that would say "princess" to set the scene, but I'm not coming up with any clever ideas.
— Princess's Mom in Maple Shade,
New Jersey

Dear Princess's Mom,
How about creating a flower tiara by planting marigolds in the shape of a crown? If you have the room to make it five to seven feet wide, it will create quite an impact.
— Natasha

I scrambled to my feet.

"Don't forget to tell Mars to keep Olive and Francie away," said Kenner. "I'll let you go first, then I'll sneak down to the guest house and wait."

I had my doubts about the plan. It seemed like too many things could go wrong, and an awful lot of it depended on Mars's performance in the car on the way home from the hospital. Nevertheless, I tiptoed down the stairs, right into Violet.

"What were you doing up there?" she demanded.

"I needed a bathroom." I hurried down to the foyer and out the front door.

Mindy paraded from the car to the house, acting like a princess. She greeted people and made sad eyes at them.

I darted to Mars, placed a hand squarely on his chest, and propelled him backward a few steps. "Kenner says you're to keep Olive and Francie away from Mindy."

"Why?"

"So they won't give anything away and alert Mindy."

"That sounds like they know . . ."

"They do, sort of. Go! Go, go, go!"

I watched Mindy play the role of shattered wife on the porch. She drifted inside, air kissing people. I hurried up the steps.

Unfortunately, she headed to the dining room. Bernie and Big Daddy had outdone themselves. My mouth watered when I saw the gorgeous platters on the table, and I realized that I hadn't eaten since the caramel banana muffin. Not only did I *deserve* to eat, but wouldn't it make me look more natural? I slathered a bagel with cream cheese, topped it with a gorgeous rosy piece of salmon, and bit into it.

Mars zoomed by me, backtracked, grabbed the bagel, and kept going. *Rotten scoundrel!*

I was about to fix another bagel, but Mindy floated over to the living room. I grabbed a cupcake because they were close by, then realized it was probably time for me to do my thing and give her an excuse to leave the gathering. Carrying the cupcake, I kept an eye on her as she waltzed through the living room. She disappeared into the den.

I had to dodge the guests to catch up. By the time I reached the entrance to the den, Mindy was gone and the door to the patio was closing.

I rushed to the window and peered outside. Mindy glanced around nonchalantly and headed straight to the guest house. I hadn't had to do a thing. I backed up a little bit, so she wouldn't see me if she turned around, lifted the cupcake to my mouth, and bit into the wrapper.

I peeled it back, and Mars came up behind me. He still held half my bagel. I waved the cupcake under his nose. "The price of observing through this window is the rest of that bagel."

His mouth twisted around. "Only if I can have half your cupcake."

"Deal."

Mars ate cupcake, and I chewed on the bagel. Nothing happened at the guest house.

"Now I need tea," said Mars.

"Me, too."

"Who's going to get it?" he asked.

"You stole my bagel."

"I returned it. Half of it. We're even."

And then it happened. Kenner stepped out of the guest house and signaled someone. Roscoe, I presumed.

It didn't prevent Mars and me from barreling out the door and running across the lawn. Kenner made us wait for Roscoe.

"Well?" Mars demanded of Kenner.

Kenner didn't twitch a muscle. He waited patiently.

Roscoe hurried as fast as he could. He entered the guest house and the rest of us followed.

Mindy's eyes flew wide open. Her arms appeared to be pinned around her sides. I assumed Kenner had handcuffed her.

"Roscoe! You're alive!" She seemed confused. "Is Audie dead?"

The bottle of Italian salad dressing sat on the kitchen counter. It couldn't have been more glaring if it had been flashing neon.

Roscoe saw it and sank into a chair. He lowered his forehead into his hand and muttered, "I am an old fool. And Audie nearly paid for my foolishness with his life."

"So no one is dead. Take these handcuffs off me so I can hug my husband properly," Mindy barked. Her voice changed. Gentle and soft, she said, "Roscoe, sweetie, I need your help. This is all a big mistake."

He heaved a deep breath. "It's my big mistake. It's too late, Mindy. I can never forgive you for trying to kill my son."

"Kill? Why, Roscoe, what kind of nonsense have they been telling you? I just came over here for a bottle of dressing. Last I heard, there was nothing illegal about that!"

Roscoe's shoulders shook. "It was about my money. There's plenty to go around. You couldn't have split it with Audie? I guess I should have recognized your greed when you bought yourself that ridiculous diamond crown."

"It's called a tiara, and they're very fashionable!"

Kenner's phone buzzed. He answered, and

acknowledged the caller, but hardly spoke at all. When he finished, he said, "Cricket and Audie are almost here."

"Is that why you're keeping me here? So Audie can confront me? I want a lawyer!"

"You want a minute alone, Roscoe?" asked Kenner.

Roscoe stared at Mindy. She raised her chin, and if anything, I'd have said she appeared defiant.

"No. I'm done with this one." Roscoe walked out of the guest house.

Mars and I went with him. The three of us traipsed to the front of the house.

Olive saw Roscoe from the porch. She ran down the steps. "You horrible old man!" But she wrapped her arms around him so tightly that everyone knew she didn't mean what she'd said.

Applause broke out. *Applause!* None of those people had any idea what had transpired, but they cheered and slapped him on the back like he was some sort of champion back from the dead.

Kenner brought Mindy to the front of the house as Cricket and Audie arrived.

Audie stepped out of the car but held on to it as though he was still weak. "What's going on? Dad?"

A police car pulled into the driveway

behind Cricket's car. Two uniformed officers disembarked. One of them helped Mindy into the backseat.

Roscoe looked as drained as Audie. Evidently, Olive wasn't letting go of his arm, so they walked to their son together. Cricket came around to the passenger side of the car.

She held out her arms. "Roscoe! Oh my gosh, I can't believe it. You're a rascal for tricking us like this. I've been beside myself all morning!"

Roscoe didn't go into her embrace. He swallowed hard. "I'd like a minute with Audie. Why don't you get a bite to eat, Cricket?"

She blinked hard and appeared surprised but said, "Of course! Audie first." After a moment's hesitation, she climbed the stairs and called out, "Who needs a drink?"

Mars muttered, "There's an offer I'd turn down."

After a brief and quiet discussion, Audie gave his permission to search the car.

It took the uniformed officer all of two minutes to locate the quilted duffle bag underneath a seat. The officer opened it, inserted a gloved hand, and withdrew Mindy's scotch decanter.

Kenner gave a little jerk of his head. The

officer understood. He bagged the evidence and went after Cricket.

There was only one problem. She was gone.

CHAPTER THIRTY-SIX

Dear Natasha,
I loved your recent TV show about reusing items in an effort to live green. I have a bag full of old pantyhose with runs. Is there anything I can do with them besides toss them out?
— Living Green in Lavender, Tennessee

Dear Living Green,
They're wonderful for tying tomato plants to stakes because they have some give and won't cut into the vines. You can also store your freshly harvested potatoes and onions in them. And if they're a pretty color or have a nice pattern, stuff a piece with lavender from your garden, and tie it off with a purple ribbon for potpourri!
— Natasha

Those of us who hadn't recently been sick fanned out to search the house and grounds.

Kenner called in more police, but I had little hope that Cricket was still on the property. If I had been in her shoes, I would have made a beeline for the woods, hiked through them, and hitchhiked when I reached the road on the other side. With her good looks, it wouldn't take her long to catch a ride.

The day had been emotionally draining. By the time Francie asked me to drive her home, I was dead on my feet and hoping I could sneak in a late-afternoon nap.

I parked Wolf's car on our street, and Natasha materialized on the sidewalk before we had a chance to step out of the car. Her hands were on her hips, and her expression was stormy. "Where have you been? You promised to repurp, and Troy made me walk both dogs twice!"

"It's still early," I protested — but not with much vigor because it was anything but early. "Don't have a cow."

Alas, Natasha's sedan waited in front of my house. I slid into the passenger seat, and she pulled into the street.

"This is all the rage, you know. It's part of the green movement to give new life to discarded objects. Don't you adore that idea? There are whole shows about it. I would love to go national with a repurp show. Leon scoped out stores for me, and said The Flee Market has the best selection. Which is so strange, because Heath recommended it to me, too. I mean, I could have just gone straight there, without having Leon check out other places. Who knew Heath would be an expert? It's a combination of new and used items, but Heath said the owner is very selective about what she'll carry." Natasha parked in front of a warehouse with a huge clock on the front.

"That's weird. There are no hour or minute hands on the clock, just a hand ticking by really fast," I observed.

"Leon told me about that. Isn't it cute? It's a *second hand* store!"

I groaned. I trusted Leon's taste, though, and hoped we could make quick work of finding something to repurp. The large piles of broken concrete near the door of the building didn't inspire me, though.

We walked into an overwhelming assortment of architectural artifacts, old furniture, linens, knobs, and light fixtures.

"Well!" said Natasha. "At least it's not too dirty." She hurried down an aisle of broken chairs.

I wandered aimlessly, wondering what someone might do with a garden umbrella whose crank had broken or a chair missing two legs.

"Sophie!" I could hear her shouting across the massive hall.

Natasha found me and tugged me to a worn-out rubber mat on which many people had wiped their shoes. "It's perfect! We'll paint it purple, and gild these ridges with sheets of that sticky-tacky gold stuff. Then a good coat of polyurethane, and we can hang it as outdoor art."

"I hope they have a mangled steel car bumper to go along with it." Apparently she didn't recognize my sarcasm.

She screeched and hugged me. "I'm so glad you're getting into the spirit of this. That's very clever."

It was neither clever nor original, but the idea made her happy. If she bought a car bumper, would the regular trash people pick it up, or would I have to schlep it somewhere to get rid it?

"Excuse me, ma'am," trilled Natasha. "Do you have any steel car bumpers?"

A tall, thin woman wearing makeup that looked like it had been applied with a spatula drifted over to us. "They fly out the second we get them. I can put you on a waiting list, but I have to warn you that they aren't cheap."

Natasha frowned at her. "Used. You do understand that we want something that has been thrown out."

"They're very hard to come by. Vintage car collectors and sculptors fight for them."

"Sophie, I believe you'll have to come up with another ingenious idea." Natasha clasped her hands. "This bed! I love it. Don't you want this, Sophie? Imagine it filled with plants. It would be a — *flower bed!*"

Wanted was the wrong word by a mile, but I moseyed over. She had her eye on an old wooden bed that had clearly been dragged out of a junkyard. *Mangled* was the only word that came to mind. It probably hadn't been much to speak of when it was new. I was not having that thing in my garden. *Not!*

"Couldn't we do something with a broken stained-glass window?" *Or anything else!*

"Stained glass." Natasha said it under her breath like it was a novel new concept.

She took off and I followed, passing a stack of yellow gingham napkins displayed in a fan. I backpedaled, and I swear my heart skipped a beat.

I picked up one of the napkins. Someone had embroidered a ladybug on a daisy.

"Those are hand-embroidered," said the saleswoman.

I opened one, searching for a name or

brand. "Are they vintage?" I held my breath. They didn't look vintage to me.

"No, I'm afraid not. I have some lovely vintage linens over here."

My heart was pounding. I would have to compare it to Wolf's pillow to know for sure, but the embroidery on the napkins looked just like the embroidery on Anne's yellow gingham pillow to me. Unlike the one I had seen in the children's store, this looked hand-embroidered. The stitches were skilled, but they didn't have that machine-stitched tightness. I tried to speak calmly. "Where do you get these?"

"From a supplier out in the country. He brings those wonderful baskets, too. They're all woven by hand, not too far from here."

"Do you have anything else like this? With embroidered ladybugs?"

She dipped into a large pile of cloths. "Here we are. A matching tablecloth. You know, I really should put this on display —"

"I'll take it."

"Wonderful. The napkins, too?"

"Yes. I'd like to locate the woman who does the embroidery. Could you call your supplier, perhaps?"

Her smile and cheery tone vanished. "No." Her voice had turned hard and huffy. "I'm sorry. If you want to buy more, I can place an order for you."

I waved my hands nervously. "I'm not trying to cheat you out of your cut. You don't understand. I think I recognize the work. I've been looking for this person."

She tucked her chin in. "And you think you can recognize the stitches?" Her voice dripped with sarcasm.

"No, it's the motif."

"Because ladybugs and daisies are so original?"

"Could you cut me a little slack here? I might be very wrong about this, but there's a lot at stake."

"What's her name?"

"Anne Fleishman."

She pulled out her cell phone and made a call. "Bobby, I have someone here who wants to know if the lady who embroiders the daisies is an Anne Fleishman."

As soon as she uttered Anne's name I realized I had made a huge mistake. If the guy called Anne and told her someone was making inquiries, she might take off.

The saleswoman hung up. "Sorry, it's not her."

My hope deflated like a pricked balloon. "What is the name? Maybe she's using an alias."

"If she's using a different name, then

maybe she doesn't *want* to be found."

"Please? This is a matter of life and death." Well, it was — sort of — Anne's life or death in a weird way.

"I suppose you need a kidney from her?"

At that moment, I wished I was tall and macho and could grab her by the throat and make her choke out the information like they would on TV. But I was neither tall nor macho, and she would have me arrested if I did that.

Natasha chugged up, dragging along three industrial garbage bins, a piece of the bed, a small bookshelf, and a stained-glass window. "Do you deliver?"

The saleslady, clearly eager to be done with me, turned her back to me and apologized to Natasha for not having a delivery service. Natasha chattered about sending Leon and someone from the production crew over to pick up the items she was buying.

Holding the napkins and tablecloth, I pawed in my purse for my wallet and promptly dropped it. I bent to pick it up and saw a corner of a picture propped up on the floor behind the counter, a picture of . . . a duck? Still hunched over, so they wouldn't notice me, I shuffled forward for a better look. No doubt about it — I had located Roscoe's mallard print.

Grinning ear to ear, I placed the linens on the counter and handed cash to Natasha. "Ring those up, too, please."

"What are we going to do with these?"

"I think they're cute."

"Oh." Her tone indicated her disagreement on that subject.

When she finished paying, I stepped behind the counter and lifted the mallard print.

The saleswoman glared at me. "That's quite expensive. Please be careful."

In a hushed voice, I said, "I happen to know the value because this print was stolen from the home of my friend earlier this week."

"Put that down this minute and leave my shop. I don't carry hot merchandise."

I calmly took out my cell phone. "No problem. I can call the police from your parking lot."

"Maria Delgado."

"In . . . ?"

"Durbin."

"Thank you." I motioned to Natasha, who looked on, appalled. "Let's go."

The saleswoman hustled around the counter and latched onto the print in my arms.

I raised my eyebrows. "I don't think so." I kept going, waiting for her to tackle me from behind. But she didn't. I had a hunch it wasn't a coincidence that Heath knew about this place.

Natasha demanded explanations on the way home, but I was so engrossed in finding Durbin and Maria Delgado on my phone that she didn't get much information from me. Durbin turned out to be a tiny town in West Virginia with a population of less than five hundred people. Unfortunately, although there were tons of Maria Delgados on the Internet, I wasn't finding any in Durbin. I was excited, nevertheless. In a town of fewer than five hundred residents, they all probably knew each other.

I asked Natasha to stop in front of my house. I unloaded the print and thanked her for the ride.

"Wait! Soooophie," she whined, "we have to get to work repurping now. I'm going to send the fellows over in the pickup to get everything."

"Okay. Call me when you have the stuff."

Natasha called an hour later, complaining that nothing had been delivered. I had to tell her I'd been called away the next day. I supposed it wasn't nice of me, but I felt compelled to follow up on the possible lead to Anne. Nina agreed to leave at the crack of dawn the next day.

It was ten in the morning when we rolled into Durbin, West Virginia. It turned out to be an adorable little town with a railroad theme in the mountains near a state park. Not all that far from Old Town, yet a world apart. We passed a feed and hardware store, a dress shop, and a diner. At the end of the block, we spied a coffee shop.

"What's our best bet?" I parallel parked Wolf's car. "The coffee shop?"

"You go there, and I'll work the feed store."

I lowered my sunglasses to look at Nina. "You? In a feed store?"

"You don't think I can flirt?"

"I'm sure you can. Have at it."

She jumped out of the car. "We should have brought Daisy, she would have helped us break the ice. Wait here."

Instead of waiting, I visited the coffee shop. The sole employee, a middle-aged woman with kind eyes, recommended the homemade ham biscuits. I bought two, along with two iced coffees, though it did seem considerably cooler and less humid than Old Town.

When I paid, she asked, "Are you from out of town?"

"How could you tell?"

"Everybody knows most everybody around here. What brings you to Durbin?"

Perfect. I couldn't have asked for an easier opening. "I'm looking for Maria Delgado."

The woman behind the counter took a hard look at me. "Are you now?"

Uh-oh. I didn't know what Anne had done, or if Maria Delgado even *was* Anne, but I knew a suspicious face when I saw one. "I hear she does some amazing embroidery."

"That she does. You looking to buy? I have a few of her pieces right there on that table."

I picked out two linen hand towels embroidered with blue delphiniums and ladybugs. "Does she always put in a ladybug?"

"Pretty much. I've never seen anything she embroidered without at least a teeny one."

I couldn't stop grinning. The woman probably thought I was deranged. Maria *had* to be Anne. I paid for the towels, and the woman gladly gave me directions to Maria's house. I met Nina on the sidewalk, lugging a forty-pound bag of dog food. Biting my lip to keep from laughing, I opened the back hatch for her.

She heaved it in. "Stop that!" But she

couldn't help laughing, either. "Be glad I didn't make up a story about needing a salt block for my horse."

She'd obtained the same directions. We hopped into the car and attacked our lunch. The ham was nicely salty, the biscuits still warm and melt-in-your-mouth flaky. If I lived around there, I would be a regular at the coffee shop for lunch.

We drove out of town, made a couple of turns, and found ourselves on a two-lane road lined by farms, fields, and forests.

"We should be there by now," Nina complained. "I bet we took a wrong turn."

"That's it."

"How can you tell? I don't see a name on the mailbox."

"The garden." I didn't have to say more. Flowers in a riot of colors surrounded the tiny bungalow. A vegetable garden grew off to the side, with eggplants and tomatoes waiting to be picked. An old pickup truck was parked on a gravel driveway. I pulled in behind it.

I couldn't recall ever having been so nervous. This was it. Either Anne was alive or I'd been about as wrong as a person could be.

Nina and I walked to the front door.

"Are you about to jump out of your skin

like I am?" she asked.

I held out my trembling hand to show her.

"Me, too. Knock already!"

I rapped on the door.

Chapter Thirty-Seven

Dear Sophie,
A friend gave me a giant four-foot-tall pot! I love the rich purple color, but I haven't the foggiest notion what to do with it. It sticks out like a sore thumb by my front door and on my patio.
— Eggplant Fan in Daisy, Georgia

Dear Eggplant Fan,
Place it in the garden in between shrubs or tall flowers. Pots are a delightful chic surprise in the garden and will draw the eye to the plants around them.
— Sophie

A woman with silver hair cut short like a man's answered the door. "Can I help you?"

She didn't look like the Anne I'd seen in pictures. We'd come all the way for nothing. I sagged. "I'm sorry to bother you. We were looking for Maria Delgado."

"You'll find her out back. I'm her land-lord. Just fixing a leak under the kitchen sink."

Nina and I exchanged a look. I couldn't stand it. The tension was worse than Christmas for a kid who wanted a bike and didn't see it under the tree.

We snuck around the side of the house. A woman worked at a rustic potting sink. Dark brown hair waved down her back, almost to her waist. She wore shorts and flip-flops. I was terrified to see her face yet anxious and excited that it might be her.

"Anne?"

She froze for a second but quickly resumed her work.

I inched around to see her face better. She tilted her head ever so slightly away from me.

"Anne Fleishman?"

She swung around and faced me dead-on with a weak smile. I'd found her! No question about it — she was the woman in Wolf's pictures.

"I'm sorry, you must be mistaken. There's no one here by that name. I'm Maria Delgado."

"I don't think so." I opened my purse and pulled out the photo of Anne and Wolf in happier times.

The smile faded. "Who are you?" It was a mere whisper.

I wanted to jump up and down and shriek. Instead I wrapped my arms around her and hugged her, probably scaring her even more.

"Woohoo!" cried Nina. She ran to us to join in the hug.

When we let go, poor Anne looked bewildered.

Nina and I babbled simultaneously about Wolf and being so glad that she wasn't dead. She must have thought us insane.

Deliriously happy, I said, "You have to come back. They think Wolf killed you."

She seemed shocked. "Why would anyone think that?" She backed up ever so slightly. "Shelby!"

The landlady opened a screen door. "Don't worry, Maria. I got your back."

Shelby wasn't menacing, she was just helping Anne like I would have backed up Nina.

"They think you're dead because no one knows where you are. Your mother and Wolf have been looking for you for years." I didn't want to alienate her by asking how she could have been so cruel to them. I wasn't sure how she would react if she knew I'd been dating Wolf, either, so I skipped over that part. "Your handbag and wallet were just found in Wolf's garden, along with a rusty knife. That confirmed their worst fears that something terrible had happened to you."

"Handbag? I never buried a handbag in my life."

"Someone did. It has your driver's license in it." Something must have rung true to her because she chewed on her lower lip, her forehead wrinkled.

"I never buried my purse. I gave it to my best friend. We swapped driver's licenses so I would have an ID that nobody would be tracking. I wanted it that way."

"But why?" I asked. Nina and I exchanged a look.

Anne's worried face relaxed a hair. "If you don't mind, it's all very personal. It's a part of my life that I would rather forget."

"Your old friend Tommy Lee Kenner is determined to nail Wolf for your murder."

She snorted. "That's impossible. I left notes. Wolf and my family know that I'm very much alive, and they know why I left. Well, kind of."

"Notes?" It didn't make sense. If Wolf and Mona knew she was alive — now *I* was confused.

"I didn't want them to worry. So I left notes on the dining room table for Wolf and my parents explaining why I needed to leave."

"They never saw them." My words came out in a hushed tone. "I don't think they ever got them."

"You're lying." Anne's voice faded. Her entire body trembled. Nina and I steadied her and lowered her to a split-log bench. Shelby bolted out of the house to help us.

I wet paper towels at the potting sink and handed them to Anne. "Hold these to your forehead."

"You okay?" asked Shelby. When Anne nodded, Shelby rushed to the house and returned with a glass of water. "Drink this."

Shelby sat next to Anne, her elbows on her knees. "I'm Shelby, and you would be . . . ?"

We introduced ourselves, but again I steered clear of mentioning that I'd dated Wolf. Anne was clearly going through an emotional event as it was — I didn't need to complicate it. She'd know soon enough.

"Your mom will be so happy to see you." I smiled at Anne.

"Then you clearly don't know my mother." Her eyes darted from me to Nina and back. "What's her name?"

"Mona, short for Desdemona," offered Nina.

Anne raised trembling fingers to her cheek. "They know my mom, Shelby. That's exactly how she introduces herself." She shoved her hands through the hair around her face. "I'd forgotten all about that purse. My mother thought I should have it because it was a status symbol that I had arrived. It was so expensive! Wolf thought it was a waste of money. I've never cared much about designers and logos and social status. It came to be a symbol of everything that was wrong with my life. I gave it to my girlfriend when I left. I had to be rid of it. I wonder why she buried it."

"Can you see why people thought you were dead?" asked Nina.

Anne's face contorted. "I don't understand. If the notes were gone, Cricket would have told them —"

Nina and I shouted, "Cricket?!"

Cricket had known all along that Anne was alive but kept quiet for Anne's benefit? "Tell us what happened."

Nina and I pulled up old-fashioned aluminum lawn chairs.

"Nothing happened. I'd just made a shambles of my life. Oh, gosh. It was a mess. I thought Wolf and I were happily married. We had little squabbles like every couple, but then . . . I found out about his affair with my best friend." She twisted the paper towels until they couldn't go further, and her knuckles went white.

"Cricket?" asked Nina.

"Evidently you know her."

I nodded. "She's engaged to Audie Greene."

"Audie? She left Wolf?"

"She actually wasn't with Wolf." I swallowed hard. Was she? Maybe she and Wolf got back together after Anne left, and Kenner didn't know about it? He said he'd lost touch with Cricket.

Anne seemed relieved. "No, no. You must have me confused with someone else after all. It must be another Wolf."

Right. Like we all knew a lot of people named Cricket and Wolf.

"My Cricket and Wolf are definitely together," she insisted.

For a split second, I wondered if Wolf had been seeing Cricket in spite of her engagement to Audie. *No, that didn't seem possible.* "Is your Cricket a bombshell redhead?"

Anne balled up her fists and pressed them against her mouth. "This can't be happening. You must be mistaken. Cricket was pregnant. They have a little boy now."

She ran inside the house and returned quickly, clutching a worn picture in her shaking hand. "Here. She sent this to me three years ago."

I took it from her hand, and Nina looked over my shoulder. A towheaded toddler with intelligent blue eyes looked like an angel sitting on Cricket's lap. He was older now, but I recognized the little fellow who had chanted "Poop, poop, poop" at the picnic and smeared his dirty hand on Natasha's dress. I shook my head. "I'm sorry. This little fellow belongs to one of Roscoe's employees."

"Are you sure? Cricket was pregnant and . . ." Anne looked away, gathered her long hair into a ponytail, and twisted it.

She had to be in a state of shock. I glanced at Nina. What would I have done if Nina confessed to being involved with Mars when we were married? "You never confronted Wolf about his affair with Cricket?"

Her eyes popped open wide. "I have spent my *life* trying to avoid conflict. It's horrible! I'm not clever that way. I don't like to argue, and I *hate* it when people twist things around. Besides, can you imagine how I would have felt if Wolf had chosen to stay with me? He wanted children, and Cricket was going to have his baby, or so I thought. He would have hated me for keeping them apart. I thought he was going to have the family he always wanted. Our marriage wouldn't have survived anyway under those circumstances. If I had stayed, he would have left me for Cricket eventually."

Evidently she wasn't quite the dumb bunny that her boss claimed. She'd certainly given that a lot of thought.

Of course, the embezzlement from Roscoe would have provided motivation to get out of town as well. Once Wolf learned of the embezzlement, that alone would probably have broken up her marriage to Wolf. He never would have trusted her again. I didn't want to accuse her of trying to steal Roscoe's money, though. She might take off. It was far more important to convince her to come back to Old Town. At least long enough for Kenner to see her and know she was still among the living. What happened after that was out of my control.

She turned her back to us, and her shoulders heaved as she sobbed. When she turned around again, she said, "I was so ashamed. Nothing was right, I didn't succeed at anything. You can't imagine the desperation. I hit rock bottom. I wasn't the wife Wolf wanted. I wasn't the daughter my parents wanted. But most of all, I wasn't *anything* that *I* wanted. I don't know . . . Maybe I latched onto that baby as an excuse to run away."

Shelby's jaw had dropped open. "Let me get this straight. Her husband never had an affair with her best friend? And there is no baby?"

"That's right," said Nina.

Shelby stared at us in shock. "And now Maria's husband is under suspicion for her murder?"

"It's been a source of gossip for years," said Nina.

Anne covered her face with her hands and moaned, "What have I done?"

Nina continued, "But when Sophie found Anne's purse buried in the garden, it sort of brought things to a head."

Shelby gazed at Anne. "Then, Maria — er, Anne — you have to go back and make it right. No matter how you feel about him or what he did, it's not fair to make him go through that."

Anne agreed to come back to Old Town with us if Shelby came along. I couldn't blame her for wanting a friend by her side. She didn't know Nina and me. It would have been stupid to just go along with us. Shelby drove her car, because Anne was a basket case, and Anne's old truck wasn't all that reliable. I was sorry they weren't in our car. I would have liked to pepper Anne with questions. Not that she had many answers.

When our little caravan headed for Old Town, Nina said, "You do realize that your relationship with Wolf is probably going to come to a screeching end. And you're bringing him the reason to break it off."

I laughed at her. "I am painfully aware of that. What do you propose? That we ditch Anne and never tell him?"

"Um, you seem to be taking it well."

"Nina, I had to come to grips with it the night you, Francie, and Mars spied on Wolf and me. Do you remember Mars saying Wolf was still in love with his wife? Mars was exactly right. Anne would have been a constant thorn in any relationship Wolf had. I don't know if they can make a go of it after all that has happened, but Anne is Wolf's wife." I sucked in a deep breath. "I don't belong in that equation. I have no business there."

She flashed me a sympathetic look. "So do you think Cricket lied to Anne because she wanted Wolf back?"

"It's possible, I guess. But if that were the case, wouldn't they be together now?"

"Maybe she chased after him, but he was too broken up about Anne to be interested."

"She might have just wanted revenge on

Anne because she thought Anne stole Wolf from her in the first place."

"I hope not! What kind of best friend would be that evil?" Nina shivered.

"The better question is why would they continue to be friends at all?"

Nina cackled. "You're friends with Natasha, and she stole Mars."

I wasn't sure that Natasha had stolen Mars. My family and friends thought so, and sometimes I even swayed that way. But more often I thought the truth was that my marriage had fizzled to a slow death on its own. Although, apparently, we still had a few sparks left in us. It made me itch to remember that romantic moment I'd had with Mars a few months ago. It had been little more than a kiss, but neither of us had stopped it. Why had it felt so right at that moment? I cringed at the memory. I was not cut out for romance with other women's men. Whatever Cricket's reasoning, lying about a baby so Anne would leave Wolf was about as low as she could get.

Nina called Kenner while I drove. "Sophie and I need to see you at Wolf's house in about an hour. Can you find Mona and Wolf and have them meet us there? The backyard would be great!"

The scene was set. Nina and I acted like

giddy children.

I had hoped to walk into Wolf's backyard like the Three Musketeers being victorious, but I feared we more closely resembled the Four Stooges.

A little crowd had gathered there. Olive must have noticed something afoot and phoned Francie, because they were both there. Kenner had been able to contact Mona because she was present, too. A couple of other cops were on the premises as well as a host of people whom I didn't know.

Anne was hesitant. We marched across Wolf's lawn, coaxing and tugging her until everyone present had turned to look at us. Mona collapsed again, but not a single person went to her aid. All eyes were on Anne. Kenner broke the stunned silence. He ran to her, grabbed her in a hug, and swung her into the air in a circle. When she landed, he held her tight and closed his eyes like he knew heaven at that moment.

Nina and I high-fived, then we caved and jogged over to revive Mona.

Anne broke through the cluster of people around her and ran to Mona. She dropped to her knees. "Mama?"

Mona clasped Anne like she had held on to her purse. "I thought I would never have the chance to tell you how much I love you. I'm so sorry, Anne!"

"It's okay, Mama."

"No it's not. I never should have pushed you to be something else. You're perfect the way you are, kind and gentle with a heart of gold. I'm so grateful that you're not dead, and that I have a second chance to make things right. That doesn't happen often in life."

Tears came to my eyes.

But one person was missing — Wolf.

Chapter Thirty-Eight

Dear Natasha,
I love an elegant garden. How can I achieve a classic look?
— Domestic Diva in Boxwood, Delaware

Dear Domestic Diva,
Less is more. Topiaries, topiaries, topiaries. Keep them neat and trimmed. Use topiaries in sets of two or three or five to make an impression.

— Natasha

If Anne noticed Wolf's absence, she didn't mention it. As insecure as she was, I suspected she thought it meant he didn't want to see her. She was the center of attention, though. Everyone clustered around her, hugging and asking questions.

Five minutes later, Wolf bounded into the yard and came to an abrupt halt beside me. "Did they find something? What's everyone doing here?"

I handed him his car keys. "I don't think you'll be needing my car anymore."

"No?" He seemed reluctant to swap keys, but he did it anyway.

The cluster of people around Anne parted, leaving her to face Wolf alone. It seemed like it was happening in slow motion. They gazed at each other, then ran into each other's arms and didn't let go.

Next to me, Nina sniffed. "It's so romantic! Just like a movie."

That was my cue to take off. They certainly didn't need Wolf's old girlfriend hanging around. "Come on, let's go."

"Already?" asked Nina.

"I have a delivery to make."

Nina and I transferred our belongings from Wolf's car to mine.

"Are you okay?" she asked.

"I'll be fine." I meant it.

We pulled into Roscoe's driveway a few minutes later. Unless I missed my guess, Violet would be in the kitchen. I opened the back hatch and slid the mallard print out. Nina accompanied me as I stepped up to the porch and around to the side where the kitchen was.

Violet worked at the stove. I rapped lightly on the window.

She opened the door, stormy as always. She didn't greet us or say a word.

"I have something for you." I handed the print to her.

"*You* stole it?" The dark eyes blazed.

"No, I didn't steal it. But I happened to find it! All that matters is that you have it back."

She slammed the door.

Nina and I cracked up. We laughed hysterically until tears ran down our faces. We couldn't stop.

Roscoe must have heard us. He and Audie appeared on the porch.

"What's going on?"

I shouldn't have looked at Nina. *Bad idea!* We broke up again. We couldn't very well tell him it was Violet who'd set us into spasms of laughter. "We found Anne Fleishman."

I wiped my cheeks with my fingers and realized that I had probably just made life worse for Anne because the embezzlement scheme would surface again. I tried to comfort myself with the thought that Olive knew about her return. She would share that information with Roscoe in a matter of hours.

"No kidding! Where's she been?" asked Roscoe.

"A cute little place out in West Virginia. In the mountains."

"Mountains, eh?" The corner of Roscoe's mouth twitched. "Sounds like my kind of gal."

Had I heard him wrong?

"I owe Anne a big apology. Wolf, too, I guess. Audie, be sure we send her a big basket of gardening things from *Planter's Punch*. And flowers. Ask your mom, she'll know what to send."

"Apology?" said Nina.

Roscoe sat down on the porch step. "One of our employees caught an unusual transaction yesterday."

Audie groaned and looked off in the distance as though he didn't want to hear about it.

"My death yesterday set off an unexpected consequence. Cricket authorized the transfer of funds from our accounts into an offshore bank. Seems Cricket was as greedy as Mindy," he snorted. "Like father, like son, I guess. Kenner and the cops caught her at Dulles Airport this morning, headed for Belize. When I died, Cricket thought Mindy would get everything, so she emptied out as many accounts as she could. Now she's singing like a canary, hoping cooperation will lead to a plea bargain, I'd guess."

"Oh no!" Nina was no longer amused. "Did you lose money?"

Roscoe grinned. "That Kenner fellow is on the ball. He thought my dying might trigger financial shenanigans and notified my banks to put a hold on large transactions. Cricket was a two-time loser."

"So Anne never embezzled from you?" I asked hopefully.

Roscoe smiled. "Not a penny. It was Cricket and Heath all along, but she did a bang-up job of pinning it on Anne and Heath. Seems when that didn't work out, she set her sights on becoming a Greene and went after Audie. The irony of it all is that Audie would have gotten everything. If Cricket had waited a day or two and married him, she would have been a Greene. How do you like that? There was Cricket trying to kill Mindy so Audie would inherit, and at the same time, Mindy was trying to kill Audie so she would inherit."

"So Cricket put the foxglove into Mindy's scotch," I said.

Roscoe sighed, shaking his head. "It nearly backfired on her. If I had been taking the digitalis like my doctor ordered and had some of the scotch on top of it — I'd have been a dead duck."

"It was a close call," said Audie. "Though I'm not convinced that Cricket wouldn't have murdered me eventually if we had tied the knot. Hey, Nina, where's Cupcake? I miss my little snuggle muffin."

"You can have her any time," said Nina. "Should I bring her to your house?"

"I'll come by and pick her up. She's going to live out here with me. I talked to my vet, and he thinks I should give an underground fence a try. I can include the pond and move the bird feeders to the side yard. That way Cupcake can roam the territory she loves" — he raised his voice — "and the birds will be safe, too." In a whisper he said, "I'm sure Violet is listening."

A muffled voice inside the house said, "I am not!"

This time, we all broke out laughing. Nina and I left in giggles.

On the way home, Nina dug in her purse and handed me a little remote control.

"What's this?"

"Your garage door opener." She made a quick phone call to tell Troy we were on our way. "They want you to drive into the garage."

"Are you serious? It's over? They're finished?"

The peak of the garage roof was visible from the street but looked cute. I turned the car into the alley behind my house. A new fence had been installed. The redbrick garage matched the style of my house, and the garage doors had faux hinges on them, as if they belonged to a carriage house.

They rose smoothly when I clicked the remote. Troy waited inside. I drove in, wondering why I hadn't built a garage sooner. No more hunting for a place to park!

We stepped out of the car, exclaiming over everything — the painted floor that would be easy to clean, the workbench along the back, the clever storage hooks.

Troy opened a windowed door on the far end. Nina and I ventured into my backyard. Except we didn't step on grass. Troy and his crew had installed a brick walkway that ran from the garage all the way to my living room. Wide enough for two people to walk comfortably, it grew to room width in the middle. The entire thing was covered with a pitched roof. In the midsection, the roof soared. A stone fireplace with an arched opening served as the focal point. A four-foot wreath of dried flowers hung above a rustic cedar mantel.

Troy ran his hand over a wooden table. "We custom built this for you. Your friends kept dropping by to check on us, so I knew you needed a super long table to accommodate everyone. There are two extension pieces in the middle. You can make it smaller for a more intimate dinner."

I couldn't get over how beautiful it was. My backyard had been transformed from a nice garden to party central. "Friends?"

He ticked them off on his fingers. "Mars, Wolf, Bernie, Leon, Francie, a couple of people who live on the block, Kenner, a woman cop — I don't even remember them all. Did you notice what we did to your living room?"

"My living room!" I looked toward my house and hurried along the brick walk. They had installed French doors with an arched top that matched the curve of the fireplace. It was stunning. I turned to hug Troy.

The vegetable garden that Wolf and I had planted was gone, as were many of the shrubs that I looked forward to seeing in bloom every spring. The rose that Wolf had liked so much had been ripped out, too, but in its place was a gate to Francie's yard.

I opened it and peeked.

"Now Francie and Duke can come over easily," he explained.

Someone let Daisy out, and she romped

toward me. I petted her. "Is that an outdoor dog bed by the fire?"

"We couldn't forget Daisy!" Troy slid an arm around my shoulders. "We're losing light. We invited a few of your friends to come over tomorrow night for barbecue. Hope that's okay."

It was better than okay.

I finally got a chance to sleep in. Some vacation! I was more worn out afterward than I was before. Still wrapped in my bathrobe, I wandered out back carrying a mug of steaming Nordic Blend coffee. Hints of cherry and chocolate wafted to me.

Daisy dashed to our new outdoor room, busily sniffing every corner. I settled into a comfy chair and stretched out my legs, marveling over Troy's incredible vision. He'd pulled off a backyard beyond my wildest dreams.

The gate behind me creaked open and Duke shot through. Francie followed at a slower pace, wearing a housedress and carrying a mug.

She eased into the chair next to me, yawning. "What a week this has been."

Troy's troops arrived to set up their barbecue around three in the afternoon. Even though Natasha and Troy had taken care of the menu, I'd baked lemon meringue pies because nothing else said summer like sweetly tart lemon with meringue.

Nina arrived first. We carried dishes outside, but someone on the production crew snatched them away from us, saying we didn't have to do anything. Another guy tested little lights along the roofline.

Francie and Duke arrived via the gate between our houses. I had a feeling it would get a lot of use. Francie had dressed in a pink sweat suit with rhinestones on the shoulders, completely out of character for her. "I hope you don't mind this gate. I said it was okay because I like to keep an eye on you."

"I think it's a great idea. Is Olive coming?"

"You bet! She and Roscoe are back together again. Can you believe it? She took him back in a flash. They're finally heading out to that bed-and-breakfast Roscoe bought in the mountains. Audie's planning to move into their house."

"What about Violet?" I asked.

"She doesn't have to worry about being abandoned. Roscoe and Olive will need her more than ever at the bed-and-breakfast," said Francie.

Nina cackled. "Just the kind of place everyone wants to relax — with Mrs. Danvers glaring at them. They can call it Manderley."

Natasha showed up carrying a coffeecake under a glass cover. She wore a white silk dress, five-inch heels, and heavy TV makeup.

"This is for Troy. I want the cameramen to get a good shot." She breezed past me.

Other neighbors joined us. I couldn't help noticing that the women wore outrageously high heels, short dresses, and low-cut necklines. It took a while for me to understand what was going on. They flocked around Troy, who flashed his toothy smile and made each of them feel special.

Bernie came without Dana.

"Where's your new flame?" I asked.

"She's busy tonight. But I wouldn't have missed this for the world. I'm very impressed with the results. Are you pleased?"

"I love it! By the way, thanks for putting up Wolf at your place. That was very kind of you, Mars, and Natasha."

"Mars and Natasha didn't even know he was there. Wolf's a decent chap. Are you devastated about losing him?"

I suspected that I would have some tough moments ahead of me, but I had done the right thing for everyone. That would teach me for dating a man with a wife — even if she was an absentee wife. What could I have been thinking? "I didn't lose Wolf. I never had him."

Natasha wedged between us. "Have you seen my repurps?" She propelled us to a cabinet near the fireplace. "Troy is featuring this one on his show!" Her sentence ended on an excited pitch.

Bernie and I agreed that it was very clever. She'd attached the stained-glass window to the little bookshelf as a door. It worked perfectly and dressed up two discarded pieces.

"Where's the bed?" I hoped she would say Troy had declined it.

"Follow me." Natasha struggled to walk across the grass to the far corner of my yard in her heels. With great pomp, she showed us an adorable bench. I'd seen it earlier in the day but hadn't made the connection. She'd used the headboard as the back. The lower footboard had been cut into two parts and used as matching arms. The slats had been screwed on to form a seat.

Leon, Natasha's assistant, showed up and wrapped an arm around me. "Isn't it gorgeous? Cutting the footboard correctly was a little bit tough, but I'm so proud if it. Did you notice that I painted it foxglove pink?"

I thanked him profusely.

"Troy turned down my trash cans and the hanging sculpture I planned. I pounded on that thing for days!" she pouted. "But he loved this bench. And you got it all for free, Sophie. Thanks to me."

"I am actually very grateful, Natasha. But don't forget that it's not completely free. I still have to pay taxes on it."

"Don't be silly."

"That's the way it works," I insisted.

Natasha turned to Leon. "Why didn't you tell me this? It can't be. Mars will know. Maaaars!" She toddled off.

Leon waved his hands in the air. "I know what you're thinking, but she pays well."

I was surprised to see Mona and Anne's friend Shelby. "I'm so glad you came!"

Mona patted my shoulder. "I wouldn't have missed it for anything. I've been by every day to watch the progress. I *had* to see the finished product." She took my hands into hers. "And I have to thank you for returning the one thing on this earth that I love with all my heart. I can't ever thank you enough."

"No thanks necessary, Mona." I wanted to ask how Anne and Wolf were doing, but I couldn't bring myself to do that. Maybe it was better if I didn't know. "Just one question. What were you doing in the woods, spying on Roscoe's party?"

She had the decency to blush. "I was following you. I thought you might meet Wolf somewhere or lead me to something, anything, that might be a clue to Anne's whereabouts. And you did! You managed to lose me on the day you dug up Anne's purse — but I found you!"

Shelby sipped a lemon slush. "Boy, that Cricket is a piece of work. She threw away the notes Anne left for Wolf and her parents and then buried Anne's purse in the backyard so that suspicion would fall on Wolf if they were ever found."

"What about the knife? Was it rust or blood?" I asked.

"Hey, Kenner! Get over here," called Shelby.

I'd never seen Kenner in shorts before. Was Shelby ogling his legs? They were fairly muscular.

"Tell Sophie about Cricket. She wants to know about the knife," demanded Shelby.

Kenner took a deep breath. It had to be hard on him, since he'd been friends with Cricket. He swallowed uncomfortably. "The knife was just rusted. Probably got thrown out by mistake."

"Tell her about the embezzlement!" insisted Mona.

"Cricket and Heath set up fake companies and paid their invoices from Roscoe's business accounts. It took them some time to accumulate the money, but the plan worked pretty well. Apparently, Heath didn't realize that Cricket double-crossed him by using his computer passwords to funnel the money to accounts in the name of Anne Fleishman, leaving a paper trail that led to Heath and Anne."

Mona shook her finger. "Which Cricket had set up without Anne's knowledge."

Kenner continued. "But the plan went south when Anne started to audit Roscoe's business. Cricket knew Anne would recognize the scheme in a flash, so Cricket had to get her out of town — and quick. Then Cricket ratted on Heath and Anne —"

"And got the credit for getting the money back!" cried Mona.

"So Anne never had an affair with Heath?" I asked.

Kenner sighed. "No. It was Cricket who was involved with Heath. But he knew a lucky break when he saw one. If Roscoe had pressed charges, Heath would have done serious time. He was more than ready to get out of town."

"I wish I'd met this Cricket," said Shelby.

"She must be a master of manipulation. She zeroed in on Anne's insecurities and guilt. Imagine sending Anne a picture of a stranger's child so she would think Cricket and Wolf had a happy family and would stay away. What a witch! It's lucky for Anne that she believed Cricket was her best friend and wouldn't lie to her. If Anne had come back, she would be as dead as Heath."

"So it *was* Cricket who murdered Heath?" I asked.

Kenner looked pained. "When Heath came back to Old Town, he discovered that his old partner in crime, Cricket, was engaged to Audie and about to enter the inner circle of Greene money. He demanded his fair share of money from her, threatening to expose her role in the embezzlement if she didn't pay. She mollified him with an expensive duck print."

"I thought Violet hid it in the guest house."

"Cricket saw her stash it there during Roscoe's picnic. But she was ready to get rid of blackmailing Heath for good the next night. She met him in the guest house with a bottle of bourbon that contained monkshood tea."

"Then, when he died, she dragged him across the flower bed, covered him with the mulch, and managed to get poison ivy in the process!" I exclaimed.

"What I don't understand," said Shelby, "is why she used that horrible monkshood on Heath but poisoned Mindy with foxglove. Why switch when the monkshood obviously worked so well?"

"Time," I said. "She had time to let Mindy die, but she didn't expect Heath to show up. She had to get rid of him in a hurry."

"The more I know you, the more you frighten me." Kenner was speaking to me, but busy looking at Shelby, who was making eyes at him.

"Sophie!" called Troy.

I excused myself and dashed over to him. Baby back ribs, chicken, and corn on the cob still wrapped in the husks cooked on the grill.

Troy gathered everyone around the table, made a lovely toast, and dinner was on!

I felt incredibly lucky to be surrounded by such wonderful, caring friends.

Daylight waned as we finished our main course. Troy flipped a switch. Small lights shone in the lofted ceiling and along the roofline, producing *ooh*s and *aah*s of admiration.

■ ■ ■ ■

I was in the kitchen putting on another pot of coffee when Francie growled at me. "Are you trying to choke us?" She held a piece of coffeecake on a napkin.

Bernie ambled in to help me.

"Not good?" I asked.

"Ghastly," pronounced Bernie.

One of Francie's eyes squeezed almost closed. "What in tarnation did you put in this thing?"

I broke a piece off, popped it into my mouth, and promptly spit it out. When I stepped on the garbage bin lever to open it, Francie guffawed at the collection of paper napkins and uneaten coffee cake inside.

"Hah! No one else can eat it, either."

"Natasha baked it." I couldn't imagine what she put in it, except for the chipotle, which burned my mouth.

"That figures," said Francie. "You should have warned us."

"But it looked wonderful," I said.

Natasha floated into the kitchen, beaming. "Troy says I'm gorgeous on camera."

Francie stared her down. "What's in the poisoned coffee cake?"

Natasha glared back. "I wish you wouldn't

use words like that about my baking. Someone might believe you."

I tried a gentler approach. "What kind of
coffee cake is it, Natasha?"

"I'll gladly give you a copy of the recipe.
It's bacon, rhubarb, and chipotle."

Francie sneered. "Ugh! No wonder it's
inedible."

Natasha tilted her head and smiled conde-
scendingly at Francie. "Oh, sweetheart, your
palate just isn't developed. You're not used
to haute cuisine."

"I am," said Bernie. "It's simply dreadful."

The edges of Francie's mouth twitched.
"That stuff is more like hot cuisine. Thanks
to you, I won't be able to taste anything for
the next two days."

Natasha flapped her fingers at Francie.
"Nonsense. You can't just eat bland food,
Francie. The chipotle will heighten your
senses and make your blood flow."

"So far it's making my blood boil."

I grinned at their exchange. My life would
be different without Wolf, but it was re-
assuring to know that some things never
change.

RECIPES & COOKING TIPS

ARNOLD PALMER

4 bags black tea
4 cups boiling water
1 cup sugar
1 cup water
1 cup fresh lemon juice
3 cups cold water

Pour the boiling water over the four tea bags and allow to steep and cool.

Mix the sugar with 1 cup of water on the stove. Heat to dissolve the sugar. Add lemon juice to the sugar mixture and add the cold water.

Mix the tea with the lemonade.

GARDEN VEGGIE WHITE PIZZA

1 pizza crust
1 medium onion
2 tablespoons olive oil
2 cloves garlic

1/2 of an eggplant (or 1 small eggplant), diced
1 red pepper, sliced
1/4 cup pesto
1 cup shredded mozzarella cheese
1/2 cup shredded goat gouda or sharp white
 cheddar

Preheat the oven to 375. (Follow directions on crust package.) Sauté the onions in the olive oil to caramelize, then add the garlic, eggplant, and red pepper. Cook until soft, but not mushy. Spread pesto on the pizza crust. Scatter the vegetables on top of the pesto. Top with cheeses. Bake 25–30 minutes or until the crust is done.

WALNUT PESTO

3 tablespoons walnuts
2 cups fresh basil leaves
2 teaspoons minced garlic
1/2 cup olive oil
1/2 cup Parmesan cheese
Salt and pepper to taste

Chop the walnuts in a small food processor. Add the basil leaves and garlic, and pulse. Slowly add the olive oil in a stream while pulsing, or add in small amounts and pulse in between. Add the Parmesan cheese and pulse. Add salt and pepper to taste, and pulse one last time.

PESTO, PROSCIUTTO & GOAT CHEESE CROSTINI

1 small loaf rustic Italian bread
1/2 cup pesto (approximate)
10–12 slices prosciutto
hard goat cheese (like Cablanca)
cherry tomatoes for garnish (optional)

Preheat the oven to 350. Slice the bread and spread pesto on each slice. Top with a slice of prosciutto. Using a vegetable peeler, peel thin slices of the cheese and add to the top. Bake 8–10 minutes, until cheese has melted. Garnish with half a cherry tomato.

Makes 10–12 servings.

THREE-DAY CROCK PICKLES

16 cups water
1 cup sea salt or kosher salt (not iodized salt)
1/2 teaspoon turmeric
1/2 teaspoon mustard seeds
1/2 cup sugar
1 cup cider vinegar
2 cloves garlic, minced
Dill
Small pickling cucumbers

Wash the cucumbers. Combine the water,

salt, turmeric, mustard seeds, sugar, and vinegar. Bring to a boil, stirring occasionally and tasting (add more salt or spices if not to your taste), and let cool. Put raw garlic into the crock or gallon jar. Add enough dill to cover the bottom. Pack the cucumbers into the jar or crock. Pour the cooled vinegar solution over the cucumbers. Cover loosely with cheesecloth, and let stand in the refrigerator for three days. Keep refrigerated.

SUNSET BOULEVARD
1 part peach schnapps
2 parts vodka
3 parts cranberry juice
1 part orange juice

Fill a tall glass with ice. Pour in the first three ingredients. Slowly add the orange juice for the sunset effect.

DANISH APPLE CAKE
1/4 cup butter
1 1/2 cups flour
2 teaspoons baking powder
1 egg
1/3 cup milk
6–8 large apples

Topping

1/4 cup butter
1/2 cup sugar
1/4 teaspoon cinnamon
1/8 teaspoon nutmeg

Whipped Cream

1 cup heavy cream
1/3 cup powdered sugar
1 teaspoon vanilla

The dough can be made by hand; however, it's a breeze in a food processor. Just be sure to use the dough blade.

Peel and core the apples, and slice. I usually quarter the apples and cut each quarter into four slices. Set aside.

Preheat the oven to 425.

For the Dough —

Cut the butter into four pieces, and place in the food processor. Add the flour and the baking powder. Pulse until thoroughly mixed, scraping the sides a couple of times.

Add the egg and the milk, and pulse into a ball. Do not overprocess, or it will be sticky.

Lightly butter a large baking sheet with a lip around the edge. Press the dough into the pan, or roll it out lightly. If it's sticky, use just a bit of flour on top to roll it out easily.

Place the apples on top of the dough in rows so that they barely overlap one another.

Bake at 425 for 20 minutes.

Meanwhile, Make the Topping —

Mix the butter, sugar, cinnamon, and nutmeg to a smooth paste. I use a mini food processor.

When the apples have finished baking, remove the pan from the oven and turn the temperature down to 325.

Drop bits of the paste topping over the apples as uniformly as possible.

Return it to the oven, and bake at 325 for an additional 25 minutes.

Meanwhile, Make Whipped Cream —

Whip 1 cup of heavy cream.

When it begins to take shape, add 1/3 cup powdered sugar and 1 teaspoon vanilla. Whip briefly.

Remove the cake from the oven, and let stand a few minutes. Cut into squares, top with a dollop of whipped cream, and enjoy your afternoon!

CARAMEL BANANA MUFFINS

1/2 cup butter
1 cup walnuts
1 cup flour
3/4 cup sugar
1 teaspoon baking powder
1/2 teaspoon baking soda
1/4 teaspoon salt
3 very ripe bananas
1 teaspoon vanilla
2 eggs
Topping below — optional.

Preheat oven to 350. Melt the butter, and set it aside to cool. Line a cupcake pan with paper liners.

In a food processor, mix the walnuts with the flour, sugar, baking powder, baking soda, and salt. Pulse until fine. Set aside.

Mash the bananas in a large bowl with a fork. Add the cooled butter and vanilla and mix.

Whisk the eggs for one to two minutes, then mix them into the butter and banana mixture. Pour the flour mixture on top and fold with a spatula. *Do not overmix!*

Spoon into the cupcake liners, distributing evenly among cupcake liners. Bake 23–25 minutes or until the muffins are a light golden brown on top.

Makes 12–16 muffins.

Topping (Per Muffin)
(best added just before eating, but Sophie also likes these muffins plain)

1 to 2 bananas
3 Kraft Caramels
1 tablespoon heavy cream

Place the caramels and the cream in a small microwave-safe bowl or cup. Microwave for 20 seconds, then for 10 seconds, checking to see if the caramels have melted. Stir. Slice the bananas, and place two to three slices of fresh banana on top of each muffin. Top with caramel.

Note:
Three caramels and one tablespoon cream make enough sauce for three to four muffins. For more, simply double or triple the amounts.

LEMON SLUSH

1 cup lemon juice
1 cup water
1 cup sugar
4 ounces lemon vodka

2 ounces triple sec
Ice

Place the lemon juice, water, and sugar in a pot and bring to a low boil to dissolve the sugar and make syrup. Cool.

Add the syrup, lemon vodka, and triple sec to a blender and fill with ice. Pulse to an icy slush.

Makes 4 large servings.

ABOUT THE AUTHOR

Krista Davis is the national bestselling author of the Domestic Diva mysteries. her first book, *The Diva Runs Out of Thyme,* was nominated for an Agatha Award. Krista lives in the Blue Ridge Mountains of Virginia with an Ocicat named Mochie and a brood of dogs. Her friends and family complain about being guinea pigs for her recipes, but she notices that they keep coming back for more.

CONNECT ONLINE
www.kristadavis.com
www.mysteryloverskitchen.com
twitter.com/kristadavis
facebook.com/KristaDavisAuthor

CPSIA information can be obtained
at www.ICGtesting.com
Printed in the USA
FFOW050850110113

9 781410 454348